# THE
# DARK
# LIGHT

Julia Bell is a writer and teacher and her novels have been published in the UK and US and translated into many foreign languages. She is also the co-editor of the bestselling *The Creative Writing Coursebook*, which she wrote and compiled while teaching at UEA. She is an alumni of the UEA Creative Writing MA and is a Senior Lecturer at Birkbeck, where she runs a successful MA programme. She also writes poetry and short stories and is the founder and director of the Writers' Hub website and the annual anthology *The Mechanics' Institute Review*.

# THE DARK LIGHT

# JULIA BELL

MACMILLAN

First published 2015 by Macmillan Children's Books
an imprint of Pan Macmillan
a division of Macmillan Publishers Limited
20 New Wharf Road, London N1 9RR
Associated companies throughout the world
www.panmacmillan.com

ISBN 978-1-4472-8303-4

· 1 3 5 7 9 8 6 4 2

A CIP catalogue record for this book is available from
the British Library.

Typeset by Ellipsis Digital Limited, Glasgow
Printed and bound by CPI Group (UK) Ltd, Croydon CR0 4YY

*Believe those who are seeking the truth.*
*Doubt those who find it.*

André Gide

# ONE

# ALEX

The first fire was an accident. I didn't mean it to burn up so quick, so fast. I don't even know why I did it. I was bored, I suppose, showing off. I set light to some chip wrappers and threw them in a pile of leaves that the caretaker had raked up next to the fence. It went up sudden and hot with a huge whoosh! that made everyone step back and nearly took Andrea Mason's eyebrows off and then it spread to the brushwood fence of the houses that backed on to the playing field, and a plume of smoke rose like a sail above the school. I got put on report for six months after that. So when it came to the second one I knew exactly what I was doing.

I squirted lighter fuel on to the cardboard to make it burn better, then rolled the recycling bin up to the side of the house so she would be sure to see the flames outside her window. I hoped it burned her face off.

It had been going on for months. *Dyke, lemon, lezzer.* She wrote it in marker pen in the toilets. *Alex Thomas is a Dyke!* And, underneath, my actual phone number. Then it was big gobs of phlegm on the back of my bag, pictures on Facebook, text messages. Kaitlin Watts and her little minion Anna Evans, they'd turned me into their obsession, probably because they fancied each other really, but what could I do about that? And then one day on the bus home she grabbed my bag and spilled my stuff out over the top deck. All my school notes and books and the magazine I'd bought because it had a picture of Kristen Stewart on the cover. *Look at her dyke magazine! Eugh, don't touch it, you'll catch something!*

I stood and watched as great tongues of flame licked up the side of the house, the paint beginning to peel, then I turned and ran.

They picked me up in the park. We weren't supposed to go there after dark on account of the muggers and prostitutes and homeless people. What a joke – there was never anyone there! It's only because adults are afraid of the dark that they tell us not to walk about in it. But I wasn't afraid of it. I'm made of the dark, me. I tattooed a moon into my thumb with a compass and Indian ink to remind myself. I smoked a cigarette and bounced my leg, so deep in thought and feeling I didn't see them till it was too late and then there was no point in running.

'Hello, Alex.'

Dick the Pig. Or PC Richards, if you read his name badge.

Sadsacks, the police, having to go round with their names on the whole time. Like they might get lost or something. He hated me. I mumbled something and pushed my hands into my pockets, jumping down off the bench. He had some woman PC with him too; that meant he planned on taking me down to the station.

'There's been a fire at the Meadow View B&B. You wouldn't know anything about that, would you?'

I shrugged. No point denying it – they knew that I knew that they knew it was me – but why let them have the satisfaction of hearing me admit it?

'Talkative as ever, I see,' he said.

Most of the time I don't see the point in talking. It's just a load of *blah blah blah* about the weather or what do you want to eat for dinner or pointless things just to cover up for the fact that no one really says what they want to say or what they mean.

'I'm going to have to ask you to come down the station.'

And he put handcuffs on me, even though he knew I wasn't going anywhere.


There were Implications, apparently, and Consequences.

Ron and Bridget and Sue the Social Worker and Dick the Pig all looked serious, and I sat there running my thumbnail into the groove of the wood on the tabletop until Bridget told me not to.

'There is CCTV *evidence*,' Sue the Social Worker said. 'You can't deny it, Alex.'

The only thing I hadn't bargained for: the camera outside the shop opposite that was pointed right at the driveway of the B&B.

'Arson is a very serious offence.'

Dick the Pig mentioned Criminal Damage and Youth Court and Young Offenders. I flinched.

'Heard that, didn't you?'

Sue the Social Worker sighed and picked at her nails. 'I *told* you, Alex. I *said* if you get into any more trouble it'll be the youth courts.'

So when Bridget laid out her solution, I didn't argue. It made sense. Go away for a bit, over the summer, take some time out, learn some new skills, start again. Go to sixth-form college in the autumn in another town.

'Of course we can help you every step of the way with the transition.'

The transition. What she was really saying was that they wanted rid. Taking me on had been a mistake, although they were too proud to admit it. There can be no failure in the eyes of the Lord.

'I think that's a brilliant idea!' Sue the Social Worker said in this fake enthusiastic way, as if they hadn't already discussed this behind my back. 'All those outdoor skills will really bring you out of yourself.'

Bridget had sold her the idea like it was some kind of holiday camp. And I guess she didn't really do her research; she'd been watching too much reality TV. People transformed by the wild. Turned from soft saps into rugged heroes by making campfires and climbing mountains. But New Canaan wasn't about outdoor skills. According to the leaflet it was a *Christian community, living by the precepts set down in the Bible*. Even more God Squad than Ron and Bridget.

'And Pastor Bevins has had great success helping people with difficult backgrounds like yours.'

'What do you think, Alex?'

I grunted. The room filled with the loud noise of everyone's silent thoughts. Being quiet makes it easier to hear what people are thinking. You can see it on their faces. Sue the Social Worker with her irritable, professional kindness, Bridget desperate to find a solution that wouldn't make her feel bad, Ron angry because I was costing him – he'd already offered to pay towards the repairs at Meadow View – and Dick the Pig looking smug, because he'd finally shown me who was boss.

'I think you're a very lucky girl,' he said, 'considering your previous. We'd be within the law to throw the book at you. But I'm inclined to be generous and I think that something like this could be exactly what you need. For someone with your background. Something to put a bit of backbone in you.' I hated the way he tried to make himself sound magnanimous, like he was doing me a favour.

'I think it would be a great solution,' Sue the Social Worker said. I knew she'd already worked this out with Ron and Bridget anyway.

'But it's either that, or I'm going to have to suggest that Mr Davis presses charges,' Dick the Pig went on. 'Then it's the youth courts.'

The decision had already been made then, and whatever fire there was in me had burned itself out.

'Whatever,' I said, not lifting my eyes from the floor.

# TWO

# REBEKAH

The rain blows in horizontal sheets under the roof of the bandstand, and against the beach a brown sea churns. The deckchair attendant has given up, tied ropes and a tarpaulin over the chairs and gone home, and only the lights on the kiosk further up still twinkle around the sign that advertises ice cream. No one has walked past in half an hour.

*Gwyllt*, the locals call it, like a greeting. *Wild*.

'*Gwyllt*, isn't it? You'll not get many coming out in this,' an old lady says, as she hurries past us in her red coat with her small, shivery dog running on in front. She doesn't stop to take a leaflet.

It's supposed to be the middle of summer but it's been like this all week.

Hannah rearranges all the jars of honey so the labels face outward. Some of them have got wet and the ink on the labels bleeds. *Hallelujah Honey from New Canaan*.

We sell honey as a way to start a conversation, as a way to start *the* conversation, because what other conversation could be more important than the fate of your soul? Although not everyone sees it like this. Yesterday a man with a blotchy face and tired, angry eyes came up and shouted in my face.

'You're what's wrong with people! You lot and your bloody magical thinking! That's what got us into this mess in the first place!' And he tore up the leaflet into little squares and threw them at my feet.

I looked at him and felt sad. I could see he'd got in so deep with the devil that he could no longer hear the truth. Mr Bevins says it happens to people who follow the broad and not the narrow path, eventually their ears close up and they become deaf to the truth. I often wonder if this means a kind of special skin grows across their ears.

A woman strides past, holding her umbrella at a right angle against the rain.

'Excuse me. Can I interest you in the word of God?' Hannah starts, stepping out of the shelter of the bandstand to hold out a leaflet, which immediately gets soggy.

'In this weather?' She raises her eyes to the sky. 'We need more than the word of God.' Then she stops and looks me. 'You're from that island, aren't you?' she says waving her hand in the direction of the sea and frowning. 'I didn't know you had children over there.'

'Young or old, we are all called to be servants of God,' Hannah says, not answering the question.

The woman raises her eyebrows. 'Others might call it something else. If anyone had an ounce of sense they'd be sending social services over there. We all know what goes on! That American! Everyone has heard the stories.'

Hannah sighs. 'Well, perhaps if you came to one of our meetings you might—'

'Don't be ridiculous!' she snaps. She stares at me again and tuts. Then she pushes her umbrella into the wind and hurries on her way.

Mr Bevins has taught us what to expect. This is what happens when you are confronted with unbelievers. He says that people don't trust him because he tells the truth. Hannah gets upset by it, but I don't. Like he says – if people weren't agitated by our message, then we wouldn't be saying anything important. That's why he chose me for Mission Week, because I am stoic, because I believe. He calls me 'a flower of the Lord'. And he gave me a vision of a special blessing that had come to him in a dream, of a light like honey shining out of my body.

The leaflet tells our story. On one side is Bible verses and on the other the account of how Mr Bevins was visited one night by an angel who told him that the Rapture will happen soon and Jesus will come down on a cloud of fire to bring an end to the world and condemn the earth to the Tribulations and take all the believers with Him back to heaven. And to have the best chance of being saved we have to live like it says in the Bible, disown all property and the evils of commercialism and set an example to others. And how he was led, all the way from Missouri, USA, to Wales, by the light of the Holy Spirit and a series of Miraculous Coincidences. One of these coincidences included meeting my father and mother, who had just inherited some money and were looking to buy a farm.

A gust of wind lifts a pile of leaflets and sends them scuttling down the prom. I make to go after them, but Hannah stops me.

'Leave them,' she says. 'You never know where God's word will end up.'

But I go and fetch them anyway. We mustn't litter. Mr Bevins says that's the reason the planet is in such a mess and the end of days is coming, because people are selfish and stupid and they've spoilt everything with all the pollution.

Before we went with Mr Bevins and built the community, we lived on a smallholding where we kept chickens and pigs and had an orchard. There's a photo of me in red wellingtons walking around a huge vegetable garden, and one that I keep in my Bible of my mother, where she's digging in the flower bed, with her hair pushed back behind her ears. She's looking at the camera and smiling, looking beautiful. I keep this to remind me that I'll be meeting her in heaven soon.

It's such a waste of time being here. We've hardly sold any honey or spoken to anyone who is seriously questioning. Usually the promenade is full of holidaymakers, but in this weather they're all sheltering in the shopping centre. Mission Week actually takes two whole weeks out of August. At this time of year everyone back home will be bringing in the harvest, cutting the barley, the oats, digging up the potatoes. Thomas and Micah counting ewes and baling the winter hay. Even in the rain there will be work to do: checking the lobster pots, changing the fuel in the smokehouse, repairing and making tools in the workshop. It's the busiest time. I'm desperate to go back. I feel useless here when I know there are tasks that need to be done at home. So much better than sitting around being shouted at by strangers. We are learning how to survive, preparing for the Rapture. Soon this bandstand and this town and all the people in it will be consumed with the fire of the End Times, and Mr Bevins will lead us to the glory.

'Only one more day, eh?' Hannah says, as if she can read my mind.

Hannah joined our Church when her fiancé abandoned her, the very day before her wedding. She met Mr Bevins on a Mission Week and was touched by his words of truth and fell in love with the island. In her testimonies she talks about how God led her. 'I was lucky! If he hadn't left me I would still be living in ignorance! I would never have been chosen!' At her first repentance meeting she burned pictures of a man in a blue suit with oily dark hair. She said she was dedicating everything to God from now on. She even built her own cabin.

I rub my arms against the cold. It's our job to stay cheerful even if it's raining set to drown us and the leaflets have all got wet.

'You'll be missing your mother,' Hannah says, looking at me kindly.

'Not really,' I say. 'Live for the Victory, remember?'

I hate it when people talk about her like they're expecting me to be sad. Sadness shows weakness. It means you don't have enough faith. We live for the life after life. That's what Mr Bevins says. What's the point of being sad when we know that heaven is only just round the corner? When we spoke to him yesterday on the satellite phone he warned us about exactly this, the backsliding that comes when you are in the world of the Antichrist. I dig my nails into my palms. 'In such a flower of the Lord, a doubt is a disappointment to him.' Isn't that what he said? I've taught myself not to be sad. I know I'll see her in heaven really soon.

By the time Father comes in the van I'm freezing, flapping my arms up and down to keep my blood up, and Hannah is humming hymns to keep us cheerful. The van belongs to the Church of New Canaan, who are our mainland offshoot and who host us during Mission Week. It has a painting of angels blowing trumpets on it and a verse from the Psalms, except whoever painted it ran out of space for the letters so it's a bit messed up on one end. If you look at it from the wrong angle it reads: *Praise Him with a Joyful Trump*. I have pretended not to notice, because the Church collects for us and gives us donations. Clothes and canned stuff, sugar, coffee, tea. A box of shoes this year. I hope there are some my size. My boots are worn at the soles; they won't last another winter.

'Hello, Father.'

Recently he seems to have got very skinny, although he's always been thin, and sometimes his head seems too big for his body, especially as he grows his beard thick and bushy, like all the men on the island do.

'I think we'll call it a day,' he says, lifting up one of the crates of honey.

As he walks back to the van, three figures appear on the promenade, rounding the corner past the kiosk, walking quickly towards us against the weather. A man and a woman and a boy with curly dark hair and pale skin, with leather tied around his wrist, who kind of swaggers. As they approach he laughs and points at our van, raising his mobile phone to take a photo.

I look at the van and cringe. I wish I could stand in front of it to stop him.

As he gets closer I can see he has a ring in his lip. People like that give me a weird feeling. I say a quick prayer for protection and wish Mission Week was over so that we could go home. Being on the mainland is precarious, like being on a narrow path on a high cliff that I could slip and fall off at any moment.

When Thomas Bragg came on Mission Week he disappeared with a woman from the Church for two nights. He said he was witnessing to her, but Father and Mr Bevins sent him to the Solitary when he got back and Hannah and Margaret remarked darkly that he'd been up to 'desperate acts'. This year he stayed on New Canaan with Mr Bevins. Father says it will be a long time before Thomas can be trusted again, that he's still too immature to be in the world without being tainted by it. But I'm not weak like that. There's nothing here that I want. Mr Bevins says I'm kind of like an angel, that I burn bright with the light, that I am a daughter of the Lord. I bite my lip until I taste blood.

I think they're going to pass us by when the man pauses and squints at us through the rain.

'Are you the people from New Canaan?'

'Yes!' Hannah says, holding out a crumpled leaflet.

'Praise God!' His face lights up. 'We've been looking for you all over town!'

They tell us that they are called Bridget and Ron and that they have travelled all the way from Essex. Ron is a member of a Church that is much like ours. It's taken them nine hours in their camper van and they've brought with them their *daughter*, Alex.

It takes me a moment to absorb this information.

She looks like a boy, the square shape of her jaw and the way she wears her jeans slung low and stands with her legs apart. When they mention her name she glances up from her phone and scowls. She catches me looking and stares at me hard, as if she's saying *So what?* She looks a little bit more like a girl then, but still it's confusing.

'What you're doing, it's amazing,' Ron says. He has a round, cheerful face which is bright red as if it's been scrubbed.

'Amazing,' Bridget echoes. 'So inspiring.'

'I don't suppose Mr Bevins is here? We've been dying to meet him,' Ron asks.

Father shakes his head. 'He doesn't come on Mission Week any more. There's too much to do back home.'

'But we speak to him every evening.' Hannah says.

'He is such an amazing example to the faithful,' Bridget says.

On Mission Weeks we speak to him every day via a satellite phone. He wants to know every detail; who we've been with, who

12

we've spoken to. He tells us his vision for our mission. He wants us to find some new recruits and he says we must keep vigilant for the influence of Satan who is all around us, remember the blood of Christ and live for the Victory.

Father says Mr Bevins is one of the best scholars of the Book he has ever known. He can quote large sections of it, chapter and verse. I often see him wandering the island, the Bible open in his hands like a map. Before he came to Wales he lived in America, travelling the country, preaching to anyone who would listen. When he arrived in London he lived on the streets, homeless, like Jesus, staying with those who would open their doors to him, and when he came to Wales he brought with him Micah and Mary Protheroe, two disciples whom he had saved. He's always telling us stories of before, of his life back in America, of his conversion to Jesus. How God hit him with the truth of life 'like a thunderbolt' between the eyes. When Father met him for the first time he said the spirit shone through him so brightly that it was impossible to ignore.

'We would be lost without him,' Father says neutrally.

Alex raises her eyebrows but says nothing, typing something on her phone. These black tablets are a sign of the end of days: the new world order of the Antichrist, who can see you and spy on you if you use one.

A few years ago a man came to visit, pretending to be from another Church. But Mr Bevins caught him taking photographs with his phone. Mr Bevins threw it in the sea and said we were going to pray over him, which we did, and then the man got sent back on the next boat. Father said afterwards that he was an undercover journalist who wrote an article full of lies about our community. And then for a while everyone was afraid that they would send someone from the mainland to evict us, although no one knew why they would. It's not as if we're breaking any laws. The island belongs to us.

'You set the standard for everyone else,' Ron says. 'It's a privilege to meet you.' He shakes Father's hand enthusiastically.

Bridget nods. 'A real privilege.'

Father smiles guardedly. Since the journalist we've learned to be careful of enthusiasm. When new people come and join us, they have to go through the days of the Solitary first to prove they are worthy. Every new member of our community has to go there for forty days and forty nights. Mother said many were put off by this, to which Father said if it was easy to join us in New Canaan then it wouldn't be a true test of faith. Like it says in the Bible, it's easier for a camel to go through the eye of a needle than for a rich man to enter the kingdom of heaven. Mr Bevins says that it's quite normal for people on the mainland to be frightened of us because we live a more spiritual life than them.

Father invites them back to the church. 'You were obviously led,' he says. 'We were just packing up.'

'The weather!' Ron says. 'It's a sign of the Tribulations. I know it.'

'That's the truth, brother.' Father nods. 'One thing though.' He points at Alex. 'We don't allow phones in the church.'

Alex makes a noise then shakes her head.

There's silence for a moment. Bridget's face changes. She looks disappointed, then angry. 'Alex we've *talked* about this,' she says quietly. 'Unless you *want* to go back.'

Alex reacts, a ripple through her body like a shock. I think she is about to shout and lose her temper but she doesn't. She shrugs. She switches the phone off and hands it to Bridget then pushes her hands into her pockets and looks at me like she hates me.

As we drive the short distance back to the church, I can't help but stare at the square line of her shoulders and the way she crosses her leg ankle to knee and fiddles with the leather braids that she has tied around her wrist. There's something about her. She gives off this fierce energy. I can almost hear it hum.

# THREE

# ALEX

I was eleven when I realized that God didn't exist, or that if He did, that he didn't care about me.

The Church home, the last one before I got adopted, which was actually OK. The best of all the places I'd been. The people were nice, and although we had to go to a Church school and Church meetings, no one was nasty or creepy. It was one of our 'family days', where prospective parents came round and met the children, and although we weren't supposed to know that that was what was going on, everyone did. I offered God every part of my little being that day. Stupid promises, like I'll be a missionary when I grow up, I promise to look after Dionne and Sharon, I promise to work really, *really* hard at school. *Please*. I knelt by my bed with my hands pressed together so hard I could feel the bones through my palms.

She had to be kind because she was so pretty. She was a model-turned-actress and she shone down on us from the cheap flatscreen in the lounge. Barry found a picture of her on the Internet all dressed up for some awards show in a glamorous evening gown and I started praying then that she would notice me and want to be my mother. My Forever Family, happy ever after. It would be like living inside a golden carriage, I would want for nothing and everything would be perfect. I'd never wanted anything so much.

She'd even been on daytime TV talking about how she was going down the adoption route, and there were sympathetic stories about her in the papers. We weren't supposed to know about it, but around the house among the older children there was gossip for weeks, about how she had been shown all our profiles and had long meetings with the social workers, that she had chosen us because she had a longstanding relationship with the charity that ran our home. For a few weeks we all felt important, noticed, like we were at the centre of what was going on, not in some rotten corner of Colchester where nothing ever happened.

Adopt them before they're seven. That's what everyone says. After seven they're spoilt, they'll never really be yours. Or there's something 'challenging' about them: disabilities, learning problems, heart conditions, behavioural issues, which makes them difficult to place.

I was eleven. I was growing, looking awkward. *Please, God, please, let it be me.*

I never stood a chance.

I practised my winning smile in the mirror. Showing off all my white teeth, like the happy children they put on the cover of the magazine they sent out to prospective families – *Children Who Wait*.

The Community Rooms had been done up with balloons and there were cakes and cups of squash. Steve had organized activities and games as if it was a party, but we all knew why we were really there.

She came with three other couples, walked in with her head down, her face half hidden by her glossy hair. You could tell from her clothes, her make-up, the very serious expression on her face, that she knew she was the most important person in the room. She was wearing a beautiful cream coat and she smelled classy, like the perfume counter in Boots.

We all froze and stared at her and I put on my winning smile and held it until my face started to ache.

Dionne nudged me. I hated her, with her braces and stupid half 'fro hair that meant she got to go to a special hairdresser once a week. I heard Steve perving over her once, going on to Sue the Social Worker, about how she was going to be a stunner when she was older, her skin the colour of creamed coffee, like Beyoncé. But I couldn't see it personally. She was up herself and she thought she was better than me because she got good marks at school. But I remembered my promise to God to be nice to her and kept smiling.

'What's wrong with your face?' she asked.

'What d'you mean?'

'You're gurning,' she giggled.

I made my hand into a fist and hit her, right on the bone of her shoulder where you can give someone a dead arm.

Immediately she scrunched up her face and started overreacting as if I'd tried to kill her.

'Owwww! Alex!' She said it really loud so that Steve came over.

'What's up with you two?'

'Alex hit me,' she whined, which made me hate her even more.

Steve made me go and stand over the other side of the room with Sharon, who had cerebral palsy and dribbled while she ate and had to wear really sad glasses. I watched as my new mother circulated around the room. She took her time, bending down to talk to Finn and help him with his Lego. Her nails were shiny salmon-pink and her skin seemed to glow with the kind of class that meant you'd never be sad or poor or sick ever again. Sharon snuffled loudly next to me. I looked at her and hated her too. I didn't want her to be chosen instead of me.

18

'You need the toilet, Sharon?'

'No,' she hooted at me.

'OK then.'

And I wheeled her to the disabled toilet, which was out the swing doors by the lobby. We were supposed to wait for her to do her business and then wheel her back in, except I didn't. I left her there and shut the door on her, knowing she couldn't get out on her own.

When I came back my new mother had moved on and I hopped from foot to foot, nervously waiting my turn. I didn't know what I was going to say, except I hoped that if I looked smart or clever enough she'd notice me right away. But before that could happen Sue the Social Worker came over.

'Alex, I want to introduce you to someone.'

And standing right in front of me, blocking my view, were this lumpy looking couple; Bridget, with her weird haircut and socks and sandals, and Ron, in a purple jumper with holes in it. I scowled at them.

'Hello, Alex,' Bridget said, reaching out a hand to shake mine, but I ignored it. This wasn't supposed to happen. 'I'm Bridget. And this is Ron. We've heard lots of good things about you.'

'Ron's a lay pastor,' Sue the Social Worker said, like that made everything OK.

'But . . .' I started to cry.

'Oh dear,' said Sue the Social Worker. 'These occasions can be a bit overwhelming. Perhaps if we go outside?'

A month later I was living in a house near Billericay with Ron and Bridget, going to church every Sunday. If they were the answers to my prayers, then God was having a big laugh at my expense.

\*

I figured out early on that they only really saw what they wanted to see. They never had kids, and at forty-six it was making Bridget depressed, so they prayed about it and went to an adoption agency and ended up with me. But by the time they got me they were so used to their ways that it was like I was a visitor rather than part of their family. As if I was lodging with them, not living with them.

Even after all that time, whenever Ron caught me coming out of the bathroom he'd say sorry and run to his bedroom and hide until he was sure he wouldn't see me. And Bridget would always knock before she came into my room. In fact, having me there didn't seem to lift her out of her depression at all. She spent long afternoons in bed with the curtains closed. Although every now and then she would seem to snap out of it enough to take me to McDonalds and say vague things about how she knew I'd had a hard start in life, but that now I was walking with Jesus everything would be much better for me. I learned quickly that as long as I was quiet and went to church on Sundays I could pretty much do what I liked.

They were the last to know that I'd stopped going to school halfway through Year 11. And when I got my lip ring Bridget didn't notice for a whole three days, until finally she said, 'Did you have an accident? You've got something funny in your lip.'

But she never made me take it out.

By the time we got to Wales I was tired and a bit carsick from all the twisty roads. The minute we got to the mountains it started to rain, a thick drizzle that seemed to settle on everything like one of Bridget's damp blankets. I felt cold just looking at the scenery, even though it was warm and dry in Ron's overheated Volvo.

When we got to the town Ron got cross because he messed up

20

the one-way system and the car park had no spaces and we had to park on a road miles away from the seafront. We got soaked trying to find the mission. It was a total joke. It was supposed to be the height of summer, and it was more like the middle of January.

The minute I saw them, my heart sank. Huddled together under the bandstand like ducks. I wanted us to drive back to Essex right then and face whatever punishment Dick the Pig wanted to lay on me. I didn't care. I got this bad feeling in my stomach like a stone had settled there, hard and indigestible. I wished I'd never agreed to this stupid plan.

A man and two women – well, a woman and a girl. The girl looked thin and cold, but her face shone in spite of the weather; pale almost translucent skin, so I could see the blue traces of veins in her face. When she looked at me she blushed, her whole face showing her feelings, and I blinked, because she'd caught me staring.

Ron and Bridget acted like they were meeting the Pope or something, all over excited and bleating. 'Oh, you're such an inspiration!' 'We love your ministry!' It made me want to puke. And Bridget made this big deal of taking my phone. Normally she didn't care.

We drive back to their church, which was in an old cinema away from the promenade. Outside were banners with Bible verses, a few sagging balloons. Inside, in the lobby were books and leaflets and a donation box and a table with an electric urn and plates and cups. There was a crash of drums and tambourines coming from the auditorium. On the doors was a poster that said *Tonight – Songs of Praise and Worship*.

There were information boards about New Canaan. *The Great*

*Revelation*, it said, and underneath this black and white photo of their preacher, who was supposed to be blessed with the spirit of God. He had wild hair and piercing eyes looking up to heaven, like an old painting of Jesus. *Pastor Bevins, Miracle Worker*, it said underneath, and, *Live for the Victory!*

Next to that was a map of the island with stuff about wind energy and self-sufficiency. There was a photo of the community, about forty people standing together in front of a church, their faces squinting into the sun. I could see the girl, Rebekah, younger then, in front of a woman with a red headscarf who held her by the shoulders.

Bridget and Ron told me to wait while they went off with Rebekah's father to talk to this Pastor Bevins on the satellite phone. Seemed like it was down to him if they were going to take me, although Bridget had made out like it was already happening. I thought about going to the toilet to scratch my arms but I counted to ten like they taught me in CBT. I went and sat on a chair by the doors. Rebekah sat next to me. She was wearing a dirty blue headscarf, which was knotted under her chin too tight, and it made her face stick out like the moon.

I smiled at her but she looked away. Neither of us spoke. I played with the zipper on my top. I went on an outward-bound course once when I lived in the home. I imagined this place would be a bit like that, except for two months rather than a week. We did survival skills, learned how to make fire by rubbing sticks together, how to make a compass from a needle. I liked outdoors stuff. I could deal with digging and harvesting and whatever, as long as there wasn't too much church.

'You OK?'

For a moment I wasn't sure if I'd imagined it, the voice was so small and quiet. I looked at her, but she turned her eyes to the floor. I knew she wanted me to say something, but I didn't. Being quiet when you're expected to speak is a good tactic. It makes people scared of what you might be thinking; either that or after a while they reckon you're stupid and leave you alone. Also there was this kind of weird feeling between us that seemed to have come from nowhere. Although I didn't want to admit it, she made me feel shy too.

'You know we're Christian?' she said eventually. 'On New Canaan.'

I nodded.

'We're in the world but not of it,' she said, arranging herself on the seat all neat and prim.

I reached out a hand and pinched her on the arm.

She flinched. 'Ow! What did you do that for?' She leaned away from me and rubbed her arm.

I shrugged. 'Just checking,' I muttered.

I never got that idea anyway. I mean, if we're supposed to be in the world but not of it, then where are we? I could never think of an answer that made sense.

'Do you walk closely with God?' She looked at me earnestly and gave me one of her leaflets. 'All around us the air is thick with spiritual battle.'

I snorted, but her expression was so sincere that I kind of felt sorry for her. I took the leaflet. The text explained all about how Mr Bevins came over from America and set up New Canaan. It was the same stuff that was on the boards except there were more photos, of a beach and farm buildings and a windmill. It made a big deal of their self-sufficiency and their special mission from God. It said that Mr Bevins *heard* God's voice directing him to go to Wales.

'What are you laughing for?'

I pointed at the leaflet. 'This.'

'Don't you ever hear the voice of God?'

'*No.*'

'Mr Bevins has a special gift,' she said, nodding at no one.

'Oh.' Suddenly two months seemed like a really, *really* long time.

We were quiet for a bit. I picked my nails, aware that she was watching me, like properly staring at me. I deliberately didn't look. 'What's that?' she said eventually, pointing at the tattoo on my thumb.

'The moon,' I said, turning my thumb to show her. 'Did it myself.'

'Your parents let you do that?'

'Ron and Bridget? They're OK.'

'Why do you call them Ron and Bridget? Aren't they your parents? What happened to your parents?'

God, she was nosy. I shifted in my seat. I wasn't sure I really wanted to tell her. Though I supposed Ron and Bridget were off somewhere telling one of the pastors anyway, so she might as well hear it from me.

'My real mother died of an overdose,' I said, swallowing a familiar sense of shame. 'Heroin.'

'What's that?'

I looked at her. She *seriously* didn't know. 'Drugs.'

'Oh. Sorry.'

'Wasn't your fault. I was only little. I don't really remember her. They found me two days later still trying to wake her up.'

These things were in my case notes, the fat file that Sue the Social Worker used to carry around with her to meetings, stained with mug rings and drips of grease from her desk lunches, then on her iPad with the cracked screen.

*Early years chaotic, mother drug abuser, father unknown . . . Alex is a lively child who loves playing with her toys and lots of cuddles! . . . Wary of strangers, would be best placed in an environment where she is the only child . . . Has difficulty relating to others, presents as detached and unresponsive . . . tendency towards living in a fantasy world . . . self harm is an issue.*

She let me read it once. 'It's only fair you should know what has been written about you.'

Fair, maybe, but I'd rather I hadn't. It made me angry, all the things other people had said about me as if I wasn't an actual person, but a specimen to be dissected and studied. And no matter how many people told me it wasn't my fault, I still wondered if maybe, if I'd been a different, better, nicer person, she might have lived. She might have fought for me, for us.

Rebekah blinked at me. 'Quite a few of our number have had drug problems or been possessed by alcohol. All who repent are welcome at the Lord's table. We don't judge.' She said this like she was offering me a favour.

'*Thanks*,' I said sarcastically.

What was it with the God botherers that they couldn't open their faces without sounding like they were patronizing you? I wondered what she'd say if I told her I was gay. Although I doubted she'd have a clue what the word meant.

I'd known since I was about twelve, ever since I had seen Carrie Matthews winning the 800 metres on sports day. Her legs were the colour of smooth peanut butter and I wanted to touch them in wonder. And I knew too, without anyone telling me, that these feelings weren't something I was supposed to share with anyone. Especially at Ron and Bridget's where no one spoke about sex, ever, and in the Church where they only talked about it as a sin.

Other girls, normal girls, liked boys. They obsessed about whether they were friends with them. About who was crushing on who. They were like Kaitlin Watts, bitchy, territorial. I didn't know what my territory was, if I even had a territory. Mostly I just felt bad. Bad about being different, bad about being the one with the tragic story that everyone felt sorry for, bad that I didn't want to dress girly, bad that I was even on the planet at all. I touched the white scars on my arms. Sue the Social Worker had been getting me help with that, but I still wanted to do it all the time.

Being gay was the worst thing some of the Church people could think of. The way they went on about it you'd think it was worse than murdering someone or being a paedophile. But if God was supposed to be all about love, how could He hate people for feeling it? It wasn't God who hated; it was people. People like Ron and Bridget and Dick the Pig and that other woman, Hannah, who kept staring at me. Her disapproval was like a force field. I got it all the time; I knew I looked a bit like a boy. I always got mistaken for one. I glared at her until she looked away.

'Is that your mother?' I nodded at Hannah.

'No!' Rebekah said this like she was shocked. 'My mother's dead. Like yours.'

I looked at her properly then, and smiled, and a current of understanding passed between us.

'She got sick.' She turned away from me like she didn't really want to talk about it and her eyes shone like she was holding on to tears, and I wanted to be nice to her and tell her I knew how she felt. That whatever anyone said about it being OK, nothing was ever going to make up for that emptiness.

'How old are you?' I asked.

'Nearly sixteen,' she said.

I sat up. '*Seriously?*' She was lying, had to be. She didn't look a day older than twelve.

'Why, how old did you think I was?'

'Maybe thirteen or something.'

'*Thirteen?*' She sounded offended. 'How old are you then?'

'Sixteen in two months.'

'Then we're nearly the same age,' she said impatiently. 'Anyway, if I don't look my age, then *you* don't look like a girl. I thought you were a boy back there on the prom. You even sound like one a bit.' She said this like she was telling me off.

'*So?* What do you think a girl should look like?' I said this more cockily than I felt.

'Well, you wear trousers. In New Canaan women must always wear skirts, and cover their arms for modesty.'

'But we're not Victorians! Girls can wear trousers too.'

'Only if they're with the devil,' she said.

I stared at her. 'Are you *serious?*'

She nodded. 'Yes. Mr Bevins forbids it.'

'I'm not wearing a skirt!' Skirts made me feel at odds with myself. Cold, mostly, but also unprotected. I couldn't remember the last time I'd worn one. Even at school I wore trousers.

'You have to if you're in our community.'

'What if you're just visiting?'

She shrugged. 'I don't know. We don't get many visitors.'

I wriggled in my seat and wondered if there was any way to get out of this. I could just run away. But I already did that once, and I knew what the streets held for girls like me. Across from me,

Hannah was standing in the porch arguing with a man who was pointing his finger at her and shouting.

'But you know the End Times are here?' she was saying. 'The days of the Rapture are upon us.'

'Well, you know what? Hoo-bloody-ray. I can't wait!' he said. 'If you're going to be in heaven, then I'll gladly go to hell! And no, I don't want one of your bloody leaflets!'

I closed my eyes. I was beginning to think this was a very bad idea. Two months. It couldn't be over soon enough.

# FOUR

# REBEKAH

The camp bed creaks as I turn over. In the other bed I can hear Alex's slow breathing, the occasional snuffle. Light from the corridor filters through the porthole window on the door, which is crosshatched with wire and glazed with frosted glass so no one can see through. I can't sleep.

I've never met anyone like her before. She seems like two people, both boy and girl, shy and confident, hard and soft. I think New Canaan will be a good place for her. I'm glad she's coming with us. Ron and Bridget made a big fuss of praying over her in the meeting, and then afterwards Father said that Mr Bevins had approved the idea that she was to come and live with us for a while and he charged me with looking after her. I have already prayed that she will see the light.

The last new people to come to us were Jonathan and Daniel, who came after Mr Bevins went on a mission to London to speak to a Church there. When Daniel arrived his beard was so thick he looked like a wolf-man, and he kept his hair long and tied it back in a ponytail. Everything about him was dirty, and since he'd stopped taking drugs he'd been seeing visions of devils following him. So they kept him in the Solitary and prayed over him for days and then baptized him in the sea. He cut his hair and shaved his beard and suddenly we could see that he was young. The lines on his face from the dirt had washed away. And Father told the story of how the whole of heaven would be rejoicing because of the one sinner brought to God, and what a miracle-worker Mr Bevins was, gone into 'the very jaws of darkness itself' to rescue lost souls.

I wonder if they've told her about the Solitary. I wonder if Mr Bevins will make her go there. It's an old stone house on the other side of the island, about a three-mile walk from the Protheroe farm, turned into a chamber of cells. It has thick stone walls and a heavy earthen roof and was built many thousands of years ago, maybe as a burial chamber, although no one really knows. It was once home to a hermit, the last person living on the island, found crawling around on all fours like a dog when some sailors stopped off to visit years ago. Apparently he barked at them and ran away. The next time the island was visited there was no trace of him, only some rabbit bones and the remains of a fire.

Father and Micah Protheroe divided it into four small cells. Each has enough space for a bed and a chair and the person gets water and soup and a copy of the Bible, but for forty days and nights they must remain in prayer to prepare themselves for our community. There is always one of the community resident there, living in silent contemplation. At the moment it's Naomi; she's been there for many years. When she came to the island she said it was her role, that she was a prophet of God and she was watching and praying for signs of wonder. As far as anyone knows, she has not spoken a word in two years.

Sometimes Mr Bevins will go there to listen to God, or he will send those he perceives are in danger of backsliding to go there to watch and pray. When he's angry Father threatens me with it, usually if I've been too talkative or too demanding. I've always been afraid of being sent there, locked up all day in the cold with no fire and nothing but the mousy scratching of Naomi and the sea and the gulls for company.

Suddenly there's a fanfare and a blink of light coming from her bed. There's a halo around her hair. She's looking at something, her phone.

'How did you get that?'

'Go away,' she growls.

She turns over so she's lying on her back and I can see she has her phone held above her face.

'You're not supposed to have that.'

She grunts.

She's scrolling through photos. I get flashes of images, the light changing against her face. When one picture comes up she looks at it for a long time.

'I don't suppose you've got a computer here with the Internet?' she asks, her voice muffled by the sleeping bag.

I shrug. 'I don't know. Maybe in the office.'

'Huh. Didn't think so.'

That makes me cross. 'The Internet is a gateway to a world of sin,' I say. 'It's not important to us. That's the point of living off the grid.'

She sighs. 'I suppose I should have known people like you wouldn't be on Facebook.'

'Is that a religious book?'

She snorts. 'A religious book! Ha!' Then she looks at me funny, sort of hard, like she's trying to see inside me. 'Seriously? This place is really freaky——'

'We're not freaky!' I say. 'It's the world that's all wrong! Everyone who doesn't believe is going to hell!'

'Yeah, exactly, like I said: freaky.'

31

This just makes me confused. I curl into the blankets. I don't want her to think I'm freaky. We're silent for a while.

'The island's really nice,' I try again. 'It's beautiful.' Which is true. On a sunny day the whole place is like heaven itself, the deep blue of the sea, the springy turf, the birds, the cliffs like cathedrals. Mr Bevins says it's easier to be close to God in such an elemental place. 'We're blessed by Him,' I say.

'What if God is a woman?' she says.

'But He's not!'

'But how do you know?' She has this way of asking nosy, insistent questions.

'Because it says in the Bible.'

'Oh yeah, I forgot. *That*. Look, if it's OK with you, I'm just going to be here for a couple of months to pick up some skills and then I'll be on my way. I don't have anything against your religion and stuff, but please don't expect me to want to *talk* about it, OK?'

'What do you want to talk about then?'

'I don't know. Maybe I don't want to talk right now. If that's OK with you.'

'OK.'

There aren't many other young people on New Canaan. I'm glad she's coming with us. I lie in the dark a long time looking at the silhouette of her shoulder, listening as her breathing softens into sleep, my thoughts whirring.

Hannah wakes us early for a prayer meeting, which I doze nearly all the way through. Alex sits next to me, twitching the whole time. Since we got up she's been sulky and silent, just grunting at me, or pretending to ignore me. I don't know what to say to her to make it better. I wonder if it's my fault. I don't want her to hate me.

Afterwards the pastor drives us down to the harbour in the Church van. The van is full of boxes, right up to the roof; some of the Church members helped us pack it after the prayer meeting. We won't be getting deliveries again for a while, unless the Church has scheduled a visit, so everything counts. The jars of peanut butter and tins of baked beans will be used up first, then the tubs of sugar and flour will slowly dwindle until there is nothing and we will be on fasting rations again until there's a delivery or a visit to the mainland in a couple of months. I wonder how everyone is doing with the harvest and if the weather there has been as bad as it is here. I long to see the land again, the greenhouse tomatoes that I have nurtured since they were tiny seedlings. I love this time of year – the harvest is like our reward for all the hard work.

The tide is high at ten and the best time to get out of the harbour smoothly is just as it is on the turn, pulling the boat back out to sea with hardly a need of the engine. It will take six or seven hours to get there, maybe more depending on the swell. It's why no one ever comes except by appointment or accident. And it's one of the hardest islands to land a boat on because of the way the tides sweep around the rocks at the mouth of the harbour.

Alex scowls when she sees the boat.

'What's wrong?'

'It's rusty!'

The *Spirit of the Sea* is an old fishing boat with a closed cabin. I suppose it does look a bit scruffy, but it got us here OK. Terry, a local fisherman who worships at the Church, is making ready, checking his radio and electrics, coiling the ropes that keep the boat secured to the jetty.

'It's fine,' I say.

Alex looks sceptical. 'What happens if I change my mind?'

Father has overheard, and he puts his arm on Alex's shoulder. 'Put your trust in the Lord, Alex. All will be well. You'll see.'

She grunts as if she doesn't believe it. 'Seriously? What if it sinks or something?'

Hannah laughs. 'Don't be hysterical. Terry does this journey all the time. Come on, give us a hand.'

Alex gives her a dirty look and mutters to herself.

We pass the boxes into the hold. The wind has dropped since yesterday, but it's still grey and gloomy with a thin cloak of cold drizzle. The hull is rusting in places, bubbling through the paintwork and scarring it. The boat dips and sways as I step from the jetty to the deck, which smells really strongly of fish. My feet slip in the wet and I nearly drop a box.

'Careful!' Father shouts. He seems really angry about something, I'm not sure what. In the prayer meeting this morning one of the congregation had a prophecy. A passage from the Book of Samuel about David and Goliath, in which David hurls a stone at the giant and kills him. There was lots of discussion about its meaning, but then we had to go. The pastor said he would pray for it to be revealed, but it seems to have made Father nervous and anxious to get back to the island.

When the hold and half of the small cabin are packed with our stuff, we stand on the harbour road pulling on our waterproof clothes.

'The time is soon at hand, Brother,' the pastor says to Father as he shakes his hand. 'I'll be seeing you in the glory before I see you here again.'

Father nods, but he doesn't seem too happy about it. 'Well, I hope so.'

'Come on. Let's not be pessimistic.'

I wonder what's happened, but when Father catches me watching he shoos me away. 'Go on, Rebekah, get ready.'

We wear bright red trousers and coats that smell of mildew from the boatshed. I have to roll the skirt of my dress up into a bunch around my middle in order to get the trousers on. There was some discussion about us being allowed to wear trousers at all, but they decided in the end that there was no alternative, although Hannah did suggest that they had solutions for these things in the Middle East, but as that would have meant buying clothes from the Internet it was decided that waterproofs would be allowed just for the length of the boat journey. Gulls circle above us, and rigging clangs as the boats in the harbour bob on the rising tide.

The pastor drives off in the van and we all jump onboard, Terry unhitches the rope from its moorings and the boat slips quickly into the tide and out of the harbour to the open sea. I huddle in the cabin with Hannah on top of some of the catering tins of sugar and flour that Terry has lashed to the sides to stop them falling over. Alex won't sit with us; she insists on standing outside with Father and Terry.

'I want to see where I'm going,' she says, pulling up the hood of her windcheater and zipping it so I can see only her eyes. 'How long does it take?' she asks.

I shrug. 'Six hours,' I say.

Immediately the boat is in the open sea it starts to dip and roll in the swell. It's much choppier than on the way over, in the calm, when the water was so smooth and clear it was almost a lake. The tins shift underneath me and I have to grab on to the ropes to stop myself from slipping off.

Before long we are out of sight of the mainland; the cliffs and the mountains disappear into the murk behind us, and ahead nothing

35

but the folds of the sea. The engine drones against the hiss and roar of the ocean as it slams against the boat. The waves are tipped with white foam, which after a while become hypnotic as we lurch in between the peaks and troughs, and I don't notice that Alex is sick until she's bending over the side of the boat, hurling into the spray.

I go out to her, the full force of the wind a shock after the shelter of the cabin.

'Come inside,' I shout, grabbing on to her arm. But she shrugs me off.

'Please make it stop,' she says. Her face is pale as milk; she turns away from me and heaves again. 'Haven't you got any tablets or anything?'

Terry clambers around the edge towards us holding a yellow plastic bucket. 'You need to sit inside, *cariad*.'

When we finally get her inside the cabin, she sits on the floor with the bucket between her knees. When I offer her a drink of water she just shakes her head and tells me to go away.

Fine then, I think, be like that. I go back outside.

All there is to look at is the sea: white foam churning under the mist that makes the horizon close in around us. Sometimes in the angles of the waves I'm sure I can see other things: the dark shapes of whales, other boats, shadows that fill me with dread. There is a sudden flutter as we cut through a group of kittiwakes rising and turning on the air ahead of us, then settling back into the water. The engine drones on and on, and in spite of all my waterproofs I am getting cold and damp and the constant cycle of tensing and relaxing is making my stomach churn too.

Minutes later I'm sat next to Alex on the floor of the boat, heaving into the bucket. Mostly water, but my stomach has finally given in. Alex is lying down, groaning.

'Don't you have any seasickness medicine?'

'We don't believe in it.'

'What d'you mean?'

'Medicines are of the world of men. We don't believe in them.'

'W-what are you on about?' She sits up. 'I want to go back. You have to take me back right now!' But she says this without much conviction because she is struck by another fit of retching.

Hannah, who seems to be totally unaffected, sits staring out to sea. 'Live for the Victory!' she says. 'Won't be long now. Look, there it is.'

In the distance, rising out of the clouds, is the shape of land. The sharp peaks of the Devil's Seat shrouded in mist, and the cliffs fringed with the white haze of sea spray. Home.

For a long while the island hangs on the horizon like a vision, not getting any closer, as if the boat is not moving forward but wallowing in the chop. The wind picks up and the rain returns, misting the windows of the cabin so that it's hard to see anything at all. The light is beginning to dim, although it's the summer and the sky never gets truly dark. It feels as if we've been on this boat for weeks not hours. I lie down on the floor, the metal cool against my hot cheeks. Alex lies next to me, curled up like a baby. Her eyes are tight shut and her cheeks are a kind of pale green. She looks really sick.

'I'm sorry,' I say. As if it's my fault that she's sick.

'How much longer?' she mumbles.

'Not long,' I say, and the next time I raise my head from the deck I see the cliffs of New Canaan looming high above us, close enough now to make out the crags and scars of the cliff-face, and the birds – fulmars and gannets and gulls – swirling above us in great numbers.

I stand up unsteadily. Father is still outside with Terry. Against the cliffs we are tiny. This is the most dangerous part of the journey. The bay is a natural harbour, sheltered by the cliffs on three sides and from the sea by a line of half-submerged rocks; to get in and out a boat has to navigate a narrow channel between the rocks and the cliffs. When the weather is rough it's almost impossible because the transition from the calm tidal wash of the harbour to the boil of the open sea would take any boat and overwhelm it or fling it against the sharp rocks. Here the sea is at its most dangerous. Sailors call this the Hag's Cauldron.

All around us the surf booms, big breakers that are more like the winter sea than anything you'd expect in the summer. I can see the narrow gap in the waves that will take us to the harbour, but the boat seems so unsteady, even at full power, against the sea that pulls us in many different directions at once. The captain keeps the boat steady and aims the prow. A huge wave lifts us up sideways, water crashing down over the side, and for a second I think we won't make it, but the engine pushes us through and suddenly we're in the calmer water of the harbour.

Once we are away from the open sea everything is quieter. The waves ripple rather than crash. Seals loll on the rocks, watching us with eyes like black moons. I can smell them too, the fishy stink of their breath. I open the door of the cabin; the noise has changed from the battering of the open sea to the lap of the water and the chug of the boat's engine.

Straight ahead rises a line of trees, stunted willow and hazel and knotted blackthorn. This island is the only one with trees, because of how this sheltered bay gives way to a hollow gorge, worn away by the water that flows constantly from the higher ground. Here in the hollow, small trees flourish away from the scour of the wind and salt. From the top of the Devil's Seat it looks like a deep gash in the landscape, filled with lush green in the summer, and in the winter a brown tangle of twigs and twisted branches.

The harbour is bigger than it looks when approached from the sea, stretching around into a narrow estuary, the mouth of the only river on the island. There is a jetty and a boathouse and above that three stone cottages – the harbour dwellings, where Jonathan and Daniel live, and a smokehouse. At the end of the jetty is a wooden board that Jonathan painted that says, *Welcome to New Canaan*, in big letters. There is no sign of anyone, which is surprising, as usually there are folk waiting when the boat comes in. No lights in the cottages, no smoke rising from the smokehouse. They must all be away at the farmhouse, which is over the ridge and on the other side of the hollow, on the flat plateau of fields we call Moriah.

Terry ties the boat to the small wooden jetty, but the tide is low so we have to pull ourselves up on to it, which is difficult because I'm still dizzy from the seasickness. Alex climbs up next to me and immediately lies down on her belly.

'Rebekah, come on!' Father hands me a box. 'Quickly.'

Terry wants us to unload fast because he wants to get going straight back to the mainland in the window of the tide.

'Where *is* everyone?' They should have known we were coming. I thought Father spoke to Bevins yesterday.

'I don't know.' He puts his hands on his hips and scans the shoreline. 'We haven't got time to worry about that now.'

Together we unload. Terry and Father pass boxes to me and Hannah and we lift them up on to the jetty. Some of them are really heavy and my arms are wrenched in their sockets, lifting the tubs of

39

sugar and flour. Alex lies in our way until I kick her.

'Ow.' She sits up.

'You're in the way,' I say. I feel sick too, but this is no time to be indulgent. I dump a heavy box of tinned fruit at her feet.

'I feel dizzy.'

'So do I,' I say, glaring at her.

So anxious is Terry to get back home that the moment the last box has been unloaded and Father has leaped out of the boat, he casts off and sets out for the open sea again. Now everything has to be carried along the rickety jetty to the boathouses, box by box.

Alex stands up and looks at the pile. 'Where's my bag?' she asks, her voice rising.

I look at the stuff; there's no sign of her duffel bag. I don't remember seeing it when we unloaded.

'The green one?' Father says. 'I thought that was Terry's.'

We all look to the boat, which is already navigating the gap in the rocks into the Hag's Cauldron, lifted up by the sea like a cork. Too late.

'NO!' Blood rushes back to her face. 'That's all my stuff!'

She runs to the end of the jetty and waves her arms. 'Come back!' She looks ready to throw herself in and swim after the boat. She waves frantically, but it's too far away now. 'NO!' When she turns to us there are tears in her eyes. 'That was all my stuff!'

'Oh well,' Father says, a bit too nonchalant. I wonder if he's done this on purpose. When people come to New Canaan they are expected to leave their old world behind. 'You can borrow some clothes from Rebekah. We'll get Terry to bring it back with the next boat.'

'When will that be?'

Father shrugs. 'A couple of months.'

'A couple of *months*?' Alex bites her lip as if she has just realized something very serious. She looks as if she might want to kill us. Instead she walks off the jetty and sits on some rocks next to the boathouse. When I walk past her, carrying heavy boxes, I can see her face is wet and red from crying. It's not my fault. If she'd helped us she might have noticed that her bag was missing. I fight a sudden surge of irritation. Why did she have to come here and make everything awkward and difficult? It's not fair.

# FIVE

# ALEX

At first I was so wrecked it was hard to put everything together. I lay on the jetty with my face pressed into the boards and my stomach wanting to come back out of my mouth. The whole world moved up and down like a wave, as if everything was liquid. If I closed my eyes my head spun so fast I thought I was going to throw up again, even though there was nothing left to come up.

I tried to lie still, aware that they were unloading the boat around me. I focused on the boards of the jetty. The green slime that grew along the waterline, the seaweed that slapped and flopped against the shore, the smell of salt and rot. For a while I didn't really care where I was; I was just glad not to be out at sea any more, on a boat that dipped like the sickest kind of fairground ride.

But when the puke feeling started to subside I was taken with another, scarier kind of feeling. There was something wrong with this place, and it wasn't just the fading light or the way the trees grew right down to the water, their roots like tangled fingers, or the ruined buildings further along the shore, or the peeling, battered sign that said: *Welcome to New Canaan. Behold the Lord your God has set the land before you*, that looked like it was done by someone who couldn't write. It was all of these things, and the fact that even though there was no one there I had this really strange impression that I was being watched. And Rebekah was suddenly being mean, even though I could tell from her face she felt as sick as me. I couldn't believe I'd ever thought that coming here was a good idea.

And then I realized they'd forgotten to unload my stuff and the boat had taken off again with my bag still on it, and I was stuck and I had none of my things, and I looked at Rebekah's father smirking at me, like he was trying to teach me a lesson, and I wanted to be sick all over again. If my legs weren't so weak I would have run at him and pushed him in the water and punched him, and I was so angry I could probably have killed him, but instead I started crying, which I hated because it made me feel small and pointless.

It wasn't so much my clothes, it was my stuff. The diary with the only photograph of my mother that I own, a blurry Polaroid of her making a peace sign, with a tie-dye scarf wrapped around her head. Some cards that people made me when I left the home. Stuff like that. I *needed* to have them; they reminded me who I was, and that made me cry even harder, and then it started to rain.

Rebekah stood next to me and held out a dirty piece of rag. 'Why are you crying?'

'I'm not crying.' I wiped my eyes with my sleeve. She was like my little shadow. I couldn't be anywhere without her looking at me.

'You don't need to cry here. You're in the blessed place.'

'What?' She seriously had to stop with all that God stuff.

'You're in the place blessed by the Lord.'

'You just said that.' She sounded like a toy where you press a button and it repeats the same thing. Sometimes I wondered if all religious ideas were like that, just the same words in a different order, repeated over and over until people thought they were true.

'You should be happy. Mr Bevins will help you.'

'Will he get a boat to take me back?'

She looked a bit disappointed. 'But you've only just got here!'

'I know, and now I want to go home!'

She folded her arms. 'You've got to give it a chance!'

'Well, you *can't* keep me here!' It was like someone had put pincers around my chest and was squeezing out all of the air. I had to take a deep breath to stop myself from panicking. 'It's against the law!'

Her father heard this and came over to us. He put his hand on my shoulder. It sat there heavily, like a warning.

'We live by God's laws here,' he said. 'No one is keeping you here, except through our Lord Jesus, your saviour.'

'Amen,' Hannah muttered.

I didn't like her. She was sneaky. I'd caught her staring at me, looking disapproving. She'd got the kind of face that looked angry most of the time, except that she really simpered around Rebekah's father. Probably fancied him or something.

'You can go back on the next boat if that's what you want. But right now we have to get that –' he pointed at the pile of boxes on the jetty – 'into the boathouse before the rain comes.' He nodded at a dilapidated wooden shack that sat above the shoreline.

I closed my eyes, hoping that it was a bad dream and when I opened my eyes I'd be back in Essex and everything would be back the way it was supposed to be.

'You're expected to be part of things here, you know. Every one of us has to do our bit,' he said.

'I thought all this had all been explained to her,' Hannah said to Rebekah's father, impatiently, as if I was not standing right in front of her and could hear exactly what she was saying. I gave her an evil glare.

It took a long time to carry all the supplies and stash them in the boathouse. Hannah seemed to give me the heaviest boxes to carry, almost on purpose.

'Strong for a girl, aren't you?' she said, tightly. I ignored her, but made a mental note to steer clear of her as much as I could while I was there.

Inside the boathouse was a small wooden dinghy with an outboard motor. Didn't look up to much, but at least it was there. If the worst came to the worst I supposed I could take off in that, set off a flare or something, get the coastguard to come and rescue me. This thought made being there much easier to bear.

We stacked everything against the walls, and by the time we'd finished I was sweaty and cold and starving hungry and my arms ached. Now the wind had picked up too, blowing the strengthening rain sideways in stinging lashes. It was getting hard to see in the gloomy twilight. Rebekah's father lit a couple of paraffin lanterns and gave one to me and Rebekah, and one to Hannah, taking a torch for himself, but the batteries were going and it only gave off a tepid sort of light.

Up above the boathouse was a small paved road with a row of stone cottages which looked tumbledown and uninhabitable, except they had new roofs made out of corrugated iron. There didn't seem to be anyone around. Beyond the row of houses the path wound up the hill through a wood. It was hard to see where it went in the dark, and where the stones petered out the path became a muddy channel and my feet slipped, and my shoes, already wet, were now squelching and soaked through. I turned back and looked at the sea. An impulse to run to the boathouse and put the boat in the water, to get away, before it was too late, nearly overwhelmed me.

But there she was again, her moon face even paler in the lamplight. 'Come on!' she said. 'Follow me!'

I stared at her doubtfully. 'Is it safe?'

'Of course!' she said, although she didn't sound convincing, and her eyes slid away and wouldn't meet mine. 'I'm sorry about your stuff.'

I shrugged as if I didn't care. But I did, very much; I just didn't want her to see. I followed her through the mud, my heart in my mouth. The trees gave us some protection from the weather, but it was dark and boggy under the canopy and the spikes of the blackthorn clawed and snagged on my clothes. As we climbed, the trees got sparser, until eventually we were on a heathland where there were sheep wandering, and above the horizon I could see the rotor of a windmill and the roof of a house, and next to it a church, but strangely there were no lights on anywhere. I didn't like this place. Not one little bit.

# SIX

# REBEKAH

Once the seasickness has subsided, I'm glad to be home. The familiar smell of the bracken and the heather, the rocks and moss, and the good earth. And I'm looking forward to seeing Mr Bevins, showing him how I survived the mission, how we brought him a new recruit, although I'm a bit hazy on the circumstances. Usually people come with us who want to be part of New Canaan, rather than because they have been brought to us. Father says we are looking after Alex for a while because Ron and Bridget cannot, and that it's all a part of God's plan.

We walk up the hill through the woods to the houses, Alex dawdling behind me, still looking queasy. She's frightened, although I've done my best to reassure her.

'Is it safe?' she asks.

What a question! She should know she is safer here than anywhere, away from all the temptation of the world of sin.

'Course!'

The farmhouse and the church and all the cabins that surround it squat in a hollow that protects them from the worst of the north winds. The farmhouse and the harbour dwellings were the only stone buildings on the island still standing when we moved here. The rest were built from scratch. Wood for the cabins and the kitchen and the church was brought over on boats, and Micah and Father and Mr Bevins and a group of men from the mainland helped to build them. I was only little then. I don't really remember it, except in strange snapshots: Father hitting his thumb with a hammer so that his nail went black; the clean, pine smell of the church when it was new; the meeting we had to bless the community; and Mother saying to me that we were lucky to live like this, joyful and free at the edge of the world.

Hurrying now, we get to the vegetable fields, and even in the dark I can see the crops have not been harvested. Rows of runner beans spill into the path, tangled and overgrown, the pods split and spoiled. Father stops to look at a row of peas that are white with mildew, pods rotting on the plants.

'What's happened?' My heart quickens. Something's not right.

'I don't know.'

'Urgh, slugs,' Alex says, holding her lantern up to show dark blobs of slime munching through a row of lettuces that are almost nothing but stalks now. I planted those as seedlings, back in the spring. This time of year it would be someone's task for the day to set slug traps and harvest what's ready. Losing crops means losing meals. It's as if nothing at all has been done in the two weeks we've been gone. My heart sinks. All the little seedlings I nurtured, all spoiled.

'Very odd,' Father mutters to himself.

The only thing that seems to have been harvested is the patch of poppies we grew for Mr Bevins by the polytunnels. There are one or two plants with flowers still to unfurl, but most of them have been taken. All the seed heads look as if they've been snipped off.

As we get closer I can make out the white planks of the church. The roof is made of tarpaper and lined with plastic sheeting that flaps loudly in the wind. But there is no light, nor sound of any singing. Next to the church is a row of simple cabins, where live

48

the Braggs, the Webbers, the Morgans, Hannah and Margaret, Ruth and Esther, Gideon and David. The last cabin is empty since the Collins family left: they went to the mainland with Terry to get supplies and never came back. Altogether, there are nearly forty of us living here at any one time.

Ahead of us is the farmhouse. Usually there would be at least a few people here. This is the hub of the community and where I sleep, in the attic with the twins. The ground floor is fashioned into two big rooms, one a kitchen in which we prepare all our food, and another a dining room, where everyone eats at a big table. Leading off the kitchen is a wooden extension called the tack room, where we hold morning meetings and store equipment and where on a big whiteboard the daily tasks are written, and beyond that are the compost toilets and a pump where we can fill buckets with water for the house and for the cabins.

We enter through the tack room. The door is swollen and it takes a hard tug to pull it open. The room is cold and the whiteboard has no tasks on it, only: *Live for the Victory!* And underneath it a scribbled verse from the Book of Revelation:

*Behold, He cometh with clouds; and every eye shall see Him.*

'What's that supposed to mean?' Alex asks. Her voice is bit higher now; she sounds more like a girl.

'Hello?' Father shouts, but no one answers in welcome. 'Hello?'

He switches on the light, but the electricity is off. This means no one has switched over the battery, either that or they've forgotten to recharge it.

We still take our shoes off and thud our way across the wooden floor to the kitchen. Father shines his torch around the room. The hearth is swept and the plates and cups are all neatly stacked, but there's no sign of an evening meal or that anyone has even been here recently, except that the huge pan that is usually hung above the fire is on the table. There is a nasty-smelling ring of muddy residue around the rim.

A chill passes through me.

'Where is everybody?' Alex asks, coming closer to me.

'I don't know.'

'This is really freaky.' She shivers. 'What's going on?'

'Do you think——' Hannah starts, but Father shushes her.

'Not now, Hannah,' he says. 'Wait here.'

He goes into the dining room, and then upstairs. I can hear the floorboards creaking as he moves about above us.

Hannah puts her lantern on the table so it casts a dark shadow across the walls. 'They must be in church,' she says.

'But we passed it and there weren't any lights on,' I say.

'They may have been in silent prayer.'

'With the twins?'

Three years ago Mary Protheroe gave birth to twins, a surprise and a happiness, especially because, as Mary said, no one was getting any younger, although there was much discussion among the men about whether it was right to raise babies on New Canaan. But if Mary was to leave it would mean losing Micah too, as no one could imagine them separated. So the farmhouse became suddenly noisy again with babies and crying, and Father and Mr Bevins found it very irritating when the crying interrupted the prayers or the sermons. Once Mr Bevins even went so far as to tell Mary that their crying was a sign of her own faithlessness, and she should be ashamed and take a tighter control over their discipline.

'Perhaps . . .' She pauses, then she looks away as if she does not want to say what is on her mind. 'Do you think they've . . . been *Raptured*?' she whispers.

This sends a cold chill through me, but she is only saying what has already crossed my mind.

'What are you talking about?' Alex asks. 'Where is everyone? This place is creeping me out.'

'Well, where else would they be?' Hannah says definitively. 'The Rapture is the only answer.'

'What are you talking about?'

'Taken to heaven,' Hannah says, her voice breaking. 'Which means we've been *left behind*.'

Alex wrinkles her nose. 'O-*kay*.'

They *can't* have been Raptured. It would be so unfair for God to leave us when we were doing his work. If only I hadn't gone on the stupid Mission Week in the first place. Maybe it was because I was so desperate to go, and I forgot to pray because I was so excited. Maybe I should have been quieter, less demanding. I shouldn't have been thinking so much about Alex. There's a scratchy lump developing in my throat. I bite my lip to stop the tears from rising.

Father comes back downstairs. 'There's no one here.' He looks puzzled.

'Hannah thinks they've been Raptured,' I say.

He tuts. 'I expect Bevins has taken them somewhere for prayer. That's all. They'll be in the church. We spoke yesterday! Live for the Victory, Hannah, live for the Victory.'

Outside the wind has got up. A heavy gust rattles the doors and I jump nervously. None of us speaks. In the silence and the dark it seems that anything is possible.

Mr Bevins has told us many times what will happen when the saved are Raptured. How planes will fall out of the sky because the pilots have just vanished and gone to heaven, how banks will stop working, money will stop flowing, food will stop being distributed. For those left behind the world will be a nightmare. There will be wars, and armed gangs who will eat people, and the world will be ruled by the Antichrist who will turn everything upside down, making the good bad and the bad good. Mr Bevins has visions of this all the time. He says God has blessed him with foreknowledge so that he can warn others. In church his prophesying is very convincing. He says that any who doubt, who don't truly put their whole heart and soul, their whole life, into believing, will be left behind to deal with this chaos for seven years before the final judgement comes.

'I'm going to look for them,' Father says. 'You stay here.'

'No!' Hannah says. 'Don't leave us.'

'I thought you spoke to Mr Bevins yesterday?' I say.

Father pauses, bites his lip. 'I did.'

'I knew it, we've been left behind!' Hannah wails.

'Hannah, don't be silly,' Father says, but I know he isn't convinced.

Alex is staring at us, her eyes wide. She looks terrified. 'What are you on about? Shouldn't we be looking for them? They can't have just *vanished*.'

If the others have been Raptured, then we alone are left to bring in the crops and run the whole farm and all the livestock and there won't be enough of us to manage. And I don't know what it is that I might have done to have been left behind. I look at Alex, her hair turned wild by the sea and the weather, and wonder if it's possible to catch her sinfulness like a cold.

'I think we should look for them first. We would have had warning,' Hannah says. 'He wouldn't abandon us, not like this.' But her face is drained of colour.

'OK,' Father says. 'You two stay here.' He means Alex and me. 'We'll go and check the church.'

We sit in front of the empty fireplace. The wind rattles the tiles, and currents of cold air snake about the kitchen like spirits. My mind races through the implications. If we have been left behind, then everything is going to get really difficult. There will be seven years of Tribulations to put up with before I can finally see my mother.

Alex curls herself up on the bench like a woodlouse when you touch it. 'I'm freezing,' she says.

There's a dirty yellow sweater thrown over one of the chairs. It belongs to Jonathan; I've seen him wearing it in the fields. I give it to her. The sweater comes down nearly to her knees like a dress.

She looks at me fearfully. 'Rub my arms,' she says. I hesitate. 'Please.'

I sit next to her and put my arms around her shoulders. Her wet hair smells of seaweed. I rub her arms until a warmth rises in my hands and in her body.

'I want to go back,' she mutters. 'I don't like it.' She's rocking backwards and forwards. 'I should never have let them persuade me.' She gets her phone out of her pocket and switches it on.

On the home screen I can see there's a picture of her and a girl with blonde hair. They are hugging and leaning into the camera and laughing.

'Thought so.' She points at the top of the screen. It says: *No Service*.

'So?'

'So that means I can't get any signal. You have a satellite phone, right?'

'Yes.'

'Well, where is it?'

'I don't know. Mr Bevins keeps it. In his cabin maybe?'

'We need to get a message out there. For once in my life it would be a relief to speak to the police.'

'You can't do that!'

'Why not?'

'Because . . .' *Because I don't want you to leave yet.* 'Because maybe we should pray.'

'What good's that going to do? Send a message to your imaginary friend to go and get help? That's *really* going to work.'

I get up and pull out my witness kit from my bag. I took this with me on Mission Week but I never had a chance to use it. I sit next to her and open the old biscuit tin. There's a wooden cross, and a bottle of holy water from the font in the church that Mr Bevins blessed, and a small bottle of olive oil for anointing the saved.

I clutch the cross in my hand and hold it over Alex's head. I close my eyes and try to think of God, although I have always found it hard to picture what He might look like. Most of the time I see someone who looks sometimes like Father and sometimes like Mr Bevins. Some of our number can hear Him speaking. I have often wondered what He might sound like. Sometimes if I listen very, very hard I believe I can hear something, a faraway murmuring over the loud sound of my heartbeat.

'What are you doing?!' Alex squirms away, but I ignore her.

'Dear God, thank You for bringing us here safely.'

'Why are you saying thank you? That journey was horrible! And there's no one here! We're not safe! I mean, I'm sorry, but I'm going back and you can't stop me.'

'Please, God, will You help her to see the light while she is here with us. And if You have taken the others, please take us too.'

I dip my finger in the holy water and flick it on her face.

'Urgh! Get off!' She pushes my arm so I spill some of the water on the floor. 'What did you do that for?!'

'It's holy water, for purifying your soul.'

She takes the bottle and looks at it. It's an old plastic one that is scratched and the label is torn, a part of it missing. '*Bottled at source in North Wales*. That's not holy water.' She sniffs it. 'It smells off.'

'It's not off! It's been blessed!'

She passes it back to me. 'Well, it hasn't made me holy. I mean, I'm not glowing or anything, am I? Look at it! You're pathetic – that crap's not holy!' She turns away from me. 'Who are you people anyway? I want to go back. I don't even have my stuff.' And her voice cracks a little and she sounds as if she's going to cry.

'I'm sorry,' I say. I pack my witness things away in the biscuit tin. She's right, it is a bit pathetic and I am suddenly ashamed and confused.

She stands up. 'C'mon. We should go and find that phone. We need to tell people that something's happened.'

'Can't. We've got to wait here.'

'Why? Because you were *told*? Don't you have a mind of your own?'

I'm about to tell her that obedience is one of our holy responsibilities when there is a noise, at first like an animal – I think it could be Job, Micah Protheroe's dog, whimpering – but then I realize it's actually a child crying.

Alex jumps. 'Did you hear that?'

I nod. I hold my breath and listen again. This time it's louder, a kind of mewling, and there's a rattle on the bolted door by the pantry that leads to the cellar.

My blood turns to cold ice in my veins.

'What the hell?'

Both of us stare at the door.

'Help,' the small voice says.

I recognize it, but I don't want to acknowledge that it is true.

# SEVEN

# REBEKAH

I draw the bolt across and open the door. Standing there, blinking into the dim light, is Paul Protheroe. His three-year-old face sooty with coal dust and streaked with tears. He looks sleepy and disorientated.

'What happened?' I scoop him up in my arms. 'Where's Peter?'

'Down.' He nods into the darkness behind him.

'Oh,' I say, trying not to sound horrified. Sometimes if the boys are naughty Mary might shut them down there, but only when there are other people around and only for a few minutes to stop them crying. Mostly she or Micah uses the rod, as it is set out in the Bible and as Mr Bevins insists, like Father did to me.

'Shit,' Alex says. 'Literally.' She points to his trousers where he has soiled himself.

'Get him a glass of water.' I push him towards Alex. He really does stink; I wonder how long he's been down there.

I take the lantern and climb down the rickety stairs.

'Peter?' My voice is deadened by the low ceiling. I don't understand. If everyone else has been Raptured, why did God not take the twins? Why would He leave them?

The cellar is really just a small space half the size of the kitchen, where we store the coal for the house. As it's summer it's nearly empty, just full of dust, except in one corner where I find Peter lying on what's left of the coal. Like his brother he's filthy, but he's fast asleep. Even when I pick him up he doesn't wake. His head lolls back over my arm and he's freezing cold. Since I've been away he's got heavier and it's a struggle to carry him back upstairs. He is so fast asleep he doesn't even wake when I accidentally bang his head against the door frame.

'He fell asleep!' I say, trying to sound bright, as if it was a regular thing. I don't know what else to do. But Alex is sitting at the kitchen table holding Paul in her lap, looking frightened.

'He's completely out of it,' Alex says. 'Someone's given them drugs.'

I sit down next to her and look at Paul. Now she mentions it, his eyes are dozy and unfocused, and he looks like he too might fall asleep at any minute. 'No. They're just tired.'

Alex shrugs, 'I'm telling you, they've been drugged. One foster home I went to, the woman used to give the kids nips of Jim Beam to make them sleep.'

'Who's Jim Beam?'

She sucks her teeth. 'Whiskey, bourbon, *alcohol*. Don't you know *anything*?'

In the past I would have been proud not to know about the world; all I needed to know was about this island and of the earth. The way that seeds grow into plants, the turning of the seasons, the path to heaven clearly laid out before us, no distractions. But since I met Alex my mind is full of questions. I want to know what she knows, to see what she sees with my own eyes. She thinks I'm stupid, and more than anyone I've ever met I don't want her to think that about me.

'Whatever's in that pan,' Alex says, pointing at the pot on the kitchen table, 'it doesn't smell right to me.'

I hold Peter tight to my chest. He's slightly smaller than his brother. They both have the same dark hair as their father and Mary's strong features, but they are quiet, watchful boys. I shake him gently, 'Peter? Peter? What happened?'

But he can't answer me.

'I *told* you,' Alex says. 'They're totally out of it.'

Then a gust of wind blows through the kitchen, followed by heavy footsteps in the tack room. I think Father and Hannah must have come back, but they haven't. The kitchen door swings open and it's Jonathan, and he's soaking wet, shivering like a dog, and his eyes are huge and black as marbles, like he's just seen something he shouldn't.

'Light the fire, light the fire,' he mutters, over and over. 'I couldn't take it any more. I couldn't do it.'

He picks up a handful of kindling sticks, but he's trembling so much he drops them on the floor. He hardly seems aware that we're in the room. I lay Peter's sleeping body on the table and pick the kindling up and lay it on the grate and set a match to it until there is a small fire. He hops from foot to foot, rubbing his arms, and trembles like a wet dog.

'Jonathan, what's happened?' I say slowly. 'Where is everyone? Why were the twins locked in the cellar?'

'Mr Bevins has seen it! The gates of heaven! We've been praying for two days. He told me to watch for signs, but I was just so cold I couldn't stay out there any more!'

I put a few lumps of coal on top of the kindling. We have to be careful not to use too much fuel. We will need all we can get our hands on in the winter. Jonathan radiates cold and wet and he smells of outdoors. Of soil and air. But more than that, he smells sharp like a spooked animal.

'I won't make it! What if I don't make it?' He babbles about heaven's gate and auras and lights in the sky, but he's not making any sense. Alex looks horrified. I don't want her to see us like this; it isn't what we're about. This isn't what usually happens here. I talk to him softly. *It's OK, calm down, everything's going to be OK.*

When Jonathan first came to the island he was still withdrawing from drugs. He would cry in the prayer services, big heavy sobs, and when he gave his testimony he could hardly speak he got so upset. He said he left home at fourteen because he was being abused, and never knew a real family until he came to live with us. He said he was so grateful to be accepted at last, that he had never felt a love so strong and true. He struggles every day and has to get extra prayers from the elders to help him with his bad thoughts. Thoughts which he says come straight from the devil, that tell him to do bad things to himself.

As the fire rises I shovel on more and more coal and he stands awkwardly in front of it, his clothes steaming in the sudden heat.

As the shaking subsides, he notices Alex.

'Who's that?' he says in a loud whisper to me as if Alex can't hear.

I put my hand on his arm and he nearly jumps clean out of his skin. 'It's OK,' I say. 'She's come here to live with us for a while. We've been away, remember?'

'You're her!' he says, backing away from Alex. 'You're the reason we've been praying all week! Mr Bevins said that a visitor would come from the mainland. It's happening . . . just like he said!'

Alex stands up, holding Paul on her hip, and backs away from him. 'You're nuts,' she says.

'Where are the others, Jonathan? Where's Mary? Why were the twins locked in the cellar?' I talk to him slowly. 'What's happened?' But I can tell he isn't taking anything in. He kneels in front of the fire, his hands pressed together, muttering prayers.

'What the hell's wrong with him?' she hisses, sounding scared.

'It's OK,' I whisper. 'He's just a bit intense.' We back away from the fire and settle back at the kitchen table, while he ignores us. I look at the pot on the table suspiciously and sniff it. It smells bitter, of mud and of something else, something chemical that I don't recognize.

Then there is the suck of the door opening and the fire draws, logs sending out sparks. Father and Mary Protheroe come in.

Mary is tall, with a strong, serious face and red rosacea on her cheeks. This makes her look as if she's just been scrubbed, especially when it flares, which it always seems to in the summer. Her hands are gnarly from all the work she does and the beginning of arthritis. She was already quite old when she gave birth to the twins, I don't know how old she is exactly, but Mother told me once that she was over forty, and that was a few years before she got pregnant.

'Where have you been?!' I ask. 'The twins were locked in the cellar!'

She raises her eyebrows at me as if I'm making a fuss. 'They needed to be safe while we were gone,' she says with a shrug, as if it doesn't matter.

'But . . .'

She gives me the kind of look that makes it clear that she doesn't want to talk about it. 'Welcome back,' she says tightly, as if she doesn't really mean it. Her hair is wet and her face is raw.

'But *why* were they in the cellar?' I want her to explain this to Alex as much as to me.

She tuts and shakes her head, she looks at Peter, lifting his eyelids and checking his pulse. 'They're fine! Take them upstairs,' she says, and then, pointing at Alex, 'and her too. She can share your room till we sort something out.'

'But where were you?' I ask. 'No one was here. We thought . . .' but I don't tell her, because now she's here it sounds presumptuous.

'Praying,' she says curtly. 'In fact, the others are still up there.'

'But the chapel lights were off. And Jonathan . . .' He's still kneeling by the fire.

'We were outside, up at the rock.' She says this like a rebuke, as if she's angry with me. Something's been going on while we've been away that I don't understand.

'Oh.' I look at the twins.

'We were praying for . . .' She nods at Alex.

'But why didn't anyone come? We had to unload the boat by ourselves. And why has no one harvested the crops? Where's Mr Bevins?'

'Because we've been praying for your mission. Every day.' When she sees Jonathan she raises her eyebrows. 'Especially *him*. You know how he takes things to heart. We're very close now, Rebekah. There have been signs, movements, the end is in sight.'

'Go on then, off you go. Upstairs,' Father says. 'Everything's OK.'

He goes over to Jonathan and touches him on the shoulder.

'But . . . what about Mr Bevins? What about supper?' I ask.

'He's deep in prayer. You'll see him in the morning. And you don't need any supper after that journey! Best to let your stomach settle!' Father says.

Mary pours us each a glass of water. 'Take this in case you get thirsty in the night.'

They seem desperate to be rid of us.

'But the twins . . . need changing.'

'You can do that, can't you?' She sounds really irritated. 'Just put the dirty clothes in the corner. I'll deal with them in the morning.' She comes over to me and smooths Peter's hair with the flat of her palm. 'They're fine,' she says, 'just a bit dirty.'

I look at her face. Something odd has happened to the person inside her body and, although she sounds like Mary and looks like Mary, she is not being herself.

It's hard to walk upstairs carrying Peter and a lamp and a glass of water. Halfway up I spill most of it down the stairs.

There are two small attic rooms at the top of the house, where the servants used to sleep. I sleep in one and the twins in the other. More often than not they will wake up in the night and get into bed with me.

'I can't believe she'd lock them down there,' I mutter to Alex. She helps me undress them and put them in clean clothes. 'Something weird has happened while we've been gone.'

'Well, *duh*,' she says, like I'm stupid.

I cringe. I don't want her to judge me. 'It's not usually like this, *honestly*.'

But she just tuts like she doesn't believe me.

Once we have the twins changed and tucked up under the blankets as best we can, we leave the door open between the rooms and go into my bedroom, which is cold and dingy in the weak lamplight. From the window I can just see the church if I stand on tiptoe. There are lights and people now. I can hear voices outside and see the floating orange glow of lanterns. They must have come down from the Devil's Seat to pray in the church. I wonder what revelations Bevins has had now. I don't know what time it is, but my stomach is grumbling. I suppose if I go to sleep now, the morning will come quicker.

Alex lies down in my bed and burrows beneath the blankets with all her clothes on. I blow out the lantern and get under the covers. Her arm presses against mine and there's a warmth that spreads between us that makes me suddenly awake. I don't know why, but there's this electric tingle, like an energy between us. I can feel it all through my body. I wonder if she can feel it too.

'In the morning,' she says, 'we're going to find that satellite phone.'

'OK.' Although I don't know how. Mr Bevins keeps his cabin locked, and if anyone saw us we'd be in trouble. She'll learn soon enough that it's hard to do anything here without being seen. And anyway, I don't want her to leave. Maybe in the morning she'll change her mind. I want her to stay here and love this place as much as I do. She just needs to meet Mr Bevins, then she'll see. The wind has dropped and the rain stilled to a constant flat drip. I close my eyes and make a short silent petition to God that, whatever has happened, He will look kindly on me and take me to be with Mother in heaven, and in the meanwhile help me to be a good example to those who are not yet saved, in Jesus's name. Amen. But all night I dream that I am locked in a cellar, running around alone in the dark in a panic because everyone has gone and I have been left behind.

# EIGHT

# ALEX

I woke with the dawn barely edging the curtains, wide awake, damp. I'd hardly slept all night, thinking, planning how I was going to get my hands on that satellite phone. I fell asleep dreaming about it. I wanted to go back and I didn't care if they pressed charges. There was something off about the whole place that made it hard to breathe. The way those boys looked, dirty and disorientated. That woman Mary said it was to keep them safe, but I didn't believe her; someone had given them something to keep them quiet.

I turned over and looked at Rebekah, who was sleeping on her back, one arm flung above her head, her mouth moving gently with the rhythm of her breath. She was so innocent it was dangerous. Anything could happen to her. I wanted to take her away from here. Someone needed to know what was going on. None of it was right.

There was noise downstairs, pans and plates being moved around in the kitchen, the sound of voices. Then feet on the stairs, and there was someone, Mary, standing in the doorway. Her face was pinched, weathered, her shoulders stooped like someone who has spent a long time carrying something very heavy.

'You're not supposed to be sleeping there!' was the first thing she said.

I opened my eyes and stared at her. 'Well, where else was I supposed to sleep?' I said, but she didn't answer.

Next to me Rebekah moved, stretching and groaning.

'Come on.' Mary came over and pulled the covers off us. 'Up.'

'Fuck off,' I muttered, before I could stop myself.

The temperature of the room dropped. Rebekah flinched, then jumped out of bed.

'And we'll have none of that language here, thank you.'

'Why not?'

'God is listening.'

'Oh fucking fuck off,' I said, even louder. Like God would have the time and the inclination to be personally offended by me. God, if He existed, never listened to my prayers. I'd figured that out a long time ago.

'*Please*.' Rebekah covered her ears.

Mary stared at me hard. '*Downstairs*. Two minutes.' She wasn't asking.

When she'd gone to wake the twins, Rebekah looked at me reproachfully. 'Don't swear,' she hissed. 'That word is one of the *worst* things you can say. When Jonathan was possessed by demons he started saying it all the time, until he was cleansed by a night of prayer. Mr Bevins strictly forbids it.'

'Oh fuck off,' I said again, just to be spiteful. 'I fucking hate this place, and she's a complete Nazi. I mean, why is she getting all uppity about where we sleep?'

'I don't know,' she said. 'I think I was supposed to make up the camp bed for you.'

Seriously, I had to get out of there as soon as possible. It would be very easy to just start screaming or something, I felt so tense. I reached about the bed and started collecting my clothes. I'd taken my jeans and sweatshirt off in the night.

'Here.' She held out a plain black dress.

'I'm not wearing *that*.' I sat up. 'Are you mad?'

'But we're commanded to be *modest*,' she said, almost whining.

I ignored her and pulled the blanket around my shoulders like a cloak. 'But I'm a visitor, aren't I? Surely there are different rules for visitors?'

'But you can't wear those —' she nodded at my clothes — 'the whole time you're here! They're dirty.'

I got out of bed and shook out my jeans, which were stiff with salt from the boat. I was aware that she was staring at me.

'What's that?' She pointed to my ankle, where I had another tattoo.

'Eye of Horus. Supposed to be for protection. Like in ancient Egypt.'

'Protection from what?'

'Evil spirits, bad people, that kind of thing.' I pulled on my jeans, covering it up.

I'd had this boyfriend who wanted to be a tattoo artist. He wanted to give me this whole back piece. He drew it out and everything, a whole tableau of mythical beasts. Dragons and unicorns and mermaids. But I'm glad I stopped him. I mean, even I knew that fourteen was too young to make that kind of commitment. One day though I was going to have a whole work of art on my body, something beautiful and terrible. Rebekah was staring at me like I was an alien or something. When I caught her eye she blushed and looked away.

'Sorry,' she muttered.

'You don't have to keep saying that! I'm starving. Is there any breakfast?'

*

67

When we got downstairs her father was waiting with Mary and Hannah.

'You certainly do look quite the d—' Mary stopped herself. 'Tomboy. We'll have to find you some more *appropriate* clothes.'

'Look,' I said, 'look, this was all a big mistake. If you can just call Ron and Bridget, they'll pay whatever to get me out of here. I shouldn't have come.'

'I pray for you, Alex,' Hannah said, her eyes fluttering. 'We all do.'

'You can't force me to stay!' I said. They couldn't, could they? All I had to do was call someone – Ron and Bridget, Sue the Social Worker.

Mary laughed, but it had an edge of falseness. 'Of course not! We're forcing no one. Whatever gave you that idea? You come to God of your own free will.'

'We're not making anyone do anything,' Rebekah's father said. 'But if you are going to live with us, then you need to abide by our rules.' He looked at my trousers. 'You'll need to take that lip piercing out too.' They sounded just like some of the teachers at school.

I wondered if they were hearing me at all. 'But that's what I'm *saying*. I'm not going to live with you. I want to go *home*.'

'We already discussed this. Ron and Bridget entrusted you to our care.'

I folded my arms. 'Yes, but I've changed my mind. This was a bad idea.'

'I'm afraid it's not your decision to make.'

'*Seriously?* So you're keeping me prisoner? Is this like an intervention or something?'

Hannah laughed as if I'd just told a really hilarious joke. 'Ha!

Prisoner!' I didn't understand why she thought it was so funny. 'We're *all* prisoners of the Lord! He keeps us safe with bonds of love!'

I glared at her.

'Come on, we need to get the breakfast ready!' Mary handed me a pile of bowls. 'Put these out on the table, will you, please?'

Hannah was staring at me, all smug like she'd won something. I should have run then, but where was I going to go? I needed a plan.

Next to the kitchen was a dining room with a huge wooden table that filled the room and about twenty chairs around it. On the wall was a reproduction of da Vinci's painting of the Last Supper, in which Jesus breaks bread with his disciples and everyone looks at him except Judas, who stares out over his shoulder at the green fields, the blue sky.

I dumped the pile of bowls on the table, but Rebekah came in and told me off.

'You've got to put them *out*,' she said, taking them and laying them around the table.

'Whatever.' I sat in one of the chairs and folded my arms. This wasn't what I signed up to. Rebekah put a spoon in front of me. I might as well let them wait on me. 'What's for breakfast?'

'Oh no!' Rebekah said. 'We eat separately. Men first, then the women.'

'*What?*'

'Mr Bevins said it was more proper to separate us, and that the men need to be shielded from the frivolous thoughts of women so that they can better contemplate the mind of God.'

I snorted. 'Yeah, whatever. I'm not moving.'

Then noise came from the kitchen and a few of them filed through. Rebekah's father, Jonathan the mad guy from yesterday –

they all had thick, wiry beards, one huge with hands like shovels that I heard called Micah, the twins' father, who looked like he could have stepped out of the painting on the wall.

As they all came in, quiet, subdued, I could sense there was someone behind them, someone who was like the engine of this place, and when he was there in the room it was unsettling, it was like the whole place belonged to him, and all the people too, and I was suddenly nervous. He was short and wiry, his black hair long and windswept and salted with grey, and his beard grown thick and straggly. He wore a dark wool suit and a white shirt like someone from another century. He looked fiercer and more angry than the man in the photographs. I don't know why, but I stood up.

Rebekah ran over to him, as if to embrace him, but he just stood still and stared at her, so she stopped and blushed and looked at her shoes.

'Why are you not in the kitchen with the women?' he said, coldly.

She looked confused and mumbled an apology and walked towards the door. I moved to follow her, but he made a gesture with his hands meaning I should sit down.

'Eat with us,' he said; his accent was a weird mix of English and American.

There was a murmur from some of the men, like they disapproved. But he sat down next to me and smiled and looked right at me, as if he could see straight through and into me. It made me feel shy and I couldn't help it, but a blush rose up my neck and spread across my face. His eye sockets were set so deep in his face they were like tunnels, at the end of which his blue eyes shone, irises rimmed with black like someone had drawn around them with a marker pen. He spoke quietly so I had to lean towards him to hear.

'It's what you want, isn't it? To be one of us.' He pointed at the others around the table. Most of them seemed old, well, lots older than me, anyway, apart from one who was young, barely any fluff on his chin, who was staring at me like I was some kind of an alien.

I didn't know what to say, so I shrugged.

'To be one of the *men*?' He said this more loudly. The young one snorted. I wriggled in my seat, and blushed even harder.

Hannah came in with the porridge. She ladled some into my bowl with a heavy splat. I looked at the grey splodge of congealed oats and suddenly didn't feel hungry.

Before he let anyone eat he went round the table and asked everyone to confess their bad thoughts. 'We need to confess any sinful thoughts that will distract us from our purpose.'

The men looked at their hands and mumbled confessions about being lazy or tired or slothful. Jonathan said he had been doubting and having dreams about taking drugs again. 'I have been thinking of leaving, like.'

Mr Bevins nodded and listened patiently to each one like a good teacher. Then when they were finished and the porridge was definitely cold, he said, 'Let us pray.' He pushed the sleeves of his shirt up his arms — he did this a lot, I noticed. Like a kind of tic. 'Oh Lord, forgive all our sinners. And bless this meal, and bless —' here he paused and grabbed my hand — 'our new arrival. The precious flower You brought to us. Help us to lead her to Your light. Help us to live for the Victory.' I stared at his clasped fingers, they were clean and neat, unlike the others whose hands were roughed and calloused and stained with dirt. Everyone had their eyes closed, apart from the young man sat opposite who was still staring at me. I stuck my tongue out at him, and his glare intensified. He pointed his fingers at his eyes and then at me, to show that he was watching me.

When Mr Bevins had finished, he took a long time to let go of my hand, running his finger across the shape of the moon tattoo on my thumb. Every nerve in my body tingled.

'You know it is written that if your hand or foot offend you, better to cut it off than be cast into everlasting fire!' He put his arm around my shoulders and pulled me towards him so I could smell damp clothes and sweat and something else, a strange muddy, chemical odour. 'She's come here to learn from us. But also to lead us home! Isn't that right?'

'Hmm.'

'I have been praying all week for your soul. I have seen your arrival in the kingdom of heaven. You are loved and welcome.'

The emotion came off him like a force field. And that force field wrapped itself around me and made my body tremble. It was strange, but when he was talking he had this way of making me feel like I was special, like I mattered. Like he could see beneath my skin and see what made me tick.

'Thanks,' I muttered.

After breakfast he insisted that I go with him to the church. So we could 'get to know each other better'. I didn't really want to, but no one protested. Rebekah's father nodded approvingly.

He took me past all the huts. They would have been nice when they were new, wood cabins with sloping tin roofs and wooden planked walls. Except now they looked weather-beaten, fixed with bits of driftwood, plastic. I wondered which one was his. I was going to make a call on that phone the minute I got my hands on it.

'I know why you're here,' he said, staring at me as if he really could see inside my head. He said I came to him in a vision. The harbinger. The one who foretells.

'You were the one who stood there in the last moments and ushered us home! The good Lord blessed me with a gift. I can see what will happen in the future.'

'No! You've got it wrong. I'm not any kind of mystical person!' I said. I didn't like the sound of the harbinger.

'I know you're sceptical right now. Perhaps you're scared. But for those who walk in the light, there's nothing to fear. I have nothing but love for you – God's love, which passes all understanding.' He smiled and laughed softly. 'Jesus died for your soul. He would die a million deaths for you! Human love pales into insignificance in comparison.'

I nodded and prepared myself for the kind of burble Bridget used to give me when she went on about God but then he said, 'I'm not like the others, Alex, I don't condemn you. I'm standing here with love, so *much* love for you.' And his eyes shone like he was holding back tears. 'I *understand* what you've been through. I *do*. You grew up with nothing. No parents to love you. No one you could count on. Everyone here understands that. That's where we've *all* come from. You've done so great to get this far. So, so great.' He shook his head. 'What happened back in Essex, it's totally . . . *understandable*. You were angry. You were lost.' I felt suddenly embarrassed. Had Sue the Social Worker been talking about me? 'I spoke to Pastor Matthews the other day. Everyone back there is praying for you so hard, that you will see the way. The Lord has plans for you. He has kept you safe all this time for a reason and brought you here to be with us.'

I laughed nervously. It was embarrassing to think that he had been talking about me, everyone passing me around like I was this big problem.

He opened the door to the church. They had built it on the ruins of the old one, with a shingle roof and pinewood walls and wooden chairs laid out in neat rows. At the front was an altar with a white cloth on it and a line of perpetual candles burning. Above that was a lurid painting of Jesus on the cross, his face twisted in the agony of the crucifixion.

'You know when I was a boy, growing up, I was lost, I had no purpose. My mamma, she could see that I was born for the glory but I wouldn't hear it. She was gifted with visions and voices, but I thought she was crazy. I was angry, a nasty sneak, I lived in sin, like a pig rolls in its own dirt! I went to church but I was so full of filth I could not bear to hear the truth. I would sit in the back carving on the pew with my hunting knife, and making a deal of snoring in the sermons. And then one day, I was out in streets of my hometown, wandering around, looking for trouble, and I came across an old hobo, sat on the sidewalk begging. You know what one of them is?'

I shook my head.

'An old tramp, of the old school, lives his life travelling from place to place, never settling down. He was blind. Both eyes were like these black holes, made me feel sick to look at them. But he said, "Son, I can see you. I can see your sin like I used to be able to see the sun and the stars and the faces of people. It stinks on you." He had a cup that he held out for change and I thought, Right, mister, if you can see me so well then see this! And I stole it right out from under his nose. I thought I was so clever! Only a few quarters and dimes, but I thought I had him beat! That stupid old man for calling me dirty and sinful! How dare he! But later that night I was in bed and I couldn't sleep, I kept tossing and turning, thinking everything over and I thought to myself, He was right. I was a bad person, the kind of person that steals from the poor and helpless, that is full of prideful thoughts when he should be clean and whole!

74

'The next day I went back to where he had been sat, but there was no sign of him. I asked around the whole town, but no one remembered seeing a blind beggar on the street, it was as if he had never been there at all and I realised then what had happened. It was Jesus himself, come disguised as a hobo! Come in the clothes of a beggar to show me the way! And from that day forward I realized I had seen a miracle! I had been saved! And I gave my life over to Jesus to do with as he willed.' He stopped talking and stared at me until I had to look away. His eyes were so intense. 'I can see it in you, you have the same ornery wilfulness. Will you let me pray for you?' he asked.

I nodded because I didn't know what else to do and because his story made me paranoid. What had Ron and Bridget said about me?

We sat down at the front and he put his hand on my head and squeezed his eyes shut.

'Bless this child, Lord. She's the one we have been waiting for.'

Here he paused and then suddenly his voice changed. It was like he was two people at once, both himself and another person with a voice that was deeper, darker. I wanted to laugh, but not because it was funny. It made me nervous.

'*Indeed she is. I bless her.* Show her how much You understand that she is a lost little girl, how hard it is to grow up so. *I love her, she is a child of My heart.* We are so full of love, so full of love. *We are full of love.* Show her that You have led her here for Your divine purpose. *She is the one who will open the door. But only when she has been purified.* But must she renounce all the sin inside her? *She must. But she must come to Me of her own free will. But if she does, I will reveal to her the love at the centre of everything. This I will show only to her.*'

When he stopped he stood up and shook himself like a wet dog. 'Did you hear that? The message?' he said. 'Don't be afraid.'

'I'm not,' I mumbled, though I was suddenly very confused. He seriously thought I had some special mission, some special message to bring them. But I couldn't see how that was true. I was just me. I wasn't special. And I didn't like the idea of being purified. What did that mean? He sounded like he was faking it.

'Here.' He touched my lip piercing. 'You're too precious to be so disfigured. Let's start by taking that out?'

I don't know, maybe on another day I would have told him to fuck off, but he had this way about him, of making it difficult to say no, of drawing you in. I wanted to please him. I guess that was how it started for everyone. So I unclipped the ring and gave it to him.

'Good girl,' he said. 'Good girl.'

And for a moment I thought it might just be possible that I was.

# NINE

# REBEKAH

By the time the women sit for breakfast there's not much left —
a splash of coffee each and a spoonful of porridge. Even Hannah
complains, makes some veiled comment about the men being so
hungry because of yesterday's prayers going on all day, which Mary
silences with a glare. Everyone looks tired. All the other women
are here, Hannah and Margaret and Mrs Bragg and Mrs Webber,
Leah Morgan, and Ruth Davis and Esther. Along with me and Mary
Protheroe and Naomi in the Solitary, that makes ten women in a
community of nearly thirty. Eleven if you count Alex, who Mr
Bevins has taken to the church for prayer.

The talk over the table turns around what there is to do. The crops
that need harvesting, the plots that need digging, all the work that
has been neglected over Mission Week. Mr Bevins said that it was
more important to pray. I don't know why he was angry with me
earlier. I feel a deep chasm of shame opening in my chest. I must be
careful to show him how hard I've worked, how much I've tried to
be good while I've been away. I look out of the window, to the blue
sky, longing to taste the air again, to smell the soft earth. But Mary
tells me that I have to look after the twins and make soup for lunch
and that Alex can help me until they've decided what to do with her.

'You do know *why* she was suspended from school, don't you?'
Margaret says conspiratorially, eyes made huge by the thick lenses
of her glasses.

'I'm not sure it's wise to bring that up now,' says Mary, taking piece of dry bread and cracking it in her hands. 'We have been praying. We must trust her care to Bevins.'

'The Lord certainly moves in mysterious ways,' Hannah says. 'They only found us at the eleventh hour, just as we were packing up.' She takes a piece of bread and chews on it, then discreetly spits it out. 'Did no one bake bread all week?'

'No,' says Mary. 'Bevins said it was more important to pray.' Hannah frowns.

'Bevins had a vision,' Margaret says. 'It's coming soon, Hannah! We're in the last *weeks*, Hannah. *Weeks*.' Her eyes bulge.

There's a small squeeze of fear around my heart. I don't want to die. I know it won't be death but a kind of transition, but it will probably hurt, and that scares me.

'To be honest, it'll be nice to have a normal day, you know?' Mrs Bragg says, like she hasn't been listening. 'There's so much to do in the garden.'

Hannah raises her eyebrows and there's a tension around the room. Something happened while we were gone, but no one is quite saying what.

Mary leaves me to take care of the twins and I wash up the many dishes from breakfast and put the porridge pot to soak and lay out the vegetables. The twins play at the other end of the table, building figures from dirty modelling clay.

I don't know why I have to stay in here. It's so unfair. Mary couldn't disappear fast enough into the gardens, and it was me who planted everything in the first place. I take a potato and try to peel it, but it's soft and spongy and not good for eating. There must be fresh produce still in the ground, so why has no one harvested it?

Mr Bevins says it's not godly to ask too many questions. 'Thinking is sinking,' he says. The faithful accept without fear or complaint the life the Lord has chosen for them, but now my head fizzes with questions. Like why is Alex here, and why did she have to leave Essex in the first place? I don't even know where Essex is, or what it's like there.

I wonder at her life, at what things she has seen and done. The next Mission Week is a whole year away. A whole year of scraping soft potatoes and looking after the twins, of putting up with Mary and Hannah and all the many, many hours in church listening to Mr Bevins going on and the cold nights of winter. And for the first time in my life, maybe the first time ever, I wonder with a sinking feeling whether I want to be here. But then just as quickly I pray, to push the thought away. This is what Mr Bevins means about trusting the Lord to give us what we truly want. We mustn't choose for ourselves; we have to wait for what is meant to be revealed.

Then the twins, bored with the clay, are playing around the kitchen table and they upset a bowl of water, sending it smashing to the ground, breaking into little pieces all over the floor, and I can't help it but something bad and angry comes escaping out of me and I shout at them.

'Will. You. STOP IT?!' I grab Peter by the arm and am about to let fly with my hand when I see his face, turned away from me, frightened, and I relent and hold him close instead. His body is trembling. 'You need to be CALM,' I say through clenched teeth. '*Please*.' Guilty now, because I have been angry, lost my temper. And being full of anger will count against me on the Day of Judgement and I'll never get to go to heaven or see Mother again. And I'm sure I can see her face looking at me, disappointed. I say a prayer for patience and let him go.

'Hate you,' he says, aiming a kick at me. Then he runs away to the other side of the room and stands by the door as if he means to run out of it, which he knows he is not allowed to do.

'Well, that's as may be, but you'll hate me even more if there is nothing to eat tonight. Why won't you LISTEN?'

And my hand raises again, but this time someone grabs it and I turn round and Alex is standing right behind me. 'Don't hit him,' she says gently.

But that just makes it worse, because now she's seen me like this, like the kind of person who gets mad at children and loses her temper and goes to strike them.

'Get off me!' I shout, and Paul starts to wail, and then I turn and see Mr Bevins. I didn't even hear him come in.

His eyes are light blue, almost transparent; and they give him the expression of someone who is looking far beyond us into a world no one else can see. Hannah compares his looks to classical paintings, though I haven't seen many so I can't say I know what she means. All I know is that we must tend to him, as a precious gift. He is the one who brings us the word of God.

He takes a step forward and stands over the table, picking up one of the boys' clay figures.

'What are you making?' he asks softly, in his deep American accent.

'The fiery furnace,' I say. Peter holds up a piece of red clay that he's fashioned to look like flames.

'Very good,' he says, rubbing his hand through Peter's hair but staring at me. 'And do you know who went into the fiery furnace?'

'Shadrach, Meshach and A-bed-we-go,' the twins say together. The name is really Abednego, but we say this sometimes on the way up to bed, because I remember that's what Mother used to say to me as we counted the slow steps upstairs when I was little.

'Who were thrown into a fiery furnace but they did not get burned,' I say.

'That's right! Obedient servants of God! Refusing to bow down to a golden idol. Even on pain of death in the fiery furnace! Even though King Nebuchadnezzar commanded that the furnace be made seven times hotter! Hotter and hotter and yet they weren't burned up! Isn't God awesome?!'

He comes over to me and grabs me by the arm and pulls me towards the stove. He takes my hand and holds it over the coals. 'Imagine!' Heat starts to sting my palm. 'And still they were not burned! They felt the flames as a cool breeze! Because they were obedient! Because they bore witness! Because they lived for the Victory!' He releases my hand and I pull it away from the fire, rubbing my thumb across my palm where it stings. He comes closer, sniffing the air. 'I can smell it on you.'

'What?'

'*Sin.*'

He stands right in front of me. He looks down at me, then pulls me towards him. Slowly and deliberately. So that eventually my face is against his chest and I can smell the damp wool of his waistcoat and feel every bony angle of his body, the jut of his hips. I freeze. I must make a murmur because he says, 'Hush now.' Then he's pressing my head against his chest. 'Live for the Victory, Rebekah, live for the Victory. You are spiritually exhausted.' He holds me for a really long time, stroking my headscarf, saying a prayer over my head until I think I'm going to suffocate.

'Amen!' He pushes me away from him. 'Tonight we will pray over you.'

There's an edge to his voice that makes me sure I've done something wrong.

'It's so easy for your mind to be polluted. Thinking is sinking, Rebekah; *remember* that.'

I know this is all because I allowed my thoughts to wander. For allowing myself to think about leaving. Mr Bevins is sensitive to these things. He can see sin where most would not. Tears sting my eyes, and before I know it I'm sobbing and asking for forgiveness and he is patting me on the head like I am Job, Micah's sheepdog.

'Enough now.' As he steps away from me his foot scrapes against a shard of broken bowl. 'Clear this up.' And he walks off. Between his fingers one of the pieces of clay that the boys have shaped into a flame.

Alex bends down and helps me to pick up the pieces of the bowl. 'You OK?' she asks.

I shrug. I think it's probably better not to speak to her too much; it's just getting me into trouble. 'Yeah, I'm fine.'

She looks different; it takes me a moment to realize that her lip ring is gone.

'What happened to your . . . ?' I point at my own lip.

She won't meet my eye. 'More trouble than it's worth,' she says. 'Anyway, it's hard to keep it clean.'

'What did he say to you?'

She sighs. 'He told me I've got to wear a dress and say this prayer for repentance.' She holds out a piece of paper to me, handwritten in Bevins's familiar tight handwriting. 'He said they spent all week praying for guidance not even stopping to eat.' She rolls her eyes. 'That I'm some kind of . . . harbinger. I mean, *seriously*? Fasting, for me? It's a bit *extreme*.'

'No, it's not!' I say, more tartly than I want to. 'Those prayers were a gift to your soul.'

'Right. You sound just like him! Don't you ever think for yourself?'

'Thinking is sinking,' I say automatically.

'Oh come on! What's that supposed to mean?'

But I can't answer that and I look at the piece of paper. It's a prayer for repentance like we say in church. I know it by heart.

'*Almighty God, we miserable sinners come to You in penitence and sorrow . . .*'

She grabs it from my hands and rips it up. It's then I realize quite how strong the devil must be in her, so much does she struggle to hear the truth, and I step back from her, afraid.

'He tried to burn your hand!'

'No, he didn't!' I say. 'He was teaching me a lesson.' And at least it wasn't stripes from the rod, which would have hurt a great deal more.

'But . . . I mean . . . *seriously*?' She shivers. 'I don't like him.'

'You don't know what you're talking about,' I say. She just wants to attack; I don't know why I didn't see it before. I must be strong, show her the way.

I take the knife, start chopping carrots for soup. I see it before it happens, but I don't move my finger out of the way fast enough. The knife comes down on my finger instead of the carrot, slicing through skin, almost touching bone. Blood bubbles up to the surface and I stare at it, at the depth of the cut, unable to move until Alex grabs my hand and puts my hand under the tap. I'm faint and I'm trembling, but I won't cry. I bite my lip and close my eyes, pray to God to help me. Sometimes I wish He would hurry and come with His chariots of fire and chorus of heavenly angels, and then all this confusion and suffering would be over once and for all and I could see my mother, who I miss with all my heart.

Alex wraps my finger in a strip of cloth that she tears from a tea towel. 'You've gone all white,' she says.

I swallow a feeling of sickness. I've still got to prepare food for thirty, then make a pot of soup enough to take to the Solitary and then scrape dishes and wash up, and how will I be able to do that now? The cut throbs violently.

'You'll be OK,' she says, and she winks at me kindly, almost protectively, and I sense the spark in the air between us. The corners of her mouth twitch when she smiles. 'See? You're laughing already.'

'No!' But I'm smiling at her, I can't help myself.

'You know, one time when we got new knives at the home, Clayton cut himself so bad they had to take him to hospital. It wasn't even like yours – he cut the top of his finger clean off. Now instead of a round finger he's got a flat fingertip. Everyone called him Flat Top after that. That's how he got his nickname.'

I stare at her. She sounds as if she's speaking a foreign language.

'I don't know about that,' I say lamely.

'Why would you know? You weren't there!'

And then I want to ask her so many questions about her life, about what she has seen and what has happened to her, but I can't because Ruth comes in, sent to keep an eye on us, I suspect.

'Mr Bevins sent me to help you,' she says, her voice clogged up with hay fever. She has a way of swallowing her words and hunching her shoulders that makes her look as if she is always very sorry about something. Then, she sees my finger – blood has started soaking through the scrap of towel – 'What have you done?!'

She makes me sit and drink some water and rewraps the cut in a clean bandage.

She came here alone and is troubled in her mind because she lost her baby soon after it was born and then her husband left her. Father says she's full of sorrow and needs to be kept busy in case of backsliding.

'More haste, less speed, Rebekah,' she says briskly, but her eyes are kind.

Very quickly she turns the pile of carrots and onions and herbs and some potatoes and few scraggy pieces of mutton into soup, then she kneads out the dough. I sit with the twins and Alex and we make a model of the lion from Daniel and the Lion's Den, except it starts to look more like an elephant and then Alex changes it into a dragon instead. When the soup has risen to a soft boil Ruth pours it into a flask and wraps one of the fresh loaves in a tea towel.

'Here,' she says, gently handing the parcel to me. 'Do you both good to get some fresh air.'

Then, seeing Alex's face, she ladles some soup into a cup and slices off the end of one of the loaves.

'Mary never makes enough for breakfast,' she says.

'Thanks!' Alex says, grabbing it from her. 'I'm fucking starving.'

Ruth flinches and I yelp.

'Sorry,' she says, her mouth full. 'Old habits.'

# TEN

# REBEKAH

The moment we're outside of the door, she wants to know when she can get the phone.

'Not now,' I say. 'We'll be seen. We can't just go breaking into Mr Bevins's cabin.'

'Well, when?'

'*Soon*,' I say, though really I don't have a clue. I know he keeps the phone in his cabin, but I don't know where or how we might be able to get at it. 'We'll have to wait until everyone's at church.'

The moment we climb the bank up towards the fields the air whips around my ears, piercing through the layers of my clothes. The clouds are rising and not rainy, but the shrill wind makes the grass in the fields quiver. It's never completely warm here. Occasionally we get a calm day where the sea seems like glass, but mostly the wind blows in from the Atlantic, harsh and persistent.

The quickest way to get to the Solitary is across the bridge at the top of the lake, over the rocks we call the Devil's Seat — and down the other side. The longer way around means going back to the harbour, then around the cliffs, as the path at the bottom of the hill is too boggy. The Devil's Seat is the highest point on the island, an outcrop of crags and boulders that form the shape of a seat if you look at it from the western side. Sometimes the peak gets shrouded by low cloud so it can't be seen. According to Gideon, the people who lived here before us took that as a sign that the devil was on his seat and no one should go up to the peak, in case they met him in person. It has become our superstition too, and common sense as well, because going up there in the cloud would be dangerous. There are sheer drops and scrambles of scree, places where it would be easy to fall and die.

On the other side the hill slopes more gently into heath where the goats are allowed to roam to chew the gorse and heather. It's a distance of about three miles and when the weather is good takes maybe an hour to walk there, though the uphill part is hard. But the ground around the lake is heavy and boggy and full of mud, even by the bridge, which Micah and Jonathan widened. I try to pick my way between the puddles and tread only on the tufts of grass, but in places the path is so heavy and marshy it's impossible to walk without slipping and a few times my feet sink up to the ankles in the mud. By the time I get to the hard rocks my feet are soaking wet.

'Shit. I'm fucking freezing,' Alex says, half laughing. She's not wearing enough clothes.

'D'you want my coat?' I offer. But she just looks at me funny.

'Then *you'll* be cold.'

'Only for a bit. Then you can give it me back.' It's a blue padded jacket the same as all the women on the island wear. Mine is old and scruffy now, with the padding escaping out of a rip in the seam. Mary was supposed to mend it while I was away, but I suppose that was something else they didn't get round to doing. The men wear mostly black trousers and waistcoats, and in the winter thick waxed coats. The women have black dresses that cover our bodies like a robe, and headscarves. Mr Bevins says we need to live as simply as possible, like people in the old days.

'No, you're OK.' She tucks her hands under her arms.

From the lake the path climbs up the hill, a sheep track that zigzags until it reaches a small plateau where there are flat rocks. Sometimes on sunny days I'd come here with Mother and lie on a slab, warm from the sun, and pick the lichen off the stones, watching as the bees buzzed in the heather, listening to the distant sound of the ocean, the high calling of the gulls. Or we would lie on our stomachs, our faces in the grass, and watch all the tiny insects going about their business, the ants and the worms and the crickets. Or put an ear to the earth and listen to the booming thunder of the wind against the ground, the distant roar of the sea. Mother said that was the best thing about living here, being so close to the elements, almost as if we lived inside the wind and the sea and they in turn inside us. How lucky we were to be in such a beautiful place, where we were safe from all the pollution, where the air tasted of honey.

Now the rock seems empty and desolate and the wind scrubs my face raw. I hurry past with my head down; I try not to remember.

From there it is another steep climb to the outcrop of the Devil's Seat. The grass gives way to scree and twice I stumble and nearly fall, have to cling to tufts of grass or cracks in the rock to steady myself. At the top is another flat stone, with one tall rock that has been scraped into a sharp pillar by the wind, and around it are boulders, strewn about as if someone has thrown them in a fit of temper. There are signs that people have been here. There's a cup and a couple of bowls from the kitchen, a piece of rag, one of the twins' dropped toys. This is where Bevins had the prayer meeting. It must have been hellishly cold because the wind is suddenly Atlantic, stronger, pushing me on my heels. I rest for breath in the lee of a boulder with Alex, who is panting, mud crusted all the way up her legs.

'Wow. It's beautiful,' she says, and her approval lifts my spirits.

From up here you can see almost the whole island and beyond that the sea that surrounds us, dark blue and tufted with manes of white foam. In the distance are other smaller, uninhabited islands, some no more than a slice of rock that sits in the ocean's boil, and then beyond that the open water to the mainland, which is a thin bumpy line on the southern horizon. Above all that, huge Atlantic clouds blow towards us, vast and mysterious.

This view fills me with a longing to fly. Instead I turn back towards the path and spread my arms and let the wind flap at the fabric of my coat.

'Come on.'

The other side of the hill is softer; once we have clambered down from the rock the ground slopes into bumpy moorland where the grass and heather are buffeted and flattened by the wind. I look at the ground beneath my feet, the barbed grass and the gritty soil, the springy clots of turf.

The walking is easier here, and we fall into step and start to march, swinging our arms. We walk side by side, in a companionable silence, our hands almost touching. Rocks lie about us if they have been blown from the top and scattered across the turf, and in the far distance I can see the red tin roof of the Solitary.

'There it is,' I say, pointing.

Alex grunts as if she disapproves.

'All newcomers go there. For forty days and nights of silent contemplation to prove they are worthy.'

She shivers. 'Well, I'm not going there!'

'I don't think you have to.' Although I'm not sure why not. 'You're like a special case.'

'Good. Because no one said anything about this to me before, and I would never have agreed to come here if I'd known. And anyway, isn't that against the law?'

I have to consider this for a moment because I know the law of the Solitary is not really written in the Bible but it is one of the laws of our community. 'No, but it's *our* law,' I say.

'Well, that's not like the laws of the country, is it? It's illegal to keep people locked up unless they've done something.'

'But we don't live by the laws of man. And the people who go to the Solitary *want* to go there. Naomi has been there for nearly two years. She prays for prophecies, for revelation.'

'Why?' Alex demands.

I don't know what to say to this. Why would anyone *not* want to pray for a revelation? A revelation from God is a blessing, something to be wished with all your heart.

'Because it's her gift.'

Alex frowns. 'This place is doing my head in.'

'Sorry,' I say. Then, realizing what I've said, 'I mean, you'll get used to it.'

'You think? I'm going right back on the next boat. You lot are seriously Upminster.'

'Upminster?'

'Two stops from Barking. Mad, bonkers, crazy. Off. Your. Head.'

'No, we're not.' But I have a strange lurch in my stomach like when I stand at the edge of the cliff and look down.

'First boat to leave here, I'm on it. And I want to find that satellite phone. I mean, you might mean well and all that, but seriously . . . your man Bevins is mad.'

She says this with a kind of determination and defiance that make me angry. She can't run away. She's can't leave me here. She can't. If she left, I know I wouldn't want to stay here any more. This thought slides through my mind so quickly I can hardly hear it, but I feel it, in the way my body begins to tremble and in the black noise that builds inside my head.

The Solitary is half underground, built in a circle. Four triangles of space like the quarters of a cake, built out of stone, with a square tin roof that Father and Micah built to cover it, because it was too difficult to build a round one. What these chambers were originally made for and by whom, no one knows.

We have to stoop to enter, but once inside it's big enough to stand up, and the clamour of the sea and the wind have gone, replaced by the deep quiet of the earth. Each cell has a heavy wooden door with a hatch through which I can look, and through which I can push food. Inside there is a bed and a desk and a drop hole for a toilet, which is covered up with a plank of wood. A small window high up in the wall lets in the light but it is impossible to see out, even standing on the bed. Naomi has the cell that faces towards the island, away from the prevailing wind. This was the only request she made for comfort.

I knock on the door before I slide the hatch open. I cannot see her anywhere on the bed, nor at her desk. Sometimes when I come with the soup she is kneeling in prayer and only nods to acknowledge me and I am compelled to stand there for ages before she finishes.

'Naomi. It is Rebekah,' I say, 'come with your food.'

But still there's no sign of her. I push my face closer to the hatch to better see into the room. Maybe she's lying on the floor, praying; she often prostrates herself, arms spread in the shape of the cross, fully penitent. Suddenly a hand appears close to my face, two gnarled fingers like grey twigs holding a scrap of paper. Startled, I yelp and stagger backwards into Alex.

'What the hell?!' Faster than I can react, Alex moves forward and snatches the piece of paper.

'"Jonah 2.3". What's this supposed to mean?'

'It's a prophecy.' I snatch the piece of paper back from her, ball it into my hand.

There's a scrabbling noise on the other side of the door and Naomi stands up, her face appearing at the hatch. Her eyes are huge, almost as if she never closes them. Her face is as knotted as bark. From under her headscarf emerge wisps of grey hair. She puts her finger to her lips as if to silence us. Then she scribbles something on another piece of paper and holds it up.

'LIVE FOR THE VICTORY!'

I step forward and give her the soup and bread, which she takes, but not before pointing at Alex and then at me and frowning. She puts her fingers on her lips again and then touches her ears and shakes her head. I take this to mean that she does not like us to be talking. Then she closes the hatch herself with a bang, dismissing us.

Alex laughs, but not because she's amused. She looks sort of horrified.

'She's just a bit old,' I whisper, as if that explains everything.

'No shit,' she says, looking at me. 'She's seriously freaky.'

Outside the sun has come out, low and blinding, but there are clouds now gathering around the Devil's Seat and rainclouds on the horizon, travelling fast inland.

'Let's walk back the other way,' I say, meaning that we should go the long way round, following the cliff path to the harbour and then back up through the woods.

We follow the goat track towards the cliffs. Here the birds roost: gulls and cormorants fly around the cliffs in a whirlpool of movement. It's quieter now than it is in the spring when they come in from the sea to nest and it's as if the whole island is made of birds and the cliffs here become a loud stink of guano. Harsh calls fill the air and at the bottom of the cliffs the sea churns, a constant boom as it breaks against the rocks. A gull hangs in the air just in front of us and we stand for a moment, the wind lifting Alex's hair, birds diving and swirling around us.

'You don't *really* believe it, do you?' she asks eventually.

'Believe what?'

'That the world is going to end, like, really soon.' She points back to the Solitary. 'All that prophecy and stuff. I mean know you're supposed to respect old people and stuff, but . . .'

I look at the birds and the sea and the whole churn of it. Father and Bevins would say that the world we see is but a mirage compared to the eternity that waits for us.

'Yes.'

'What crap! I mean, look at these rocks. They've been here for millions of years. Why would it all come to an end now, just because *you* want it to?'

This sounds like temptation to me.

'We know not the hour or the day.'

'But that's not true!' she says. 'I could make myself die right now. I could just throw myself down there.' She walks towards the edge, making my heart leap.

I put my arm out to stop her. 'Don't do that.'

'I'm not going to, silly. I was just saying I *could* kill myself. Then I would know the hour and the day.'

Since we have been here three people have been lost from the cliff tops. One when I was very young, before I can remember. The other two were newcomers. One was a woman who believed she could see the devil in everybody. Father said they were accidents, although I have heard Mary Protheroe and others refer to them differently.

I'm not scared of dying. Mr Bevins has taught us all to expect the transition from heaven to earth as if passing through a burning curtain. And once on the other side, all will be peaceful and gorgeous. It's avoiding the Tribulations that is most important. During the Tribulations people will go mad and there will be raping and pillaging and torture.

'But aren't there things you want to *do* before you die? Like a bucket list.'

'A what?'

She sighs. 'Things you want to see or do before you kick the bucket. A bucket list.'

'Oh.' I'm still not sure I understand what she means. 'I suppose.' I haven't really thought about this. Everything we do is about preparing for heaven, not about living our lives as they are now.

'There are so many things I want to do!'

'Like what?'

'Like . . . I want to go surfing in Hawaii! And ride elephants in Thailand and . . . Oh! Go everywhere! Don't you want to see the world?'

I shrug. Bevins teaches us that the world is full of danger. That there are demons and agents of the Antichrist waiting to destroy us everywhere, that being here is the only safe place. I've never thought of the world as somewhere I could visit. I've only ever thought of it as somewhere to be avoided.

And then Alex turns towards me and looks at me strangely, a smile twitching across her lips, as if she has just thought of something amusing. 'Have you ever kissed anybody?'

What a thing to say. 'No!' I giggle.

'Don't you want to do that before you die?'

'I don't know.' I wish she'd be quiet.

'Are you embarrassed?' She's testing me, I know she is. 'Your ears have gone red.'

'*No!*' I say, wanting her to change the subject. She's being deliberately provoking. The sun disappears behind a bank of cloud and the wind starts to pick up. I shiver. 'Shush.'

'Aw, you're shy. Don't be shy. Kissing is nothing to be scared of.'

'Have you kissed anybody then?'

'Course! Loads of times.' She puts her hands in her pockets all nonchalant.

I wish I knew how to be confident like that. There's this awkward silence between us, where what I really want to say is, 'Kiss *me* then,' like a challenge, but I don't because I'm scared and the thought stays in my head and I know it's making me go bright red. Sometimes I feel so see-through it's painful. 'Come on. We need to get back.'

But Alex stands still. 'I don't want to go back,' she says quietly. 'I mean, not back with you. Sorry. Coming here was, like, a mistake. I'm serious. You've got help me find that phone.'

'But you can't leave!' I blurt out before I have a chance to think. Then, flustered in case she thinks I'm trying to stop her. 'I mean, not till the next boat comes and that won't be till next month. You heard what Father said.'

'I can't wait that long!' She reaches into the pocket of her jacket and pulls out her phone.

'You know if they find that they'll think you're a spy.'

She shrugs. 'That's just stupid. It's fucked anyway. There's no reception and the battery's about to die.' She stares at the blank screen a moment and then says, 'Maybe it was my fault.'

'What was?'

She shivers. 'Everything. He said . . . she never wanted to see me again.'

'Who did?'

'My mother. Bevins said I was sick. And because I was sick, that was why she died.'

'You don't look sick to me.'

She smiles bitterly. 'I think he meant sick in the head. In the soul.'

'Oh.'

Then I realize that there is a fat tear snaking down her cheek.

'Oh. No. Don't cry.' I don't know what to do. I touch her arm.

But she turns away from me and sniffs and wipes her sleeve across her eyes. 'It's OK,' she says. 'It's OK.'

'No, it's not. You're crying.'

'I'm just cold.'

'If you want that satellite phone, we'll have to make a plan.' I say it before I realize what I'm promising. If I get caught breaking in to Mr Bevins's cabin I can't imagine what will happen. 'We can't just go and get it; someone will see us.'

'You'll help me?'

I look at my shoes, the scuffed, muddy leather, the holes in the toes. Something in me gives, and I know then that I'd do anything for her. But I don't say that:

'Yes.'

She smiles at me then, properly. 'You're cute, you know that?'

No one has ever called me cute before. She has this way of being confident, like she *knows* stuff about the world, like she knows me. It makes my insides flip over.

But then she's distracted by something behind me. She squints into the distance. 'Someone's following us.'

I turn around quickly, but can see no one behind, just the rocks of the Devil's Seat towering above us.

I stare until my eyes hurt, but nothing emerges, just the bright hum of the wind in the grass, the constant smash of the water against rocks.

She shrugs. 'Maybe it was nothing.'

But as we walk towards the harbour and the old lighthouse my back starts to prickle. I keep turning around, just to check.

A shower blows inland on the wind, the rain sudden and harsh. We run to the lighthouse, Alex pulling her jacket over her head for protection. The lighthouse is dangerous now; Micah has built a fence to keep the goats away. Bits of masonry and mirror keep falling from the top, and on the western side, where the winds are worst, it has a gaping gash where the bricks have split and crumbled. I look over the fence. It's made from rolls of chicken wire, which in places have sagged so low as to make them pointless. I can see goat droppings on the grass on the other side.

Alex steps over it. I am about to tell her it's dangerous, but she won't listen to me anyway. I step over too and we walk around it, looking up at the damage. One more winter storm and it will be rubble, the bricks have moved since last summer and the structure is unravelling from the top like a dropped stitch.

'It stinks in here!' Alex says, peering and then stepping inside, disturbing a whole colony of birds, who rise from the top in a messy squawk.

I wait outside. 'Be careful! It's dangerous!'

As if to prove my point a slither of crumbling plaster hisses down the wall.

'Come on, hurry up.'

'Who used to live here?' Her voice echoes inside the walls.

'The lighthouse keeper, some farmers. A missionary. That's who built the houses at the harbour. Before that, I dunno. Vikings or something. Hermits.'

She seems impressed by this. 'People were so hardcore back in the day, weren't they?'

'I suppose so,' I say, like I know what she means. Her hair blows across her face and she suddenly looks really beautiful, like she could be an angel or something, both a girl and a boy.

'Are you OK?'

I realize I'm staring and my face flames. 'Uh, sorry, er, yeah.'

She steps towards me and touches my cheek. 'You're blushing.'

There's a heat in my body so vivid I can't believe she doesn't feel it too.

'I want a bucket list too,' I say, lamely.

She looks at me from the corner of her eye and then squeezes my hand and we walk along like this back to the path. All I can think about is how I want to walk with her off this rock and into the world and know the things that she knows, and my thoughts are so loud I'm sure she must be able to hear them. And my mouth is dry and I don't know what to say. When we get to the path there is bright flash, the reflection of the sun on glass, someone with binoculars, higher up. Instinctively I let go of her hand.

'There!' Alex says. 'I told you there was someone following us!

Whoever you are – we can see you!' She waves her arms.

I wonder who it is, until a figure emerges from behind a boulder and starts to walk towards us. My stomach cramps. Thomas Bragg, followed by Job, Micah's dog. He's wearing dark glasses and he takes his time, swaggering almost, towards us.

Job reaches us first, barking and putting muddy paws up the front of my dress.

Thomas shouts at him, but it seems to make no difference; Job carries on grinning and slobbering, as if he's pleased to see me, though I know he's sniffing my bag for food. Micah has had him since he was a puppy and he trained the dog himself to round up the sheep.

'What are you doing?' Thomas asks, not smiling. The dark glasses make him look mean.

He stands in front of us and glares at Alex. He has the kind of heavy face that makes him seem fat even though he's thin, like we all are. Since he went off with that woman at last year's mission, he's moved back into a cabin with his parents. Father says he will have to work hard to prove that he is worthy of being trusted again. Lately Bevins has been keeping him close. They are often seen walking together discussing passages from the Bible, striding around with the book open in front of them like a map.

'We were just—' I start.

'I didn't mean you,' he snaps. 'I meant *her*.' His face is red and he seems really agitated.

Alex shrugs. 'We were just looking at the lighthouse.'

'Yes, we were looking at the lighthouse,' I echo. 'Nothing was happening.' But Thomas isn't interested in talking to me.

'No, I mean, what are you doing *here*?'

'I don't know what you mean.'

'He said you were a harbinger.'

'Who said?' Alex stares at him, all the time squaring her shoulders, clenching her hands into fists.

'Bevins.'

'Don't be ridiculous!'

'Well, why are you here then? Why aren't you in the Solitary?' He's almost shouting.

'Thomas, calm down,' I say, but he ignores me.

'Bevins said you would corrupt us. I saw you; I know what you're doing!'

'And what were we doing?'

'It's just like Mr Bevins said!'

'What is?' I'm confused, I don't know what his problem is.

'I'm not talking to you!' He swats at me with his hand. 'Have you forgotten yourself?'

Women aren't supposed to speak to men unless they're invited, but somehow Thomas doesn't count. He's only a few years older than me. I remember him as a boy, still young enough to play with me, hide and seek in the barn, beachcombing on the north shore. He used to be okay.

'You're unnatural!' he says again, his voice too high, tinged with hysteria.

'Thomas, you're being rude.' I feel embarrassed. I don't want Alex to hear this.

He shrugs. 'I don't like her,' he says, as if she isn't even there.

'But we have a message from Naomi.'

'Show me.'

I hold out the piece of paper, which he snatches from me.

'Why didn't you tell me?'

'I'm telling you now.'

He looks at it. I still don't understand why he's being so aggressive.

'Well, come on then, we'd better get back. Come on.' He gestures to the path, and we walk in front of him, all the way with him and Job behind us.

'What the hell's going on?' Alex whispers at me. 'Who is he?'

'I'm sorry,' I say. 'I don't know what's got into him.'

'If he touches either of us, I'll end him,' she hisses. 'Seriously. I will.'

I look at her, shoulders set, fists balled, muscle twitching in her cheek, and I don't doubt her. It makes me like her even more.

# ELEVEN

# ALEX

The tack room went quiet the minute we walked in. A shiver pulsed through my body. The room was muggy and full of people and mud and piles of carrots and potatoes and courgettes. They all turned to look at me. I tried to hang back behind Rebekah, but it was as if I had some glowing spot on my head or something. Rebekah was the only one I felt safe with in the whole place. She was naive, but she wasn't angry or spiteful. She stood up for me against Thomas, and said sorry when he was nasty to me. She didn't blame me. I wished I could take her away from here, show her the real world, show her what she was missing, let her decide for herself. She deserved that, at least.

Thomas elbowed his way past me, in his stupid, pretend-important way. He thought he was someone special, but Mr Bevins was using him, I could tell.

'A message from Naomi!' he announced, opening his hand and throwing the crumpled ball of paper on to the table like he was the one who had been there and heard what the freaky woman said, not us. Something about his attitude made me angry. Who was he to make out like he was in charge? I hated him then, as I knew he hated me.

The paper was damp with his sweat.

Hannah peeled it apart. 'Jonah 2.3.'

One of the other women, a thin and willowy shadow called

Margaret, pulled out a pocket Bible and looked up the verse.

But before she could find it Hannah said, from memory: '*For thou hadst cast me into the deep, in the midst of the seas; and the floods compassed me about: all thy billows and thy waves passed over me.*'

Margaret put her hand over her mouth and started to cry. 'He sends us comfort!' she said.

'Praise be to God,' said Thomas.

'Praise be to God!' everyone repeated loudly. Thomas whooped and stamped his foot. Idiot.

'What are billows, do you think?' Hannah asked of no one in particular.

'Holy pillows?' I muttered. I couldn't help myself.

Rebekah snorted, but no one else laughed. We looked at each other and I grabbed her hand and squeezed and she squeezed back, but she then she let go like my hand was a hot coal when she saw Mary staring at us.

'Has Bevins seen this?' one of the men asked, a touch of irritation in his voice.

Thomas shook his head. 'Not yet.' I hated the way that he took the space in the room as if he was the one that was in charge when Mr Bevins wasn't around.

'Before we all get carried away, *he* needs to verify this.' The man seemed angry. I guessed it must be Thomas's father. He looked a lot like him, with the same fat-thin face and doughy expression.

Thomas narrowed his eyes. '*I* am the appointed deputy!' He was really big on trying to prove he was the favourite.

'Thomas!' one of the women, his mother, said. 'Honour your father.'

But Thomas shrugged. 'I have one Father, and he is in heaven.'

There was a hush around the room. Mr Bragg's face was going

purple but he didn't say anything. There was obviously some kind of situation going on between the two of them.

Then Mr Bevins came in. I could sense his presence even before I saw him. The room was suddenly quiet, expectant. He stood in the centre of us, smiling benignly, hands raised, palms open as if he were like the blind beggar in his story.

Thomas snatched up Naomi's prophecy and gave it to him.

'She gave *you* this?' Bevins asked.

'No, them,' he mumbled, reluctantly pointing to me and Rebekah. I think Thomas wished it was him. He wanted to please Mr Bevins the most out of everybody. I wished it had been him too. I didn't want Mr Bevins to notice us. I didn't want to be in the path of those eyes. I felt his gaze burning right through me.

'And how was she?'

I didn't know what to say so I kept my mouth shut.

'OK,' Rebekah answered.

'Did she say anything? Was there any other message?'

'No. She just gave me that.'

'See!' he said. 'I told you she was the one!' He pointed at me as if that prophecy had something to do with me. 'That she would set off a chain reaction. It's in motion! The countdown has started! The time is upon us! I must now discover the hour!'

It sounded like craziness to me, except that everyone was drinking it in. Some were nodding, some had their eyes closed and hands raised to the ceiling. I didn't know what to do.

'Praise Him!' Hannah said.

I stared at the table, at all the grooves made by scratches and weathering, at the grain of it, the whorls and rings, the knot marks. I could almost hear the tree that made it creaking in the wind, the shudder of a chainsaw, the—

'I asked you a question!' I looked at him. I hadn't heard any questions. 'What do you think of our paradise?' he said, slowly, like I was dense.

I flinched, then nodded. 'Really nice,' I said, like a sap. In my head I wanted to tell him to fuck off, to let me go home, but what came out of my mouth was something else. That was the effect he had on people. 'Great.'

He nodded. 'Great and *nice*,' he said. 'Yes, it is nice. But not *too* nice – lest you get too comfortable. Life is a short dream, Alex. You don't want to get too *attached* to it.' I nodded, even though what he was saying sounded like riddles. He turned the piece of paper over in his hands thoughtfully. 'Didn't I say? Didn't I say that this would happen?' A few people murmured and nodded, as if they were encouraging him. 'It's uncanny. So soon after the vision. And now this . . . and the girl . . .' He looked at me again as if I contained a puzzle or a secret and shook his head. 'We should be in the church on our knees! Thanking God for revealing His mysteries!'

'Yes!' Thomas leaped up and punched the air.

But Mr Bragg blinked and cleared his throat. 'Mr Bevins, if I may . . .'

'*What?*' He looked suddenly irritated.

'Some of us have been talking . . . Everyone is very *tired*. The crops . . . The farm needs working. We can't be at church all the time. People are exhausted. They need to rest, to eat, to sleep.'

There was a silence that lasted a beat too long, then a long-suffering sigh. 'They need to sleep?!' He sounded incredulous. 'When the hour is at hand? We don't need sleep! We need to be walking on the high wire to the glory. It could be weeks now, *days* even. Brothers, we are so lucky to be here.' He made his eyes big.

'How long since we've had a word from Naomi? How many *years* have we been waiting? And now this in the same *week*!'

'But people will be able to think better in the morning.'

'No better time to think about God than the present!' He folded his arms.

'No one doubts you, Bevins, but . . . The people, we, *I*, need a rest tonight. Maybe you can read to us from the Book of Jonah, before we retire. That will sharpen our minds and in the morning we can gather . . .'

There was another long pause, like the vacuum suck before an explosion. I thought Mary looked scared.

'You're telling *me*?' Bevins's eyes narrowed. 'You're telling *me* what to read to *you*?'

Everyone looked at the floor. Mr Bragg had gone red.

'You know this is how it starts! With a little rest, a little *weakness*. And before you know it, you are so far down the path of backsliding no one can save you. You know what it says in the scriptures! I was sent by God to keep you to the path, keep you *safe*, so that you will live for all eternity. That is my calling. I work so hard for you, so *hard*.'

'But . . .' Mr Bragg looked scared; his chin wobbled and his voice became high-pitched. 'There's so much to do on the farm that we don't have time to spend all day in church.'

'Pffffft,' Mr Bevins whistled through his teeth. 'There's the struggle, my Brothers, right there. See how it starts, with just one little doubt, and then it all falls away and before you know it the whole of eternity is lost because you were *tired*.' His eyes narrowed. 'We've had such exciting news! And all you want to do is sleep! Who are these people? Who among you is coming to the church?'

'I will!' said Thomas, first to put his hand up. He looked at his father with contempt.

Mr Bevins smirked. 'Of course there's no *pressure*, Brothers — those of you who would rather follow the doubter here, there is no shame in it, in admitting that you are backsliding, but . . .'

'But, Mr Bevins, you know, my heart.' Mr Bragg touched his chest. 'I need to rest.'

'Indeed I do know the weakness of your heart, and it is wretched and faithless. You can rest.' He nodded at Jonathan and another man who came up behind Mr Bragg and took him by the arms. 'In the Solitary.'

'Please! No! I have a weak heart. Dee, tell him.'

But Mrs Bragg was turned away from him, shaking her head. 'I told you that you were backsliding, but you wouldn't listen.'

'See?' Mr Bevins said. 'Even your wife can't bear to look at you.' He nodded at the men. 'Love the sinner, hate the sin, and he is so full with sin right now I can't even see him. You need to spend some time in prayer and private contemplation. Take him away.' And he waved his hand to dismiss them.

'No!' Mr Bragg said. 'This isn't right! This isn't what we came here for!' He struggled, but the men were much taller and stronger than him, nearly lifting him off his feet as they dragged him out of the room. I tried to catch Rebekah's eye, but she was staring into space, her hands clasped in front of her, same as they all were.

When they'd taken him, Mr Bevins asked again, 'Who is with me? Who will come and pray?'

One by one everyone put their hand up. Even me.


The church smelled of damp and dust and it was cold. Bevins stood at the front with his eyes closed for a long time. Everyone was standing, stiff and obedient, for ages, until the twins started to fidget. I was right at the back with Rebekah and the other women who were all praying silently, their heads bowed.

Once the boys started to make a noise Bevins opened his eyes and stared at Mary. She looked flustered, but it wasn't her fault. Children can't be expected to stay still for that long. She shushed them, then made a bed for them under the chairs out of her coat, where they curled up and slept. I could see through the windows that it was already getting dark. I wanted to look at my phone to find out the time. But I didn't dare get it out in front of everyone. At some point Jonathan and the other man came back from taking Mr Bragg to the Solitary. The door closed behind them, and they took their places down the front right next to Mr Bevins, but he didn't even open his eyes or acknowledge that they had returned.

After ages, he inhaled loudly through his nose and brought himself up on his tiptoes. He pushed back his sleeves and stretched his arms to the sky and started speaking, except it was in a language I didn't understand. Then others started to join in until the room echoed with the babble of everyone speaking a loud mumbo-jumbo.

I prodded Rebekah. 'What are they saying?'

'They're speaking in the spirit.'

'Sounds like baby talk,' I said, too loudly.

'*Shhhh*. It might be a prophecy,' she whispered. 'Someone will translate it.'

The noise went on and on, someone even started clucking like a chicken, Jonathan started laughing. I'd been in church before where they'd had a kind of free prayer, but it wasn't like this.

Then Bevins lowered his arms like a conductor, and the noise stopped and he smiled at everyone benevolently, then stared at me. I looked at the floor.

He motioned for people to sit. He said he'd had a message from God, 'something important that needs to be heard'. He started talking about sin. About the temptations of the flesh and how easy it was to be led astray. He talked about adultery and the abomination of homosexuality. He talked a lot about homosexuality. He said the word *sexual* like it was a disease. He got very red in the face, describing how God would punish the 'deviants and sodomites' — how he couldn't bear to look at sin, how he must turn his face away. 'It's these among all other sins that have ruined this world for the rest of us!' He talked about how you would end up in hell if you did any of these things, although it wasn't really clear what he meant by 'things'. But he described very vividly exactly how painful it would be when the fires of hell were burning you, melting the flesh from your bones, charring your skin like a barbeque, boiling your brains inside your skull, and the pain and torment that would last for eternity. I felt sick. I knew he was talking about me.

After he'd finished speaking he insisted we all knelt to pray. I watched Rebekah beside me, folding herself up on her knees, clasping her hands together and resting her forehead on them. She was muttering a prayer under her breath. I wanted to interrupt her and ask who she thought she was speaking to, I wanted to grab her hand and pull her away from all of this, I wanted to shout loudly and tell them all not to listen to his madness, but I caught Mr Bevins staring at me like he could see straight through me and I quickly closed my eyes and pretended to pray.

# TWELVE

# REBEKAH

Mr Bevins went on a long time tonight. Hours. I have no sense of the time, except I know it's late when we get back to the farmhouse. We take the boys and put them in their cots. Peter is whining and clingy. I sing him the song of Noah, about the animals, and then tell him the story of Jonah swallowed into the belly of the whale, until eventually he quietens. Alex squats in the doorway and watches. When they are asleep I go into my bedroom, leaving the door ajar so I can hear in case they wake up.

I sit on my bed and Alex sits next to me. She's so close I could touch her hair. Being so close to her does something strange to my head. Like I'm going too fast or something, and all the nerves in my body tingle and I feel like I must be blushing all the time. We're quiet for a moment. Then she whispers. 'You must be so *bored*.'

I draw my knees up to my chin and pull my dress down over my legs. I'm hungry and my bones hurt with cold.

'You don't even have music or books.'

'We do! And anyway, we won't need them where we're going.'

'And where is that, exactly?'

I don't know how she does it, but she has a way of asking questions that are impossible to answer, and all the things that have always seemed so easy to talk about, fall away from me. I want to her to see that I'm not stupid, that I do know about the world. I prayed hard in church that she would see the light. I want her to go to heaven to be with me. I want her to be with me; I want her to meet my mother.

I show her the encyclopedia Mary gave me. She told me to read from it and study it when I am not reading the Bible. *The Encyclopedia of the World 1973*. It's old and smells of rotting paper. Everything about the world in one volume. In the margins Mary has written notes, links to Bible verses, comments. There are colour plates to illustrate some of the key features. The nervous system, the chambers of the heart, the countries of the world, even the history of the kings and queens of Britain and Europe. Just opening the book makes me excited.

Alex flicks through it. 'This is a bloody antique!' she says. 'Where are the fossils and dinosaurs?'

I shrug. I don't know what she's talking about.

'And reproduction? Someone's ripped out the pages,' she says.

'Oh.'

I hadn't noticed this before.

'Look.' She throws the book down next to me, pointing to the places in the index where it says: *Dinosaurs*, *Darwin and Evolution*, *Fossils* and *Human Reproduction*.

'Maybe they fell out,' I say.

She snorts. 'Right. Someone *made* them fall out, more like.' She flicks back through the book until she gets to Ancient Egypt. Here Mary has written: *Worshipped False Idols! Satan's Lies!* and a list of verses. There is an illustration of Egyptian symbols, and one that is an eye, the same as Alex's tattoo. She points at it and laughs.

'Look,' she says. 'My tattoo! "The eye of Horus is an ancient Egyptian symbol of protection, royal power and good health",' she reads. 'See? I told you it was for protection.'

'"Also known as the eye of Ra",' I continue, but then I look

111

at Mary's margin notes. She has circled the word Ra and in the margin written: *Another word for Satan!*

A fear rises in me. Alex has the symbol of Satan on her. 'Why did you come here?' I say, my voice a hiss. 'To torment me?'

'I'm not tormenting you!'

'Yes, you are! Why aren't you listening?'

'Ha! Like you, you mean?'

'Yes.'

'Because I'm not *stupid.*'

I flinch from her, then snatch the encyclopedia and bang it shut. Her criticism stings like a slap.

'I mean, don't you hate it?'

'Hate what?'

'Being told what to think all the time. I couldn't stand it – no one tells *me* what to think.'

'I'm not told what to think! I'm here because I'm chosen! Don't you *want* to go to heaven?'

She shakes her head. 'I don't believe in it.'

'You don't believe in heaven?!' How can she not? I can't believe she's so ignorant.

'I think we make our own heaven and hell here on earth. I mean, don't you listen to music or anything?' she asks.

''No,' I say, not really knowing what she means. 'We sing hymns and sometimes Micah Protheroe plays guitar, but we're not allowed to play the music of the world.'

'Don't tell me –' she shakes her head – 'it's the work of the devil?'

I nod. 'The devil can get in through music,' I say.

'How, exactly?'

I don't know the answer to this, though I assume it must be through the ears.

She gets her phone out of her pocket. 'I've got some amazing hip hop on here.' She switches it on, but then has to hide it right away at the sound of footsteps on the stairs. I stand up. It's Mary. She comes into the room and, seeing Alex sitting on my bed, flinches.

'Right,' she says. 'Where's the camp bed?'

'I was just showing her the encyclopedia,' I say, holding up the book.

'Well, that's nice, but I need you to get some rest now.'

Suddenly I feel really awkward. I jump up and help Mary put the bed together, threading the poles through the canvas, shaking out the spare sleeping bag. When I'm done, Mary waits by the door with her hands on her hips for us to get into our own beds.

'Come on, chop-chop.'

She stands there watching while we both get under the covers. She takes the candles away and pulls the door to, although I can hear her breathing outside for a long time. When I finally hear her feet on the stairs, I sit up.

'You asleep?' I whisper.

But Alex doesn't answer. I lie on my side and nuzzle into my pillow. I wish she would wake up and talk to me, because even though I'm exhausted, being alone in the dark with her makes me wide awake. I lie there not sleepy at all and wonder if Mother can see me, and if she thinks about me if she can, or if she is so busy with her business in heaven that she has forgotten all about me. I'm sure she would like Alex if she met her.

In the middle of the night something wakes me. It's Alex, sitting bolt upright, shouting, gasping for air.

'You OK?'

'I had a nightmare,' she says groggily. 'That I was still here, and then I realized I was.'

'Come here,' I say, and she gets out of her bed and comes and lies next to me. Her body trembles. 'Don't let anything bad happen to me,' she mutters. '*Please.*'

'It's OK,' I say, putting my arm around her. 'Nothing's going to happen to you. I promise.' But even as I say it, doubt creeps around the edges of my mind. Even in the warm hollow of the bed, in my heart there is the cold glitter of fear. When her breathing has calmed and she's asleep I get out of my bed and into the camp bed. Something tells me that Mary wouldn't be OK with us sharing again.


Mary wakes us before the light has even had a chance to colour the sky. I can only have had a few hours' sleep. I feel sick and groggy.

'What is this?' she asks, pulling the covers off me. 'Why aren't you in your own bed?'

'Wha' time is it?' I say blearily. I'm sure I've only been properly asleep for about five minutes.

'You had your lie-in yesterday. There's too much to do to be lazing around all day. And I don't know why you're not in your own bed.'

Alex puts her head over the covers. 'It hurt my back. So we swapped.'

'Hmph.' She looks unconvinced. 'We'll have to sort out something more permanent for you – I think probably you should be sharing with Ruth.'

No! She can't do that. *I'm* supposed to be looking after Alex. *Me*, not Ruth.

'You heard Bevins yesterday. We have to be constantly vigilant

114

and help each other keep to the path. Now hurry up.'

We get dressed and fumble our way downstairs. I don't say anything to Alex, but I can't quite work out what we're supposed to have done wrong. I can still feel the bony tremble of her body in my arms. She likes to act all tough, but actually she's small and scared; I can see that in her. She catches me staring and pulls a dumb face, and then an even dumber one, which makes me laugh. I don't think I've met anyone, ever, who made me laugh like she does.

After prayers, Mary gives us bowls with a smudge of porridge and a cup of weak, milkless tea. Bevins says that being hungry is good for us, it keeps us sharp and spiritual, makes us consider our souls and not the corruption of our physical flesh. Sometimes after a service or prayer meeting or something I am so full of light that I'm not hungry at all. But this morning my stomach growls and clenches.

The men have already eaten and gone to their appointed tasks. Alex complains loudly about the fact that it is the women who are expected to clean up the piles of dishes that Hannah brings in from the dining room.

'It's not fair! Why can't the men help?'

'They have their appointed role, just as we have ours,' says Hannah. '*Blessed is the woman who follows the directions of a man.*'

Alex looks sceptical. 'But what if that man's a wanker?'

Mary blinks. Margaret crosses herself.

'Alex, we're daughters of Eve. We carry her wayward genes. We're the ones who threw away paradise. Don't forget that,' she says.

'I don't believe this shit,' Alex mutters.

Something in me wants to laugh hysterically because everything

115

is so tense and prickly. Hannah and Margaret won't even look at her. They are behaving like she's infectious. Every time she speaks they freeze and raise their eyebrows.

'But don't you miss *stuff*? Like a dishwasher and a washing machine?' she asks. We have to wait for the pot of water on the stove to heat up before we can wash the dishes.

'We came here for a simpler life. To get away from the temptations of laziness. Keeping busy is good for the soul – even small tasks like cleaning can be meaningful if done for the glory of God,' Mary says.

'*A good woman looks well to the ways of her household*,' Hannah says.

'*She girds herself with strength*,' Mrs Bragg replies.

It's a prayer that we say sometimes in church, when Mr Bevins wants to lift up the spirits of the women.

Alex sucks her teeth and scowls. 'Whatever floats your boat.'

Mary gives her one of her cold, steady stares. 'You may come to see in time, Alex, that you are more like us than you think.'

When we're finished with the washing-up the dawn has started to streak the sky red and purple and Mary tells us that today we are to work in the kitchen garden.

'What if I don't want to?' Alex says, but there isn't much fight in her voice.

We go to the tack room to get ready. Alex is still wearing the same clothes that she came in; her trousers are filthy with mud all around the bottom and her shoes are soaking. Mary says she will give her a new pair of shoes only if she agrees to wear a dress.

'Fu– get lost,' she says.

There is a tense silence, then Mary laughs. 'The Lord certainly moved in mysterious ways when he sent us *you*.' And she goes back into the kitchen without pushing her point.

Alex laces up her shoes getting mud all over her hands. Her feet squelch when she walks.

'But you can't wear those the whole time. You'll stink,' I say.

'Like you, you mean?' She points at my headscarf. 'Don't you ever take that off?'

I put my hand up to my head. I can't remember the last time I shook out my hair from its braids. When Mother was alive she would undo it all and boil up water on the stove once a month and rub sweet-smelling shampoo into it, or when there wasn't shampoo she would mix an egg and then rub it into my scalp. Then she would dry it very slowly before the fire, brushing and brushing until the hair was fine and soft, and then she would braid it into fine plaits and then tuck it all up again inside my scarf. Now I just tie a headscarf over it every day and don't think about it.

'No.'

'Well, that smells.'

'Fu—' I stop myself. But I can't believe what I nearly said.

'What did you just say?' she says, nudging me.

'Nothing.'

The day is high and cloudless. It's going to be hot, a late summer present after all the rain and wind. We follow Mrs Bragg and Hannah and Margaret past the cabins and the church to the kitchen garden. It's supposed to be protected from the sheep and the goats by a fence that Micah dug into the earth to stop the rabbits. But they still manage to get in. They've been here in the night – almost a whole row of carrots has been dug up, and they've messed up the earth around the gate.

Mrs Bragg wails when she sees this. 'I *told* Daniel to come down here with the gun last night!' She starts to cry.

'Now, now, Anne. Live for the Victory!' Hannah says.

'I'm just so tired . . . If only Brian was more reliable . . .'

She turns away from us and I can see her shoulders are trembling and she makes a little snuffling sound and everyone's pretending not to notice because Mr Bragg is backsliding and that means she is looked on with suspicion too.

The Braggs came with Thomas in the second year. They were family friends of the pastor on the mainland, and in the early days they often gave testimony. Mr Bragg said he was like the man who found that it was easier for a camel to pass through the eye of a needle than for a rich man to enter the kingdom of heaven and it wasn't until the bank took everything that he realized how poor he had been all along.

'The moment I became poor was the moment we became rich!'

He'd been running a property business and couldn't pay his debts, and then the bank came and repossessed everything. When they came to New Canaan it took Mrs Bragg a while to adjust. Hannah calls her 'Lady Muck' sometimes because she has a tendency to complain, and we have prayed over her many times in church because she often struggles with her thoughts. But it's Mr Bragg who is now in the Solitary for backsliding.

'You two —' Hannah turns to us — 'go and help Gideon in the polytunnel. There's lots of weeding that needs doing. And you —' she points at Margaret and Ruth.

There are four polytunnels, each with different crops; in one tomatoes, in another cucumbers, aubergines and chillies, in a third sweet potatoes and tender squashes, and the fourth is used for sowing and growing on. This is where Gideon lives most of the time, tending to his trays of seedlings. He has an old armchair in which he sits, pulled up to a potting bench which is covered in soil. His fingers are swollen and gnarled and he struggles to take tiny pinches of soil and seeds and get them into the pots without spilling them all over himself. He mostly speaks the old language. In years gone by his family owned this island, and he can remember coming here as a boy with his father and grandfather.

He grunts at us when we come in. His face is crazed with deep lines. He's something of a law unto himself, but no one minds him much as long as he goes to church. Mr Bevins is often blessing him, holding him up as an example of the old faithful. But I have heard him talking to Father about him differently; if he could, he would send him back to the mainland, but there's nowhere for him to go, except into a home and 'it's not clear who would pay for that'. So he stays here.

'We've come to help you this morning,' Margaret says, loudly and slowly.

Gideon nods. 'Oh yes,' he says.

'Is there anything that needs doing right away?'

He nods again. 'Oh yes,' he says again, but does not elaborate.

'What would that be then?'

He shakes his head. 'I don't know.'

Ruth sucks her teeth. 'You two go and pinch out the tomatoes and do some weeding.' She waves at me and Alex. 'Margaret and I will –' she looks at the mess – 'tidy up in here.'

The air is hot and humid and almost immediately I'm sweating. The tomato plants have grown into a tangle, pressing against the plastic as if urgently trying to escape. We have to squeeze ourselves between the plants to get down the row. It doesn't look like anyone has done any work in here for ages, and heavy bunches of tomatoes are ripening and splitting on the vines. They weren't even red before we went on Mission Week.

'It stinks in here,' Alex says. The air is fuzzy with the smell of tomatoes.

I give her a bucket and tell her to pick the ripest tomatoes.

'But they're rotten.'

'Not all of them.' I point at some that seem whole, only to see that they are split up the back. 'Well, never mind, pick them anyway. Mary will know what to do with them.'

But she doesn't do as I say; instead she gets her phone out of her pocket again and switches it on.

'Put that away! If anyone sees it, you'll be in trouble.'

'It's dead now anyway.' She shows me the black screen. She bites her lip and shoves it back in the pocket of her hoodie.

'Why do you always want to look at it anyway?'

She laughs bitterly. 'You wouldn't understand.'

'Why not? I can understand a lot of things.'

'Yeah, but you're like . . .' She turns up her nose.

'What?'

'Them.' She nods her head outside the polytunnel.

'No, I'm not!'

'Of course you are! You were born here, right? You don't know anything about the world!'

This stings. I don't want her to think I'm so ignorant. 'They said the Rapture would come before I got older so there didn't seem any point in learning,' I say. Until I met Alex, nothing else had ever occurred to me as a possibility.

'That's sad.' She was snarly, but now she looks as if she pities me.

The idea that there are other places to be, where there are new people I could meet, sets fire to something in my head. I could leave here. One day I could actually, literally, *leave*. The idea bursts into flame like paper thrown on embers. I don't know why I never realised it before.

'It's what people do, right? Leave home. Everyone on this island left home once. *They* chose to be here; you didn't.'

'No, no, no . . . but . . .' I don't know what to say to this. 'But I *can't*. I don't know how.'

'Get me that satellite phone, and I'll show you how we can leave.'

*We?* 'You mean I can come with you?' The possibility of the world is suddenly close. Life, away from here. My heart bursts.

'Rebekah, if the authorities knew what was really going on here, they would make *everyone* leave. What happened to the twins is not OK; that's child abuse.'

'No, it's not!' But my voice comes out too high, unconvincing even to me. 'Mary was just trying to keep them safe!'

'What, by giving them drugs and leaving them alone all day? They didn't even have any water!' She touches my arm. 'Are you OK? You've gone all white.'

'But what if I leave and the Rapture comes while I'm gone?' The idea of being left behind on earth while they are in heaven paralyses me.

'Oh, come on! You know that's not true!'

'Do I? I don't know.' It's as if a door in my head has been opened only to be slammed shut again almost straight away. It's so confusing. 'We should get on with it.' I pick up my bowl and start pulling tomatoes off the vines. *Thinking is sinking*.

We work silently for a while, hot and sweaty in the muggy heat. We fill five bowls with tomatoes; they are mushy but still useable, and I can see I'm going to spend all day tomorrow in the kitchen

121

with Mary, making chutneys. Alex has given up and is sitting on the floor with her head resting on her knees.

Then something from the corner of my eye: the fuzzy silhouette of a figure glimpsed through the translucent plastic, then suddenly he's there inside the polytunnel.

'There's been a miracle!' Mr Bevins announces, his eyes flashing. He stands very still and watches us, his head raised just slightly, chin jutting as if he is alert to something in the air. He takes a deep breath. 'Something smells bad in here.'

I cringe. There is a high tone to his voice. I don't like him to be so close to us.

'What?' Alex asks.

He looks at the bowls of tomatoes. 'I don't know, but when the devil is near I can *smell* him.'

He kicks over one of the bowls and tomatoes spill out on to the ground.

'Look at these.' He shudders. 'Don't you sense it? There's something unholy in here.'

Alex snorts, then seeing his expression turns it into a cough.

'We are in a constant battle. All around us devils and angels.' He stamps on the tomatoes. 'Give me the other bowls.' He tips them all out and then stamps on them too. Seeds and pulp explode everywhere, all our hard work, the whole season's crop destroyed. Mary will go mad – she's been saving jars especially for the chutney.

'We must pray. Come here, Rebekah, come here.' He beckons me towards him and grabs hold of Alex by the wrist.

His face is deadly serious. He holds my arm so tight it hurts and starts to mutter a prayer for protection. I look at the tomatoes at his feet all mushed up into a slimy, seedy mess. Can tomatoes be possessed? He's sweating as he prays, his eyes squeezed tight. I glance at Alex, who is smirking as if she wants to laugh. I daren't catch her eye in case she makes me laugh too, and then he will get angry and I don't want him to send me to the Solitary.

'Amen!'

Eventually he lets us go and raises his eyes to the sky and sighs. 'We must be so vigilant. In these last days he will do anything – *anything* – to tempt us away from the truth.' Bevins crosses himself and then puts his arms around us both in a hug, pulling us close to his bony chest.

Alex struggles to get free. 'Get off.'

He turns away from me. 'Alex, Alex, it's new and frightening to be confronted with the truth, I know. I *know*. But you will see that I am only here for *your* good.' He smiles at her, and holds her face in his hands, staring into her eyes. 'God loves you so *much*. He has chosen *you*.' I can see he has tears in his eyes. He smiles and she sort of smiles back awkwardly, as if she is sorry for him. 'Come with me, both of you. There's something important I need to show you. To show all of you.' He gestures to the sky. 'Come on.'

We follow him outside and out of the kitchen garden until we are standing by the church, where the whole community is waiting. Everyone is gathered, screwing up their eyes against the sun. Thomas stands so close he is almost touching him. Only Father is not there, which is strange. Bevins jumps up on top of one of the crates that lie by the gate to make himself taller.

'Brethren!' he says. 'Pray with me now.'

In order to see him up there I have to squint. He is a dark shadow in the sky against the dazzle of the sun. I close my eyes against the glare.

He says if we are to witness a miracle then we must be prepared to see it, to receive the word of God.

'This is no time for work! Soon there will be no need for this kind of earthly toil, no need for clothes, or food, heat or light. We will walk among the angels, like one of them. Imagine that! Imagine!'

I squeeze my eyes tight shut and try to imagine, but all I can see is the mush of squashed tomatoes and the scuffed brown leather of Mr Bevins's boots. He talks of all the heavenly creatures and eternity, which means for ever and ever after we are dead, and the burning flames that wait for the sinful, the idea of which makes my stomach sink to my feet. Then he stops abruptly and I look up. I can see Father walking across from the barn towards us.

'Bevins!' His voice is tight, angry. 'I thought we weren't gathering until this evening?'

'But there is further proof! Another sign!' He looks at Father then and pauses. 'The mainland makes you weak, I know.' He sounds concerned. 'It's so hard to be in the darkness without being tainted.' He shakes his head. 'But the time is *now*.'

'Bevins, the crops . . . the winter . . .' Father looks up at the sky 'We must make hay while the sun shines. Surely this weather is a sign?' he says, speaking slowly and clearly.

Bevins takes a breath and shakes his head. 'Is that saying even biblical?'

'No!' Thomas shouts.

'While what you say might be perfectly rational and logical to *you*, what it sounds like to *me* is the words of the *devil*.' He stares at Father, hard. 'Do you want to follow Brother Bragg to the Solitary?'

Father shakes his head. 'But, Bevins . . .'

Mr Bevins waves his hand to dismiss him. 'Something has happened,' he says. 'An amazing thing. Another sign. And I want you all to see it. Come.'

# THIRTEEN

# REBEKAH

We follow him. In single file down the path that leads to the farmhouse, then out across the fields along the sheep track that leads towards the north shore. Men first, women behind. Mary has the twins, who can walk for a while but soon need to be carried. Ruth takes Peter and Mary carries Paul, but it makes us slow, and before too long the main group are much further ahead of us and we are dawdling behind.

Alex walks beside me, her hands hidden in the sleeves of her hoodie.

'Why do we have to walk behind the men? It's like something out of the Dark Ages. That Mr Bevins is a total Nazi,' she mutters.

'He's come with his own struggles, Alex.' Hannah is hovering around us. I feel like we're being watched. 'We respect him because he's been chosen by the Lord. He is gifted. He has the ear of God. To have someone like him help us prepare for the end is a blessing! We live for the Victory!'

'Whatever.'

Hannah sighs. 'I pray for you. We all do.' Then she falls back and starts chattering to Mrs Webber instead about what this new sign might mean.

Alex pulls the hood of her jacket over her head. 'You don't really think it's coming, do you?' she asks me.

'What?' My mind has slid off somewhere else. I look at the

wraps of leather and beads around her wrists and wonder if I could get away with wearing one, if I could hide it under the sleeves of my dress. I could make one from garden twine or scraps of leather from the sewing bags.

'The end of the world? The Rapture.'

'Oh. Well, it won't be the end of the world for us,' I say. 'Not for everyone. Just the beginning for some people. All the true believers will disappear, leaving the rest of the world to the Tribulations.'

I tell her Bevins's vision, how everyone that is not a true believer will be left behind to deal with the seven years of war and Tribulations that will come with the reign of the Antichrist. It will still be possible to get to heaven; it will just be harder than before, and the Christians will have to live like outlaws, hand to mouth, from the land like we do now. 'This is just like a preparation. We need to live outside the boundaries of temptation if we are going to get called, but we're also learning how to survive, in case we don't.'

'But how can Bevins know?'

I look ahead at Bevins, who is deep in conversation with Father and Micah Protheroe. He has his arms around their shoulders, almost as if he is pushing them forward.

'He's a prophet. Ever since he was a child he knew he was chosen to do the special work of God.'

'But anyone could say that.'

'Yes, but not everyone *does*.' I don't get her argument. 'He's gifted.'

Mr Bevins often bears witness about his journey to the Lord. He tells the story of the blind beggar who was really Jesus in disguise, and how he was brought up in a small one-bedroom house with only his mother, who was sick in the head. He said he was often beaten and left for days with no food, but that the Lord looked after him and saved him and that when he was older he realized that it was for the specific purpose of leading God's people to glory, to help us to get ready, to prepare. I tell Alex this story, but she has her arms folded and she looks sceptical.

'I know, he told me that story. But *seriously*, so what?' she snorts. 'He's not any more special than you are.'

'But . . .' She's gone and done it again. All the answers that I'd give people on Mission Week about Bevins being a special prophet of God sound wrong when I try to say them to her.

'What's over there?' She points to a stone that stands in the field beyond the sheep troughs. 'Is that the graveyard?'

I shake my head. No one knows why the stone is there. Carved all over it are strange marks, whorls and lines and circles within circles. Some of the lines are so indistinct and full of moss it's hard to know what they might be. Mother said it was made by people who lived on this island long ago. Hannah and Margaret look at it fearfully as if it might contain spells and say it's a symbol of the times when the world was covered in a great darkness, although I don't remember that bit in the Bible.

'I want to see it,' Alex says, walking away from me and leaping the gate into the field.

I follow her. 'We'll get left behind.'

She shrugs. 'It's not like you can get lost on an island this size.'

I suppose it can't hurt for a few minutes. Mary and Ruth and the other women are busy with the boys and Hannah is ahead of us, deep in conversation with Mrs Webber. The stone is bigger than you expect. The distances are deceptive — from the path it looks close by, but it's a long way across the field. The stone is at least the size of two men standing on each other's shoulders.

'Wow,' she says, looking up at it. 'Neolithic.' She traces the lines of one of the circles with her fingers.

I don't know what she's talking about, but she sounds like an expert.

'Stone Age,' she says. 'Don't they have that in your encyclopedia?'

'God made the heavens and earth in seven days,' I say.

I don't really know what the Stone Age is. In my head I have some idea of the galaxies forming, the world coming together in some big crash like a sudden wave that comes in and then goes out, leaving things washed up on the beach. One minute there was nothing, the next there was a whole world, seas, animals, people.

'You sound like them,' she says, pointing at the group disappearing over the horizon. 'It's evolution. People growing more civilized as we evolved from our monkey nature.'

'Monkey?!'

'Yes, human beings evolved from apes. But you don't believe in that, do you?'

This makes me uncomfortable. I have never heard anyone actually say that they believe in the Big Lie before.

Mr Bevins goes on about evolution all the time. He says it's another reason that the Rapture is coming soon, because people have started believing in false theories that have led them away from God. 'But that's not in the Bible.'

'But the Bible is just a story written by people thousands of years ago. A *story*. A story isn't a fact. A fact is a fact. It's scientific.'

'But . . .' I don't know how to argue with her. 'The Bible isn't a story. It's *history*.'

'No, it's not!' She shakes her head in disbelief. 'It's *impossible* for it to be literally true. It's a story from thousands of years ago. Like Shakespeare or whatever. I mean, you've got to admit it, Bevins is kind of *extreme*.'

Her words frighten me. I look at the stone with its mossy engravings and feel a cold terror at the idea that everything I've ever believed in is nothing but a *story*. 'Come on,' I say. 'We'd better catch up.'

The main group has disappeared over the ridge of the field. Mary waves at us to come back to the path. Even though the island is only five miles across from north to south and nearly seven from east to west, the ground is rough going and we are crossing at the widest point. The fields are protected by stone walls that were made by the crofters, but in places they are crumbling and slowly sinking into the ground. We clamber over them, sheep running away from us in panicked clumps.

'Baaa!' Alex says, chasing them and laughing. 'Sheep are so *stupid*!'

Once we get past the fields the land gives way again to moorland which leads straight to the sea and the long stretch of sand that is the north beach. Blue-grey sea appears over the lip of the horizon. Around here there are birds' nests and burrows for puffins, although this time of year they are all out at sea. Alex stumbles into a puffins' burrow, kicking up a whole mess of moss and twigs. It even still has some broken eggshells in it.

'Oops.' She stops to look at the mess. 'Did I kill it?'

'No. It's old. From the spring.'

A buzzard flies above us in the blue sky, wings tipped, then turns and dives into the heather, rising again with something – a mouse, a vole – squirming in its talons. The breeze seems to be getting colder and stiffer. The weather here can change faster than you can sneeze; a breeze turns into a gale and a storm can blow in and it can be sunny again all in an afternoon. I look at Alex, her face set against the wind, her eyes squeezed to look at the horizon; she looks older than me, braver. Then she turns and smiles, and something tugs in my chest.

I want very much to know what she knows. There is so much that she understands that I don't, and I want to know what that is. I want to know everything.

'Rebekah, come and help us.' Mary is now right in front of me. She hands Peter over to me. 'Help carry him.' Peter mithers and nuzzles his face into my neck. He's heavy now, too heavy to be carried such a long way, but too little to walk. Mary rubs her back.

'Where are we going anyway?' Alex asks.

'To the beach,' Ruth says, putting Paul down and letting him run on a little on his unsteady legs. 'Just over there.' She points to the place where I can see the others, grouped together, looking down at the beach. 'There is a miracle apparently. Thomas found it.'

I carry Peter on my back, zigzagging along the path until I make him giggle.

'Silly Becca!' He squeals. 'Silly!' He tugs at my hair.

As we get closer to the cliffs, the land stops abruptly and falls down into the sea and the beach comes into view, a long curve of sand with rocks at either end where seals live. In the middle of the beach there is the surprise of a new mass, dark against the sand.

'What the hell is *that*?' Alex asks.

We stop and look down at the beach. It looks like a long rock, black and glistening, except for the familiar shape of its tail. The men are already gathered round it.

'I think it's a whale,' I say. Sometimes you can see them offshore in the water, slick shapes rising against the waves. Once I saw a whole pod of orcas breach the water, around the cliffs by the Solitary, chasing seals, turning the water red with the blood of their kill. Naomi's prophecy echoes in my head and a shiver runs through my body.

'Jonah!' Mary crosses herself.

Alex runs ahead of us. 'Wow! Is it still alive?'

'Of course not!' Mary says irritably. I have seen dead dolphins and seals on the shore, but never anything as big as this.

'Whale,' Peter says. 'Whale!'

The cliff slopes down into dunes, which give way to beach. Peter and Paul, excited, their tired legs forgotten, run on ahead. At the high-water mark is all the rubbish that gets pushed up the beach, driftwood, knots of fishing line, rope, broken lobster creels, plastic bottles and torn bits of tarpaulin, even a doll's head and an old shoe crusted with salt. Occasionally we come and collect it, and Micah sees if there's anything we can use and buries the rest in a pit. There is a dead gull trapped in the fishing line, half rotten, its wing already a skeleton.

'Eugh.' Alex jumps over it. 'Disgusting.'

As we get closer we can smell the whale. It's not bad yet, but it's a fishy dead smell that on a hot day will quickly turn to a stink. Seagulls scatter as we approach. There are great scars and tears on its flesh. Crabs scuttle about in the sand near one open wound. It's huge. Taller than me, even though it's ploughed into the sand, its enormous mouth open. The low tide laps about its tail, Alex gets her shoes soaked going to look. Its blue-black skin is rough with barnacles and wrinkles and beneath that the layer of white blubber that sailors used to melt down for candles. Daniel told me all of this. He knows more about the seas than anyone here, as he used to work on the rigs. He has faded tattoos on his forearms that say *Love* and *Mother* and *Sinner* in uneven blue letters. He said he did them himself in the days when he used to live in darkness.

Mr Bevins has gathered the men together in a circle and is saying prayers. He opens one eye and looks us but he does not stop. He is saying something about how God has sent us this as a sign that the Rapture is nigh.

The whale is on its side, and its slack mouth seems to be smiling sadly. I think of Jonah. How frightening it must have been for him, trapped in the dark, inside the belly of such a huge beast.

'Do you think he was afraid?' I whisper to Alex, looking into the grey darkness of its mouth, thinking out loud.

'What, the whale?'

'No. I meant Jonah.'

'Which Jonah?'

'Inside the whale when he got swallowed.'

'Eh? Who got swallowed?'

'In the Bible – Jonah and the Whale. He got swallowed by a whale because he had been disobedient to God.'

'Oh!' She gives me one of her are-you-stupid looks. 'Rebekah, if you got swallowed by a whale you'd, like, *totally* die. You'd *suffocate* or drown if you got swallowed by that thing.' She says this really loudly. Mary prods her and Mrs Bragg turns round and shushes her.

Looking at the size of the whale, I know she must be right. How could anyone survive inside for three days?

'Well *that* was one of God's miracles,' Mrs Bragg hisses, giving Alex a look like she should know better.

Alex tuts at her. 'Yeah. Like maybe Santa lives at the North

Pole and there are tooth fairies too.' She's still talking loud enough for people to hear.

Mr Bevins finishes his prayers with a booming *Amen!* Some at the front are crying.

Hannah wipes her eyes. 'We are so blessed,' she says.

'Indeed we are! What do you say to that?' Bevins says, looking at Father. 'After all your doubt?'

Father still has his eyes closed and his head bowed. He mutters an *amen* and looks up at Mr Bevins.

'Forgive me,' he says.

Mr Bevins bounces on his toes. 'See how the sinner repents in the face of God's miracles!' He goes over to Father and gives him a big hug. 'God loves you and forgives you,' he says. 'Being prepared for the End Times is why we are alive! This is what we strive for, and just when the road is rocky and difficult he sends us this encouragement, Brothers and Sisters!'

He points at the whale as if he himself has made it appear.

'This! This is the sign! For so long – so, so long – I've been carrying all your hopes and dreams, and here is the divine confirmation! In a week's time He will come and claim us for his own! We must prepare, Brothers and Sisters! Let there be nothing else in our heads apart from the glory! In five days on the stroke of midnight, He will come. In the last weeks I've been visited by so many visions and prophecies which have gathered like dark shadows in my mind, but today, all is revealed! As clear as day and night! Naomi has seen it too. I prayed with her only this morning before we found this miracle and she gave me a verse which points to the hour and the time. Our faith is rewarded!'

He beams as if the light of heaven itself is shining through his eyes. Sometimes there is something so passionate, so convincing about him that it's hard to ignore. I think about Mother up there in heaven. But after all the years of longing, it's an anticlimax to think that this will happen now. I look at Alex, who is idly drawing patterns in the sand with her shoe. Squiggles and hearts. And I know that there is something else I want now, more than to go to heaven, I want to leave the island with her and explore the world that she knows, understand the things that she has seen. Maybe I'll get left behind, but maybe I don't care, if it means I get to be with her. I don't want the Rapture to come. I'm not ready.

# FOURTEEN

# ALEX

'Walk with me,' he said.

The minute he'd stopped speaking Bevins came up to me, all sneaky and pulled me away from Rebekah. I didn't like to be separated from her. When we were together I felt I was safe. I think she had begun to understand this too and she stayed close to me until Mr Bevins tutted with impatience and told her to run along and join the women.

'It's OK,' I whispered to her, squeezing her arm.

I felt sorry for her. It wasn't fair to keep her here like this, growing like a mushroom in the dark, so utterly ignorant about the world. She might know about the sea and the tides and the weather and the crops, but what did she know about life? Her father seemed to ignore her and spend most of his time following around after Mr Bevins, and ever since she was a little girl she had been taught it was all going to end anyway, so what was the point of asking for more from her life? Now Bevins seemed convinced it really was about to happen. That the end was indeed nigh. This was not good.

Then Bevins put his arm around me, pulled me close. 'You brought this,' he said, pointing at the whale. '*You* made this happen.'

I laughed. 'No, I didn't! How could I?'

It was a great lump of dead blubber, huge and stinky, rotting and collapsing in on itself. It had nothing to do with me. Or with anybody. It was just what happened when things washed up on the beach, dead. It was unusual, but it wasn't anything special. A dead animal, that's all.

He laughed too, but not because he thought I was funny. 'Child, child, child. The world is governed by laws beyond our understanding. Everything is a sign, and every sign is a message. We only have to know how to read it. Don't spurn your gifts.'

And he pulled me closer, which made me tug away, except I couldn't because he was determined, strong, and because right next to me, as if from nowhere, there was Thomas, pressing into me. Squashing me between them, as if they'd like to crush me.

I could see the others in front of us in a line, Mary and Rebekah and the boys at the back. Rebekah turning every now and then to look back, but Bevins waited until they had climbed the brow of the hill and then it was just us, and I was scared.

'So, what d'you think of young Thomas here?' he asked, in a kind of insinuating voice, nudging me.

I didn't know what he meant. Or rather, I did, but I didn't want to think about it.

'Do you find him attractive?' I didn't even want to look at Thomas. His doughy face and bad teeth, his hot breath on my cheek.

I shrugged.

'He's an example of one who lives in the light. He is walking with the Lord. If the world was not going to end, would you lie with him as his wife?'

I felt Thomas's arm muscles tighten. I didn't like the way this conversation was going. 'Would you give yourself to him? Would you carry his children?'

They walked deliberately slowly. All the while Bevins going on about what me and Thomas might do together if we were married in a holy union sanctioned by God. It sounded like muffled porn talk to me and I could tell Thomas was getting excited. His breath grew heavier on my cheek, his thigh pressed hard against mine as we walked. I was afraid they were going to make me do something I didn't want to do.

'He needs to know that if the time was right, he could marry someone. That he could marry *you*. What do you say?'

I felt trapped, muddled. 'Don't I get to choose?'

'There is the problem.' He tutted. '*There* is exactly the problem. Women need to learn to submit to men. Don't you want to be saved? Aren't you going to walk through the gates of heaven with us?'

I felt like he was testing me, like he was testing both of us. And for a second, before I saw the desperate expression on his face, I felt a small flash of sympathy for Thomas; Bevins was controlling him, the same way someone might pull the strings on a puppet.

Then he dismissed Thomas with a wave of his hand. 'Off you go now, Thomas. Go and make sure the church is ready.'

And Thomas moved away from me, though I could still feel the press of his body against mine. He walked awkwardly for a few steps, then started to run, his shoulders hunched as if he was embarrassed.

When he was out of earshot Bevins said, 'Listen now, listen. You see how excited he gets? You see how he is like a wild dog? You know that this is because of you? Because of how you are *dressed*.' He pointed at my jeans. 'You can see the very shape of your legs through those.'

I wanted to laugh. If *my* skinny legs were a turn-on, then they really didn't get out enough.

'He can't help himself. It's what happens when men are confronted by women, which is why it's so important for you to be modest. To show that you know how to submit to a man, who in turn submits to God. Such is the natural order of things. You should talk to Margaret; she was like you. Before God brought her to us she lived in wickedness, like a prostitute.'

He let go of me and we walked along side by side. *Prostitute?* I thought. What the hell was he on about now? I could see the roof of the farmhouse and the cabins.

'Humanity has lost its dignity, Alex. Out there, on the mainland, people live like animals. Corrupted, base, impure. Anything goes! Everything is permitted. But here we keep God's laws.' He pats the cover of his Bible. 'We keep to the path laid out for us. Will you do something for me? For Thomas?'

He looked at me pleadingly.

'What?'

'Will you wear a dress? Like the others? A headscarf?'

I didn't want to say yes. All my instincts said no *no* NO, stand up for yourself, tell him to go to hell. But another part of me was frightened; I thought of Mr Bragg dragged off to the Solitary and wondered what he might do if I refused.

'I can't vouch for Thomas if you don't. He is made so excitable by your presence. Will you?'

He was asking me, but I didn't really have a choice.

'OK,' I said.

He put his arm around me again. 'Good girl,' he said, his voice breaking. His eyes glittered with tears. 'There is nothing more holy than a woman who keeps herself modest in the name of the Lord.'

*

138

When we got to the church everyone was waiting. The low talk gave way to silence as we walked through the doors.

'Brothers and Sisters, I bring with me the sinner who repents!' he said, holding my arm above my head, like the winner in a boxing match. He led me up the front, but not before he had whispered something to Mary, who immediately rushed off and returned a few minutes later carrying a bundle of black cloth.

'Here.' She held it out to me.

But Mr Bevins took it and bunched it up around the neck and put it over my head. The cloth fell over my body like a sack. I wanted to take it off right away. But I couldn't. I felt the hard stares of everyone looking at me. I just stood there stiff as a stick.

Then he took a headscarf and tied it around my head. 'No . . .' I mumbled, but it was too late.

'Praise Him!' Hannah said, and a few others muttered prayers until the room became loud and discordant.

'See He has sent us sinners who repent!'

I stood there up the front, hot and ridiculous, aware that everyone was staring, especially Thomas Bragg, who smirked at me while Bevins went on and on about how the time was now, how we had to give thanks, how we had to prepare. He was sure that he had the date and the time. More sure than he had ever been. 'Next week — next week the moment will be upon us and all our earthly suffering will be ended!'

Eventually he started leafing through his Bible and motioned for me to sit down next to Rebekah. She raised her eyebrows at me as I sat down, the cloth bunching around me like a heavy curtain.

'You're wearing a dress!' she said.

'In case you didn't notice —' I hissed at her — 'I didn't have any choice!'

'You look weird.'

'I *feel* weird.' I did. I felt like a fake version of myself. Like I was in a play or something and all I had to do was say my lines.

'I've got a plan,' she said, pointing at the doors. 'In a minute, follow me.'

Mr Bevins asked everyone to sit. Then he read us the story of Jonah who was swallowed by the whale.

When he had finished, Hannah stood up, hands raised to the ceiling. 'Oh Lord, thank You for this encouragement, for this sign that You are near,' she said. I watched her in prayer, eyes squeezed together the tightest, hands lifted higher than anyone else's. She was showing off.

Bevins said we needed to kneel and contemplate the last days. To become still so we could be even nearer to God. There was the hush of a deep concentration and I closed my eyes, except I couldn't concentrate. This was all getting too weird too fast. The end of the world wasn't going to happen; it was a load of mad rubbish. Wasn't it?

I didn't know how long I'd been sitting with my eyes closed; for a moment I wondered if I'd fallen asleep. One of the twins was whining and wanting to play with their toys, which dropped with a loud clatter on to the stone floor.

Rebekah poked me. 'Come on,' she said in a ticklish hiss close to my ear. She stood up. 'You need to pee.'

'No, I don't,' I said. And then it was her turn to give me a you-must-be-stupid-look. '*Oh*. OK.'

We stood up, and the women turned and stared.

'She needs the toilet,' Rebekah said to Mary, who raised her eyebrows at me but said nothing. Everyone else was still praying, their eyes closed, and no one seemed to notice us. But I knew

Bevins was watching. He had eyes in the back of his head.

Once we got outside Rebekah raced away from me, towards the cabins. 'Come on, we've got to be quick!'

I tried to run, but I kept tripping over my dress. 'I fucking hate this thing!' I said, trying to flap my arms free of the material.

'Why are you wearing it then? You look ridiculous!' She laughed at me.

'Because I was scared, OK?' I tore the headscarf off my head. 'Of what they might do.'

We both looked at each other, suddenly serious. 'Let's get that phone,' she said.

His cabin was close to the church. Rebekah tried the door but it was locked. We went round and peered through the window. Inside was a bed with a blanket folded on it and on the walls were pinned sheets and sheets of paper with writing on them so dense that some of the pages were almost black. Some seemed to have red lines connecting them, and bits of string pinned between the pages.

'Wow, look at that.'

On one piece near the window I could see the words *His salvation comes into the world as a dark light*, written over and over in biro so the paper was dented by the marks of the pen.

I ran my fingers underneath the rim of the window.

'I could probably force it. If I had something to lever it with.' I looked around me. 'There,' I said, pointing at a stick lying in the grass. 'Pass me that.'

Rebekah gave it to me and I tried to drive it under the window frame. There was a splintering sound, but all that broke was the stick. Panic rose through my body.

'Too rotten.' I stepped back. 'I don't care if we get caught. We need to get a message out there. Someone will come and help us. Find a stone, find a stone!'

I looked about but all I could see was dense tufts of yellowing grass. The dress and my panic seemed to make all my actions slow and difficult. We were running out of time — Mary would soon realize that we had gone out for more than a bathroom break.

Finally I found half a brick underneath the cabin, I picked it up and threw it at the window, but the window wasn't made of glass, instead some kind of cheap plastic, which cracked and bent, and the brick came bouncing back at us, narrowly missing Rebekah's head.

'Careful!'

I was shaking now, adrenalin making me clumsy, dithery. I tried again, holding the brick in my hand and ramming it into the window. This time the plastic splintered and broke into jagged pieces, making enough of a space to climb through. I tried to jump up, but the material of the dress, hot and heavy, kept snagging, so I pulled it off and climbed through the narrow gap, landing on his desk, sending papers flying everywhere.

I looked around me. I couldn't see anything that looked like a phone.

'What does it look like?' I shouted to Rebekah.

'Like a small suitcase,' she said. 'You have to open it up to get it to work.'

'Shit.' We didn't have any time for all that.

There was nothing much in the room, just papers everywhere, a spare suit hanging up, and by the bathroom bunches of poppies all hanging upside down, drying. There were piles of letters next to the bed, some of them, I noticed, addressed to Rebekah. I took one and stuffed it in my pocket.

I knelt down and looked under the bed. 'I can't see it!' But then – there it was: a grey case. 'Found it!' Oh, please let it work. Then I realized it was fastened with a combination lock. Oh hell no.

'It's locked!' I wailed, but Rebekah didn't respond. 'It's locked!'

I looked up, but the face at the window wasn't hers.

# FIFTEEN

# REBEKAH

I have never seen him look so angry. His face is ashen, his mouth set.

'*What* do you think you are doing?' he shouts. He gets a key from his pocket and opens the door. 'This is private property!'

Hannah and Thomas and Father are all there. Hannah gasps when she sees the mess.

'Vandalism!' she says.

'No!' I hear Alex scream, and the sound of a struggle. Thuds against the wall of the cabin as she kicks against them. Thomas and Bevins drag her out. 'Let me go! Let me go! I want to go home!'

Bevins's face is flushed and greasy with sweat. 'See how she lies!' he says. 'See the wickedness!'

Hannah shakes her head thoughtfully. She picks up the dress and holds it in a bundle under her arm.

'Oh dear, oh dear,' she says, smirking almost like she is pleased. 'The devil will out.'

'Leave her alone!' I say.

'You need to watch who you associate with,' Hannah says, pursing her lips at me.

When they come out of the cabin they are holding Alex between them. Father has her under the arms and Bevins and Thomas hold her legs. She is kicking and wriggling.

'Get. Off. *Me!*' Her face is red and she is crying, but they are too strong for her. They pin her to the ground.

'Don't hurt her!' I move to stop them, but Hannah puts her hand on my shoulder and pulls me back.

'Be still, child. It's not you,' Bevins says. 'It's the devil in you. I know how hard he struggles.'

He tells Hannah to get Mary and Margaret and Mrs Bragg. 'She must wear the dress.'

'Fuck off! I'm not wearing your dress. I want to go home! This is illegal what you're doing! Let. Go. Of. Me!' she shouts, voice hoarse with panic. 'Someone needs to phone the police!'

Bevins shakes his head and they hold her even more firmly. 'See how hard the demon tries to make itself heard?'

'Leave her alone!' I shout, but this time it's Father who is angry with me.

'It's not your battle,' he says. 'She is leading you astray. If you say one more word. One more word . . .' He doesn't have to finish the sentence. I know what he is threatening. Stripes from the rod which has been dipped in oil to make it hurt even more, like it says in the Bible. I stare at him and don't move, my heart full of anger.

The women come back and Bevins tells them that they must undress her and make her put the dress back on. The men turn their backs to us. Alex wriggles even more, but four women are much too strong for her. As they pull her trousers off there's a shriek from Hannah. 'Dear God! What's that?' She's pointing at Alex's tattoo. 'The mark of the beast! The eye!'

'What?' Alex kicks her legs. 'What's wrong?'

They pull the dress over her head and Bevins looks round. When he sees the tattoo on her ankle his face twists and he crosses himself. 'See, Brothers. I told you that he walks among us, even to put marks on our flesh. You can't come in with the eye of evil on your body. This is why it's all going wrong for you. This is why you are so confused. We must pray that demon out of you.'

'What are you on about? It's for protection!'

'It says that in Mary's encyclopedia!' I hear myself say, then bite my lip. I must be silent, I must be silent. I bite my lip till I taste blood.

Mr Bevins puts his hands over his eyes. 'Cover it up!'

Hannah takes her scarf from around her neck and passes it to Bevins. He kneels down and wraps it around Alex's ankle. 'Come, we are going to pray for you. I will ask God to have mercy on you. In these last days we will save you.'

He gestures to the bundle of Alex's old clothes that Hannah is holding. 'Make sure you burn them,' he says.

When we get back to the church everyone is talking restlessly, but the room goes quiet the moment we step through the door.

Everyone stares at Alex. Bevins leads her to the front, where he makes her kneel at the altar. He puts his hands on her head and begins to speak: 'Here, Lord, is a powerful sinner. So vile and ugly in her thoughts . . .'

He goes on and on about sin. About how awful and terrible Alex is, about how he is asking God to cleanse her and accept her as His own.

Then suddenly his voice changes, and he stands up, holding his arms to the sky, and starts to speak in a deeper, older voice that sounds like someone else entirely.

'*These days are My days. Not like any other days you have seen. Do not look to yesterday. Look to the future, because this new way is not the old. Those who do not want to give up their sin and are fearful, like Gideon's men. You must not let anything pass your lips that is not blessed. In these last days you must be purified. There are many that would try and divert you from your course. You must hold strong for Me. For these last days, all around will assail you, but you will stay strong.'*

And then he folds on to his knees, clutching his hands together as if he's holding a sword. I know what's coming now. If the spirit is visiting with us, many will fall to the floor laughing or crying. I did it once. I fell off my chair in the middle of a prayer meeting and Mother said it was because I had been slain in the spirit, although I didn't feel anything except that my elbow hurt where I banged it on the floor.

'There are among us still the signs of the devil, Satan clothed in the robes of a stranger. One who is come among us as a wolf in the clothing of sheep.'

He touches Alex on the shoulder and she cries out.

'Get off me!' She tries to stand up, but he pushes her back down.

'And now the spirit is strong amongst us we will defeat this demon in our midst that wants to tempt us away from the glory.'

Then he pushes her forward, hard, so that she falls. 'See how the devil falls away in the face of the spirit of the Lord!'

'You're hurting me!'

'It is not I who is hurting you!' he roars. 'It is the demon inside you!' And he presses her down to the floor, placing his hands on her back.

She struggles now. 'Get off me! Let me go!' She starts to kick with her legs. 'Pervert!'

'It's a strong one!' he says. 'Listen to it squeal. Be still, child. Be *still*.'

And then Father comes over to help him and Mr Protheroe, and together they hold her legs and her arms so she can't move.

147

She has started crying now, a loud yelping, still writhing to get out of their grasp. They pray for her in tongues. Watching them, I am frozen. I can see the beads of sweat on Mr Bevins's brow and Alex's hot, angry face. I am afraid for her. What if they hurt her more than they're doing already? I close my eyes and try to pray, but the voices have swollen to a loud dissonance and I can't think with everyone swaying, muttering, making strange noises, and Alex screaming to be let go.

They carry on for ages, praying in the spirit, until Alex stops shouting and crying and instead is quietly sobbing. Bevins declares a great victory against the forces of evil and stands up stiffly. 'The visitation of the spirit only comes in times of great darkness,' he says. 'To cast out demons and help us to stay strong until the moment of great Rapture is upon us. Let none of us be found wanting. There is nowhere to hide from the truth of the Lord. Nowhere to hide.'

He throws his arms open to the ceiling. Alex is curled up on the floor, her hands over her eyes, breathing hard. I look at Father, who has his eyes closed and is raising his arms to the heavens and I wonder again what it is that he sees up there. I close my eyes and go into the empty part of my mind, which is neither sleep nor waking but more like waiting, where I am in a kind of trance in which the world outside seems very noisy. As if each blade of grass had its own sound, each crackle of a leaf a percussion, each breath of wind its own note, which means I can bear to sit on this chair, still and quiet for a long time, so nothing bad can touch me.

By the time Bevins is finished it is already night. As we emerge from the church the light has faded to a fine line on the horizon and all around has turned to shadows. Everyone is exhausted and my head aches and my mouth is dry. After they finished casting her demon out, Alex fell into a sobbing sleep on the cold floor of the church and Mr Bevins left her there and started going on about how there was so much to prepare for. He said the men were to help him, that the countdown had started, beginning tonight. That we had to say goodbye to New Canaan, imagine we were putting something to bed. And then the twins started crying and became restless, and Mary stood up and said we needed to get them back to the farmhouse and get them fed. But Bevins made her wait another hour while he gave another rambling speech about how it was more important to be right with God than to be fed.

Now Mary walks ahead, quickly, the twins pulling on each hand, whining that they are hungry. It's a relief to be out in the air again, although it's now cold and a thin drizzle has set in and I am soon soaked through. The other women walk ahead, carrying the lanterns and talking about the Rapture and about what exactly will happen in the final moments.

'It's faith that makes the difference,' says Hannah. 'Faith is what allows you to make leaps of the imagination, to really *see* God.'

Mother used to say that death was just a momentary thing, like passing through a door from one room to the next. That one of the joys of having faith was that there was nothing to be frightened of.

'Do you think it will hurt?' Ruth asks.

Hannah laughs. 'Of course not! He is come to take us home!'

Margaret thinks there will be a fire that will consume us, though it will not be painful because we are faithful. It will be like the saints in the fiery furnace – though the fire burns hot we will feel it like a cool breeze. Unlike the fallen, whose flesh will melt like the wax of a candle, and their screams be heard all the way from the very depths of hell.

Mary Protheroe chides Margaret as she describes this. 'There are children present,' she says.

Margaret narrows her eyes. 'They are not too young to hear the truth, Sister,' she says piously. 'Or to be possessed by demons,' she adds pointedly. 'You yourself have said it.'

'Well, do you think it was appropriate for the service to last all day?'

'When the men call the faithful it's not for us to challenge it.'

'But the boys!' Her voice catches in her throat. 'There's no need for them to sit all day in church! They need to eat, they need fresh air, they need to play. We can't live on prayers.'

Hannah turns, her sour face looking even meaner. 'I don't like the tone of your voice, Mary.'

'Hannah, I will *not* starve my own children any longer for the sake of the meetings! Or lock them in the cellar!' She sounds as if she's about to cry. 'I'm sick of this!' she mutters. 'It's got nothing to do with God!'

'*Lies!*' Hannah thunders. '*Mary*. You're forgetting yourself.' Hannah's voice is dense with warning. 'You should address this with your husband. It's our duty to be faithful, even into the last days. Aren't you grateful? We've been called to know the hour and the day! Our faith has been rewarded with certainty. You should be preparing yourself for the glory!'

Mary snorts. 'And how many times have we heard this?'

'It's *different* this time. They have the chapter and verse. It's been confirmed in *three* separate prophecies. How can you deny the signs and wonders?'

Mary mutters something under her breath, stooping to pick up Paul, who is complaining about having to walk the distance back to the farmhouse.

Alex walks quietly beside me. Silent, trembling, clutching her arms around herself.

'You OK?' I say, touching her on the shoulder, but she shrugs me off, chewing her lip. I'm afraid that she's angry with me. I feel like it's my fault she got caught. 'I'm sorry.'

'You could have warned me they were outside!' she hisses.

'I didn't see them till it was too late!'

'*Now* what are we going to do?'

'I don't *know*!'

I want to talk to Father, to ask him if he is *sure*. It's all happened too quickly. Now the moment has come, perhaps I will be found wanting. Will I be left behind? I'm not ready for the final judgement. But when I tried to ask him after church he just smiled at me weakly then brushed me away, told me not to worry myself. He's staying in church with the elders, for a vigil, praying for directions, visions of what we should do next. My head spins.

Alex is walking so slowly she is almost standing still. 'Come on, we've got to get back, it's raining.'

'I don't want to go with them. This place is bullshit,' she whispers. 'They want to kill me.'

'Don't be silly! No one wants to kill you!' But her words hit me somewhere deep in my stomach and I don't want to show her that I'm afraid. I know what they did was not right, but I don't know how to say it. Instead I say, 'Well, if you didn't have a demon in you, then it would not be necessary to chase it out!' I can hear the words come out of my mouth but it's as if they belong to someone else.

Her eyes grow wide. 'You saw what they did to me! You think that's OK?'

'No, but . . .' I say, ashamed and confused.

'You're just as bad as them!'

This hurts. I'm not like them, I think. I'm not. But that's not what I say. 'You've been sent to tempt me away from the glory and then I'll never see my mother again! You're disgusting. I wish you'd never come here!'

She stops and looks at me. I can see the hurt in the twist of her lips. I wish I could take the words out of the air and stuff them back into my face before she can hear them, but it's too late.

'Screw you,' she snarls, and she runs on ahead of me.

'Come back!' I shout, but my words fall into empty space. All I can see is the jagged silhouettes of gorse and hawthorn and the dim lights of their lanterns just visible on the track ahead.

When we get to the farmhouse Alex refuses to look at me or sit next to me. Her face is the colour of the mashed potato. I feel terrible for what I said. I didn't mean it. What I wanted to say was, *I'm afraid too*. But the words came out wrong. Another black mark against me on Judgement Day. I remember Father said once that when the Rapture comes we will see all our actions played out as if in a film and will have to watch and be accountable to God for everything we've done. This thought makes the blood in my veins run cold. I am sure I am not good enough for heaven and I will die in fear and torment and burn forever in the lake of fire.

Mary boils up some goats milk and gives it to us. The warmth of it radiates through my body with the comfort of a hug. I'm so hungry I don't care that usually I can't stand the strong flavour, and when it's finished I wish there was more.

Alex stands up and asks to be excused. 'I need to lie down,' she says.

Mary nods. 'Of course. Rebekah, you can put the twins to bed in a moment.'

In the kitchen I can hear her heavy footsteps climbing the stairs.

'So young. So much sin,' Hannah says, shaking her head.

'Hold your judgement, Hannah. There was no need to make such a spectacle of her. She's only a child,' says Mary.

'A child with a demon, nonetheless,' says Hannah. 'She broke into Bevins's cabin! She was possessed!'

'Hmmm,' Mary says. 'So they say.'

'What do you mean?'

'Well, she's obviously upset, but that's not the same as being possessed.'

'But her tattoo!' Margaret says. 'It's the sign of the devil!'

Mary brushes her hand in the air. 'Or perhaps it's just a tattoo.'

'It's not for us to question, Mary,' Margaret says with a dangerous voice, as she stalks out of the room.

Mary gets up to see to the dishes, but she's angry. I can tell by the way that she clatters plates in the sink. It's unusual for her to be this outspoken. Ruth sits quietly with her hands in her lap and stares into the empty space as if she's waiting for something to happen.

I take the twins upstairs. The attic is quiet. Through the doorway to my room I can see the shadow of Alex's body in the camp bed, her back to me.

The twins are restless and will not settle; they have already slept too much in church. They demand one story after another and Paul keeps getting out of bed wanting to play. All the while I can see the shape of Alex's back in the bed and all I want to do is to press myself into it, to feel the warmth between us, tell her I'm sorry, promise that together we'll make another plan.

I can hear noises downstairs, doors opening and closing, the heavy tread of Micah climbing the stairs. It's odd that even though the Rapture is supposed to be happening really soon, no one seems excited about it.

Finally the twins fall asleep and I get up stiffly and creep into my bedroom. I go over to the camp bed and gently touch her sleeping figure, only something is not right. It's too soft . . . too . . . I realize I'm not pressing into a human body but into pillows and blankets rolled up.

I look round the room, but it's obvious she's not here. She must have sneaked out when no one was watching. I go back downstairs, quietly in case I wake anyone. If Mary finds me I will say I was thirsty and wanted a glass of water. But the kitchen is empty now and there's no sign of anyone in the tack room. I push the door, but it doesn't budge. I wonder for a moment if it's locked, but it's just swollen and stuck to the frame and it won't give without forcing it, which will make a noise. I press my shoulder against it and the wood squeaks loudly. I hold my breath, but no one comes. I push again, and this time it opens with a quiet pop.

The night is black and there are no stars. I can't see even my hand before me, although I know I'm still in the yard from the crunch of my feet on the stones.

I stand still and listen. In the dark you can hear further than you can see. Across the yard is the barn where the chickens are kept and the bales of winter hay. In the spring the sick lambs are put there, especially the ones who come early and need feeding from a bottle. I have seen the lambs being born, small and wet and covered in slime. Hardly able to breathe, eyes half closed, almost dead, until their mother licks them into life. Father says we are the lambs of God, that we are in His flock, that He cares for every one of us like his own. If this is so, then I can't imagine he will leave Alex behind. Surely we're on hallowed ground, here on our island, and all will be saved, even me, who has had bad thoughts against Mr Bevins, and Alex too, in spite of her tattoo.

I pick my way across the yard until I reach the barn. I feel along the wall to the door; it's ajar. I slip inside and stand and listen to the silence, small snuffles from the chicken coop, the creak of a beam, the thin whistle of the wind. I can just make out piles of hay against the skylight. I'm sure I can hear something breathing.

Suddenly there's a hand across my face, an arm across my chest. I scream but make no sound. I use my elbow to try to escape, bring my arm back, hard, into ribs.

'Ow!' Just as she lets me go I realize it is Alex. 'That hurt!'

'Sorry.' I'm relieved that it's her, though I can't see her, only the outline of her hair.

'How did you get out?'

She flashes on a torch, blinding me. 'Front door. Did they send you to get me?'

'No! I wanted to say sorry. I didn't mean what I said. It was my fault you got into trouble.'

She laughs. 'It's all right. I get it. I have this kind of effect on people. I know. People hate me.'

'*I* like you.'

'Whatever.' She jumps away from me up the tower of hay bales. 'Come up here,' she says. I can't see where she's gone, only the beam of her torch flashing through the air. Mary is always cautioning the boys against playing in the barn. The bales are dangerous, she says, they are big and heavy and should one fall on us and crush us we would likely die. I hesitate. 'Come on.' She shines the torch so I can see the way – she has made a path through to the top.

The hay is prickly, but at least it's warm. They make hay from plants which have dried in the sun, turn them into bales using the machine on the back of the tractor. This is last summer's hay and it smells sweet, of sunshine and warmth and of my mother. I want to drink it in, hold it inside me forever in case I should ever forget.

I climb up, digging my feet and hands into the bales, and when I get to the top I'm breathless. 'You don't deserve what happened to you in church.'

'They'll kill me. You know they will. This dress.' She shudders. 'I wish I'd never come here!'

'But the Rapture is coming! Don't you want to stay for that?' I suddenly, urgently, want her to be saved. 'At least be here when it happens and we can go to the glory forever and be with Jesus and all the angels.'

She's silent for a moment. She has planted the torch in the hay, its beam shooting upward between us. She looks puzzled, not unkind. 'I'll take my chances.'

I don't know what to say to that. She's brave, I think. She'll stand there at the gates and she'll ask questions, she'll rage. She won't be taken meek as a lamb like me.

'I'm sorry.' I reach out my hand. She takes it and squeezes it. 'What I said before, I didn't mean it.'

'What's happening here is wrong. You do know that, don't you?'

I don't know what to say to this. All I know is that when I'm with her the world seems to make sense and doesn't give me a headache the way it does in church or when I'm thinking about the end of the world and what a bad and sinful person I really am, or when Mr Bevins is praying over me. I don't feel sinful when I'm with her. All this and more, but I can't say it. Words seem to be stuck somewhere between my thoughts and my voice, and all I can do is smile at her until she wrinkles her nose and laughs and sticks her tongue out at me. But instead of making me happy, something in me is then suddenly very sad, and I don't know why. I swallow down a hard lump in my throat.

'What are we going to do?'

She turns and looks at me seriously. 'I don't know.'

I feel the fear again, a hard twist in my guts.

'Come here.' She puts her arm around me and I curl myself into her. We lie back in the nest that we've made and she pulls some sacking across us like a blanket.

'We need a plan.'

I think about this for a moment. 'I know.'

'Can't we get the boat out?'

'How would we make it?' I say, shivering. In that small boat, against that rough sea. I don't want to tell her that I don't know how to row. 'It'll be dangerous.'

'No shit.'

I press my body into hers. If only we could stay here like this forever, then nothing bad would ever have to happen. She knits her fingers in with mine, so our arms are twined like branches growing together. Along her arms are silvery traces of scratches.

'What happened to your arms?'

She flinches like she's embarrassed. 'I got sad,' she says. 'It made it easier to deal with.'

I trace my finger along the length of one scar that runs nearly all the way up her forearm. 'Sad about what?'

'My mother. I don't do it any more.'

'You did it to yourself?'

'Well, yeah.'

'Oh.' I can't imagine wanting to hurt myself like that. 'It's not your fault,' I say.

'That's what everyone says. But it doesn't feel like it sometimes.'

We lie there in silence. I wish I knew what to say to make her feel better. 'Can we just pretend?'

'Pretend what?'

'That we're not here? Just for now? Can't we make a plan in the morning?'

She leans on her elbow and looks at me. 'Where would you rather be?'

'Everywhere, anywhere. I want to see everything! Monkeys and elephants, Africa and all the world's tropical places.' I imagine lush forests like the pictures in the encyclopedia, and from the shampoo bottle when I was little. 'I'd like to see forests and cities, Paris, New York . . . maybe we can go together,' I say.

She touches me on the nose with her finger. 'Yeah, why not! I want to go to America. To New York and San Francisco. We can hire a car and drive it coast to coast.'

'Oh, and I want to go to Zanzibar.' Because it's the most exotic-sounding place I can think of.

She laughs.

'OK. And what do you want to do in Zanzibar?' Her face seems too close all of a sudden.

I'm not really sure how it happens, because there's no pause or gap between the action of her getting closer and us kissing and I couldn't tell you which one of us started it because that seems to be what we really wanted to say to each other all along and there's a tingle that runs through my body and I feel sort of dizzy.

'Is that what happens in Zanzibar?'

'Dunno.' She laughs. 'I've never been.'

We don't say anything for a while, just lie there in the dark, quietly. My body trembles. No one has kissed me like that before. 'Was that sinful?' I ask her.

'What do you think?'

My whole body tingles, suddenly alive. And in my head it's as if someone has flipped a switch to illuminate a dark room, and I can't help myself but I start to cry. It comes out like a sneeze and then a snuffle and then a loud sob.

'Hey.' She leans on her elbow and looks at me. 'Hey, it's OK.' She takes the sleeve of her dress and wipes my cheek with it. 'I hate this freaking dress.'

'You look really weird in it,' I say, half laughing, half crying. It's true, she does. It makes her look awkward and small when she is strong and powerful.

'No weirder than you. Anyway, what did they do to my clothes?'

'I don't know. I think Hannah took them. He said to burn them.'

'I found some letters in his cabin.'

'Letters?'

'Yeah, addressed to you. I took one. It's in my trouser pocket.'

I can't think who would write to me.

We lie quietly for a while, spooned into each other until it starts to get colder. 'What are we going to do?' I ask. The question is a persistent nag. We can't just stay here.

'We're going to make a plan!' she says brightly, but there is something brittle in her voice. And she starts to talk about the boat and how if we can just get out to sea we will be spotted by someone, eventually.

'But you get seasick,' I say, remembering the journey to get here.

'S'OK. I can deal with that.'

But I'm not convinced. There's a shadow in my mind that has the shape of a coming thunderstorm that won't be outrun, and we are holding hands so tight my fingers have started to numb.

# SIXTEEN

# REBEKAH

I wake suddenly. It's light, and I'm cold under the hessian sacking, and my clothes are damp. Alex is already awake. She turns to me and presses a finger to her lips. I feel kind of shy looking at her now. There's noise in the barn. I slowly roll on to my belly and peep over the edge. The front door is open and Micah Protheroe stands there whistling at Job the sheepdog.

He is herding sheep into a pen made out of hay bales, the one we normally use for the sick ewes. The sheep are panicked, bleating and trampling over each other.

'What are they doing?' Alex mouths at me.

'I don't know.' I can't imagine why he's doing this. We don't usually bring them in until winter. Maybe the weather is going to turn. The sheep are our life. Wool for clothes and bedding, meat to eat and lambs to sell in the spring. My heart pounds in my chest and I press myself into the hay.

When all the sheep are in the barn, Mr Bevins comes in and stands there with Micah Protheroe and Jonathan and Daniel and Gideon.

'Let us pray,' Mr Bevins says. The men close their eyes and bow their heads.

'Bless us, oh Lord, for our faithfulness. See that we are doing this out of thanks for Your divine prophecy. Thank You for showing us the time and the day. We are striving to be ready. In Your name . . .'

'*Amen*,' Jonathan bellows loudly at the end.

Then Bevins starts talking about how the Lord will be happy with this sacrifice as the evidence of our commitment, but that it is not enough.

'We must be cleansed. We must cleanse the whole island! All the goats and chickens! All the greenhouses! We must leave nothing behind! And we must fast, keep our bodies pure, our spirits pure! When we enter the gates of heaven we want there to be not a mark upon us. We will have one last feast, one last supper, then I want everyone in the church on their knees waiting for heaven.'

There are grunts of assent, loud *amens*.

'And the girl. Let us pray for guidance: Oh Lord, guide our hands in these last hours, as we look to make righteous our house.'

There is a long silence. 'Righteous, amen,' says Micah.

'In Your blessed house,' echoes Jonathan.

The hay is making my nose itch and I suddenly want to sneeze. I hold my breath until my face turns purple and I need to cough and I can hear nothing but blood in my ears.

I want to talk to Father, ask him if he is *sure* the Rapture is coming. We have been good, we have already prayed and fasted, we have been lucky to be given such a sign from heaven that the Rapture is near, but surely we do not need to take it so far? So soon?

At last I hear the sound of the door banging, bolts being pulled across, and I breathe and sneeze and cough all at the same time.

'Shhhh!' Alex nudges me in the ribs.

I lie and listen to my own breath. The barn smells of the sheep. They rustle and bleat.

'They're going to kill them,' says Alex.

'What?'

'The sheep.'

My heart sinks. 'Don't be silly.'

'Weren't you listening? They're going to kill everything. We have to get out of here.' Her eyes are wide with fear.

'What about me?'

'You're going to the Rapture, remember?' she says, raising her eyebrows sarcastically.

'I don't want to go.' Saying it aloud suddenly makes it true. 'I want to go with you.' I can deal with the Tribulations, I am sure of it, especially if I am with her.

'Right,' she says, 'but you know it's not going to even happen? And then everyone here will *starve*.'

Her words give me a chill. I shiver.

We wait a little longer, until we are sure there's no one around, then climb down from the top of the hay.

Alex peers through a hole in the corrugated iron. 'They're still in the yard,' she says quietly.

I don't know how we're going to get out of here without being seen.

'Isn't there another way out?' She looks carefully around the barn – there's a hole in the roof, just above us. 'What about up there?'

'Don't be silly. We'll die. It's too high.'

'Not if we use that.' She points at a wooden ladder that is leaning against the hay. 'Come on.' She leaps back up into the hay and grabs the ladder. If she plants it in the top hay bale it just reaches the gap in the roof. Before I can say *be careful* she has climbed up it and through the gap and all I can see are her legs sticking out. She reappears almost straight away.

'There are men in the field,' she says. 'They're building a

massive bonfire or something. We can't go now, they'll see us.'
She jumps back down.

'Shit,' I say.

Alex laughs. 'What did you say?!'

'Nothing.'

'You totally just swore! You so did!' She sounds triumphant.
'Say it again!'

'No! It came out by accident.'

'Go on, say it again.'

'Shit!' I whisper. 'Shit, shit, shit, *shit*.' Five times. I wonder if
I'll have to do some kind of penance for that. But it's not like I'm
saying God, or Jesus, or the other bad word beginning with *f* that
Alex says. Anyway, something in me doesn't care. Like the tear in
a piece of fabric suddenly made worse from pulling, I can almost
hear the rip. I start giggling, and I can't stop; it's a relief, like inside
me is all this tension, fizzing out over the edge.

'Shhhhh.'

I hide my face in the crook of my elbow. But I'm not laughing
because it's funny, but because if I don't laugh maybe I would
scream.

We sit in the hay and wait for ages. Alex makes a plan. We're
going to make our way down to the harbour and take the boat, get
it out to sea, then let off a flare or something. 'We just need to get
someone's attention.'

'But what if nobody comes?'

'Well, that's where you've got to have faith.' She winks. 'Or
you can always stay here?'

'No way!'

She goes up the ladder again to look. I don't know what time
it is, or even if anyone has noticed we're missing. Part of me

wonders why no one is even searching.

'It's OK, they've gone,' she says, hoisting herself up. Her feet clatter on the roof, the noise echoing around the barn. I climb up the ladder, careful not to look down; the height makes my muscles tremble. When I put my head out into the air the wind is suddenly cold and fresh. I can see that Alex is right – in the field they have begun to build a huge fire out of scraps of wood and brush.

'If we leave the ladder, they'll know you were in here,' I say.

Alex is crouching down. She holds her fingers to her lips. 'Too late,' she says. And I hear a noise beneath me. Someone has opened the barn doors. 'Quick.'

I climb up the last rung of the ladder and step out on to the roof. It doesn't seem very safe. There are large patches of rust where the metal looks too thin to stand on, and it makes a loud creaking when we walk.

I follow her, half running, half sliding, until we gather so much momentum it is inevitable that we're going to fall off the edge, and suddenly I'm in the air and falling and I can't help but cry out in fear. Then the bounce of soft soil, grass, the smell of peelings, eggshells. The compost heap. I land awkwardly on my wrist.

'Wow,' I say. 'How did you know that was there?'

'I didn't.' Alex laughs. 'I must have a guardian angel. Or maybe that's the devil in me.'

'More likely the devil.' The voice is stark. Loud and startling. Mr Bevins. With Father and Thomas. Oh no.

Bevins looks at us, from one to the other the air around him seeming to crackle. He says nothing for a long time. Staring at us with his intense blue eyes, he looks more like a wild animal than a person.

'Rebekah, are you a servant of the Lord?' he asks eventually in

165

a quiet voice. 'Do you believe in your saviour who died for your sins? Do you believe you are blessed with the gift of eternal life?'

'Yes.'

'And you renounce the devil and all his works?'

'Yes.'

I look at Alex. Run, I want to say. *Run*. She moves, but Thomas grabs her. Holding her by the arms so she can't run, although she struggles.

'Well, that's not what you are doing, is it?'

He turns to Alex. 'You. Come with me. We need to talk.'

'No!' I hear someone say. Then realize it's me. 'You can't take her!'

Mr Bevins spins round and stares at me. 'And why not?'

'Because she's done nothing wrong!' I say. 'She just wants to go home!'

'So why were you in there then?!' He points to the barn. 'If you want to go home, then why aren't you helping the women? Your home is not here! Your home is with the Lord in heaven.'

'To hell with the Lord in heaven!' I say, before I can think. 'I'm sick of this place!'

Mr Bevins flinches. 'Rebekah, what is the fifth commandment?'

I bow my head. 'Honour thy father and mother.'

'Are you honouring your father now?'

'No,' I mumble.

'What did you say?'

'*No!*' I shout.

I look at him and then at Father, whose face is angry and serious. It's as if he has forgotten that I'm his daughter. Instead I am like some piece in a puzzle which must fit where he wills it. I dig my nails into my hands. I hate him, and even more I hate

166

Mr Bevins for carrying Father along with him.

Alex starts to struggle again, kicking out and biting Thomas on the hand. 'Let me go!'

'See, she's all Satan's,' says Bevins impassively. 'And you –' he stares at me – 'she's corrupted you.'

'Leave her alone!' Alex says.

He shakes his head. 'Too late!' He comes towards me as if he is going to hit me, but he only brings his hands together with a loud slap that makes me jump.

'Take her,' he says, nodding at Alex, 'to the Solitary. And fetch Jonathan. And *her*.' He looks at me and shakes his head. 'You will need to deal with her –' he looks at my father – 'bringing despair on the house of the Lord. How easy it is for those of faith to be tempted away. It is as it was written . . .' And he goes on and on, spouting out verse after verse, white flecks of spit gathering at the corners of his mouth.

I catch Alex's eye. *It's OK*. I mouth at her. *I'll help you*. She nods, like she understands.

# SEVENTEEN

# ALEX

They pushed me through the door and slammed it shut behind me. The sound of my voice bounced off the walls. *Please.* I banged on the door with my fists, bruising my knuckles, I scratched the floor, I tried to climb to the roof, but there was nothing to stand on to get me high enough up. *Let me go.*

'What you have,' he said, 'is a demon! We have to break it!'

'Fuck off! You can't keep me prisoner!'

'It's not you that speaks, Alex, it's your demon. Just submit. And you won't ever have to be afraid again. Jesus is here to help you cast out his enemies! All you have to do is believe. *Believe.* The world we live in is not real, Alex. It's nothing but a mirage, full of phantoms! You can't see it but I can see the glory that waits for you on the other side. You're a miserable sinner, all you have to do is believe it and repent and you will be forgiven. Repent!'

I turned away from him, and put my hands over my ears, my fear giving way to a kind of blank exhaustion. I don't even know when they left, except suddenly there was no one outside the door and I realized the loud shouting sound was all in my head.

There was a crappy bed which was really just some planks laid out over some bricks and a thin blanket. In the corner there was a bucket for a toilet and a bottle of water, but it looked murky and smelled wrong and I didn't want to drink it.

*

But then the day died and it got dark and there was no light and I was thirsty and all I could do was lie under the blanket with my eyes closed. And then I prayed. *Dear God, if You're there, then get me out of here. I'm sorry I never really believed in You.* But I felt unconvincing and half-hearted. If there was a God, then He would know that, wouldn't he? That I was only doing this because I was desperate and that I'd never really believed in Him anyway.

Then, in the morning, they came to get me.

# EIGHTEEN

# REBEKAH

We walk together over to the lake. I can see the clouds, the rocks of the Devil's Seat reflected in the water. The wind blows across the surface making the reflection shimmer and distort. As we get closer I can see my own pleated shape, my hands clenched into fists. Next to me my father, thin, ghostly. I wonder why he wanted to come here. I can't believe they caught us. We should have waited till it was dark at least. I should have reasoned with Alex, I should have realized they would be looking. But something about being with her makes me believe that everything is safe, that anything is possible, even when it's not.

Father holds me by the arm so tightly it hurts. 'Rebekah . . .' He starts, then stops.

'What?'

He shakes me roughly. 'You will *not* disrespect me in front of Mr Bevins.'

'Or what?'

He looks troubled. 'Or there will be consequences. You will be left behind. Is that what you want?' He lets go of me and stands looking out at the water with his hands in his pockets. I think of what that man said on Mission Week about wanting to go to hell if we were the kind of people that would be in heaven, but I hold my tongue.

He sighed. 'I know it's hard for you sometimes since . . .' He doesn't even say her name. 'But we're so close to the end now.'

I want to tell him that I don't care how close we are, that I want a chance to get away from this place, that I want to see the world with Alex, before it all burns up. I want the kind of life she has – exciting, carefree. That it's not fair. He had his chance to make his choices. Now I want mine.

'I haven't been paying you enough attention, I know, but there is so much to do here before we go. And you've been spending too much time with Alex.'

'No, I haven't!' But I bite my lip. 'What is he going to do to her?'

Father tuts. 'No one is going to *do* anything to her. We are just going to help her get to the glory. No one left behind.'

But what if I *want* to be left behind? I think. Maybe they will all get Raptured and me and Alex will be left behind and we can run away then. Then there won't be anyone to stop us.

'Will we see Mother?'

He won't look at me. 'Rebekah, you really need to behave. She . . .' He stops. He looks as if he is about to say something else, but thinks better of it. 'Mr Bevins has been sent to us to lead us home. Where have all these questions come from all of a sudden?'

'Nowhere.' I mutter at my shoes.

'Come on, Mary needs you in the house. There's lots to do.'


When I get back to the house it's obvious everyone has been talking about me. No one will look me in the eye. Father tells Ruth and Margaret to look after me, that 'she must not leave your sight'. So they are more like jailors now than Sisters, which means one of them sits with me all the time when I'm not helping Mary with the chores. Today the women are clearing out the tack room and cleaning all the boots and doing all the laundry. A pointless job if we are to be Raptured, especially as it takes so long to heat the water, but apparently Bevins wants the place pristine.

Hannah says she's relieved that Alex has been removed from among us. 'At last we can concentrate on the task in hand instead of being distracted by that she-devil.'

I'm not to be left alone even for one minute. Even though no one has said why, I know it's because they want to stop me seeing her. I know Bevins has her there with the others on shift, praying for her, but I don't see why. She has no demon in her any more than I do.

Hannah and Margaret read Bible verses and chatter about what will happen to those who don't go to heaven in the Rapture and how they will suffer horrible torments at the hands of the Antichrist, who will rule over the whole world for seven years.

'He will come from Islam or China,' says Hannah definitively.

Alex: thoughts of her are like a constant beat that pulses beneath all my other thoughts. I feel sick thinking about what Bevins will be doing to her. I don't want her to be hurt or afraid. My mind races through plans. I will go and rescue her, and I make silent petitions in my head, asking God to permit the weather to be fine enough to get the boat out and to help me navigate the sea and I promise to be a great witness, even in the Tribulations. Once we're free we will go travelling together and see the whole world, tropical forests and deserts and cities and Zanzibar. And I think about how I want us to kiss each other again and sleep warm and nested next to each other, until it all becomes such a whirl of colour and ideas that the fragile egg of my heart is almost ready to burst.

While we are cleaning the men are still building the huge bonfire in the field, like Elijah the Prophet of God in the Book of Kings.

Margaret reads the story while we clean. How Elijah shows King Ahab who is the one true God. When Elijah goes to King Ahab, he makes all the false prophets try to set their sacrifices on fire, dancing and cutting themselves and scattering blood on their pyres, but nothing happens. Elijah makes his altar wet, even digging a trench around it and filling it with water and he prays that God will accept his sacrifice. Suddenly the fire of the Lord comes down and consumes Elijah's sacrifice, a fire so hot that even the rocks are melted, proving to the false prophets who is the one true God. And afterwards Elijah takes the false prophets to the brook of Kishon and kills them all, smashing their heads with stones until the river runs red with the blood of the unbelievers.

'The Lord's justice,' Margaret says, her eyes greedy with revenge. 'This is what will happen to all the unbelievers when we're gone. All the people who ever laughed at us, or took the name of God in vain!'

'Amen!' says Mrs Bragg.

In the afternoon, when my back hurts from scrubbing mud off smelly old boots, Mr Bevins returns with Mr Bragg, who has just come out of the Solitary. He is thinner, paler, conspicuously sorry, loudly telling anyone who will listen that Mr Bevins has saved him and how grateful he is to be ready for these final days.

I watch Mr Bevins carefully. I hope he will say something about Alex, and where she is, how she is, but he doesn't and I daren't ask, in case he singles me out for special prayers and attention. Instead he inspects our work. He takes some of the boots that Ruth has cleaned and says that they aren't shiny enough.

'Do it again,' he says. 'All work done for the Lord must be perfect.'

Ruth's face pinches but she doesn't say anything.

When Mr Bevins goes no one says a word, but we start again on the boots, polishing them, one by one, until I can see my face in the shine.

For supper Mary has cooked up a thin soup with some vegetables and scraps. Mr Bevins has said food is impure, that there is no need for it now we are going to go to heaven. A plan is formulating in my mind. In four days, according to Mr Bevins, the Rapture will be upon us, but I won't be Raptured. Not with them. They can go without me, I have decided, and then Alex and I will be free to be together. With no one watching us or interfering.

The world: out there beyond the sea. I will read Mary's encyclopedia from cover to cover, so I know what to expect. I will know what it is that Alex knows. If Alex has lived out there, then it surely can't be so bad. This island is not my world; though I live here, it's Mr Bevins's world, and Father's. After all this time, my home suddenly seems to me like a foreign country. I long to leave it behind.

When the men come in to eat there is a fuss in the kitchen about who will get to serve. Apparently it's Hannah's turn, but she's not back yet. The women used to argue about this all the time, until Bevins insisted on a rota. Now Margaret has worked out that there won't be enough meals for us all to have our turn before the Rapture so someone will have to stand down. I listen to their dreary discussion, knowing Alex would think this was hilarious. I'm not going with you, I think. Idiots.

I play with the twins, who are scribbling with pencils on an old book that Mary has found. Paul draws shapes that he scrawls over and over until they are just hard black marks on the paper. He says they are devils, at which Mary frowns.

Everyone is here except Alex and Naomi. I feel as if I have my heart in my throat. I *have* to know where they have taken her. I think I will ask Mary if I can catch her on her own, but I needn't have worried. Hannah soon tells everyone.

'She's gone to the Solitary to pray.'

*No.*

'The sin has begun its journey out. But the demon is a tough one. It's so deeply embedded.'

The women nod, seriously. All except Mary, I notice. All day she has been quiet and withdrawn, watchful.

'How has it been drawn out?' Margaret asks.

'There has been a confession. Of *unnatural* passions.' Here she stares at me, hard. I blush and look away.

'Like we didn't already know,' mutters Margaret.

'Indeed,' says Hannah. 'But Bevins is pleased. He says we are winning. Tonight we will be holding a vigil. Don't worry, we will carry her over the threshold.'

I feel like all of this is being directed at me. I look down at the paper and realize I have pressed through with the pencil, leaving a jagged gash on the page.

I am pointedly not invited to the vigil. Neither is Mary. When I try to speak to Mr Bevins he looks at me as if I'm not there and walks on past me.

When everyone else is gone the kitchen is quiet and calm. Mary and I sit at the table almost too exhausted to move.

'Will she be OK, do you think?' I ask.

'No more or less OK than any of us.' She rubs a hand across her face and smiles tiredly. 'It's not much of a life for you up here. Your poor mother. She . . .' Mary looks at me thoughtfully. 'I'm sorry,' she says. 'You know I have only ever been trying to keep you safe.'

I nod. 'What is an unnatural passion?'

Mary flinches, squeezing her eyes together. 'Nothing for you to worry about, I'm sure.'

'But . . .' There's a question in my mind but I don't know how to formulate it. About passions and Alex and nature. The words slide around uneasily in my mind. All I know is that I want so much to see her and lie down with her, safe and warm, it's like an ache. I am going to get away from here and I am going to see the world. The real world, the one that I can see with my own eyes, make sense of with my own words.

Later, when the twins lie sleeping. I get the encyclopedia and open it on page one.

A for *Animal*.

The word animal comes from the Latin word *animalis*, meaning 'to have breath'. . .

# NINETEEN

# REBEKAH

I'm woken by gunshots. At first I don't know what they are, though the sound is loud and close. The sky is not yet fully light, and the clouds are already thickening, threatening rain which will surely soon come. I look out of the window, down into the yard, and see Mary Protheroe standing outside the barn holding a torch.

Through the small barn windows is the orange light of lanterns. I can hear the bleating of panicked sheep, and then another blast of a gun. There are voices shouting. Then another blast and a flash which makes me jump.

Mary shouts something and knocks loudly on the door and Micah comes out. He is wearing overalls that are red with blood.

I can't hear all of what she is saying, but she is pointing at the barn and then at the house. 'This is madness! I will *not* starve my own children! I will not—'

She's answered by a stinging slap that makes me flinch and immediately draws red stripes across her cheek. I drop the curtain. Peter wakes and comes into my room, sleepy. 'What's going on?'

'I don't know,' I say.

'Why is Daddy shouting?'

'I told you, I don't know.'

'Is he cross with us?'

'*No.*'

'I'm hungry.'

'I know.'

Then there are more gunshots. He furrows his face. 'What is it?'

I have no answer for him, so just grab hold of him, press his body into mine. He is thin, the bones of him press into my chest. 'It's OK,' I say, even though it's not. 'I'm going to make it OK.'

We have a hundred head of sheep and forty goats. The gunshots seem to go on and on, until it gets fully light and the rain starts again, an endless, persistent downpour. Peter falls asleep again in my arms, but I stay awake, watching the weather getting heavier and closer until the clouds are so low and dense I could almost pull them out of the sky.

Downstairs, Mary is in the kitchen raking over the fire, trying to coax the embers back to life, her face still red with the marks of Micah's hand.

Hannah and Margaret sit at the table discussing how when we are in heaven after the Rapture there will be manna to eat like there was in the days of Moses, which fell from the sky and kept the Israelites alive through their days of exile. Although no one is sure what manna really will taste like, Hannah says it will melt in the mouth like a delicious honeyed wafer, it will keep us full up all day and will make us glow with a special force.

'Are you sure you are not thinking of Ready Brek, Sister?' Mary says, arching her eyebrow.

Hannah presses her hands together and looks pained. 'Sister,' she says. 'Sister, we would all have to be deaf and blind not to have witnessed what passed between you and Micah this morning. Would you like us to pray with you?'

Mary stands up and puts her hands on her hips. '*We* may be able to fast, but the boys have no idea why they cannot eat. Would you starve your own children?'

'If the Lord commanded it. Think of Abraham and Isaac.'

Mary turns up her nose. 'That story is unnatural,' she mutters.

I have always thought the same. Father often tells the story of how God commanded Abraham to sacrifice his beloved son, going so far as to build the pyre and trick the child to lie on it before God sent a ram to be sacrificed instead. Isaac, the child, so trusting, followed his father without knowing what intentions Abraham held in the name of God. Father is always using this as an example of true obedience and faithfulness, but I think it's frightening, horrible.

'God was only testing him.'

'*Only?* Hannah, you have not had the blessing of children so perhaps it is hard for you to see. Would *you* take your beloved child and be prepared to kill him? Is *our* God really so bloodthirsty?'

'Our God is the God of the Bible. It is not for us to judge Him. Such vanity!' She tuts and her face seems to wither. 'And I would trust that my God knew better than I, that there was a *plan.*'

Mary shakes her head. 'But what kind of God would want to torture me in such a way? I myself would rather die first. Micah may be my husband, but I will not respect him in this madness.'

Her words echo around the kitchen. Hannah shifts in her seat and purses her lips, presses her fingers together into a bridge.

'Sister, you know that Bevins warned us that there would be demons pulling us away from the truth. The girl has already—'

'Never mind that! What do you suggest I tell the boys when they come to me hungry? I can't feed them on prayers!'

'And that the demons would come in the female form.' She narrows her eyes. 'Beware of your words, Mary.' Hannah's voice carries the sharp edge of a threat.

'You even *sound* like him!' Mary says. 'Can't you *think* for yourselves?' She throws a bowl into the sink, which smashes into pieces.

But Hannah doesn't get a chance to answer, as Father comes into the kitchen with Micah and Jonathan. They are carrying chickens, their necks floppy and broken. Mary makes a strange, strangled noise as they lay their still-warm bodies on the kitchen table.

'On Monday we will have our last supper. A feast!' says Father, looking around at us, his eyes glittering. 'And then a fast to purify. The time is near, Sisters. Let us be ready.'

But then Bevins comes in.

'What's this?' he says, pointing at the chickens. 'Why are they in the kitchen, and not on the pyre?'

'I thought . . .' Father starts. 'You said . . . that we would have a feast, a last supper . . .'

Bevins shakes his head. 'No no! You misunderstand me. There will be no feasting! We must prepare, keep our bodies holy even unto the last! Now is the time for fasting, not feasting!' And he picks up the chickens by the legs. they dangle dead and lifeless from his hand.

'Oh.' Father looks unsure, his face reddens. 'I thought . . .'

Bevins puts a hand on Father's shoulder. 'What do we know about thinking? Thinking is sinking! Thinking is of the body, of the flesh. In these last days we do not think, we *believe*.'

'Yes, Bevins, I'm sorry. I must have misunderstood.'

'I think you did.'

He tells us all to close our eyes and leads us in a prayer. I half close my eyes and watch Father. He has his head bowed, his eyes squeezed shut. After Bevins is done we all look at each other as if we're not sure what is supposed to happen next, and then Hannah is the first to speak, asking him some long and pointless question about what exactly will be the manna that we will eat in heaven.

'Will it be like wafer, Pastor Bevins, or more like a kind of flatbread?'

'I can tell you, Hannah, that heaven will be exactly the way God wills it.'

I go over to Father and pull on his sleeve, but he just mutters at me and shrugs his arm away. When Father tells the story of the day he saw the light, he tells it as if it was a story from the Bible itself. He was driving his car to work one day when it broke down on a busy road. He managed to push the car to the edge of the road and someone finally stopped and offered help. Except it wasn't just a someone, it was Mr Bevins, who gave him a lift to work and a leaflet about the Church. And at that meeting Father said he felt the hand of God upon him, and he knew from that moment on that he was where he was meant to be, that he had found his special purpose in life. I wonder sometimes at my special purpose in life and whether it is the same. It seems a shame for the Rapture to come so soon, before I've had a chance to find out. I tug again on his coat.

He turns to look at me. 'What is it, Rebekah?'

Now that he is looking at me with his full attention, I stumble. 'I-I-I was – I, well . . .' I am aware of Bevins standing behind me, listening. 'Are you *sure*?' I look at his belt, where the key to the Solitary swings from one of the belt hooks. I wonder if I could just reach out and grab it.

He looks surprised. 'Sure of what?'

'That the Rapture is coming?'

His eyes narrow. His faces grows serious and unsmiling. 'As I take breath, child. It has been revealed in the Scriptures.' He taps the cover of his Bible. 'And Bevins has *seen* it. We can't argue with that.'

'But *how* has it been revealed?'

'Through prophecy of course. You heard Bevins bearing witness. You read Naomi's note.'

'But what if he's wrong?' I can feel Bevins's eyes burning into the back of me. The fire of them turns my face red.

'He is not wrong.'

'But —' *How do you know?*

Before I can ask, Bevins has pushed me aside to stand next to Father. 'Are you calling your father a *liar?*' he says, staring at me. 'Child, you know full well that those who will not stand with us stand against us.'

I shake my head. 'No! I was just asking . . . I am thinking about the twins. The boys are too young for fasting.'

Father rolls his eyes. 'Have you been talking to Mary? We will take care of it. They will not go hungry.'

He rests his hand on my head and I nod, although I am not reassured; something in me does not believe him, and I am angry that they are so dismissive. As if getting food to eat is a petty concern. When they walk away I realize I have had my fists clenched so tight my nails have dug deep grooves into the palms of my hands.

The afternoon is spent reading the Bible while the men take the bodies of the sheep and the goats and the chickens they have killed and bury them. They have kept alive ten sheep and ten goats for a sacrifice on the night of the Rapture. They begin to dig a trench too, like Elijah's, but it's raining too hard and they come and sit inside, the boots we cleaned yesterday now all caked in mud again. We can hear them singing and then saying prayers. The rain will not last, they say; it will blow over by the evening.

'Perhaps we should start our own singing,' Hannah says. 'Who would like to start?'

There is silence in the kitchen. I notice Mary makes a face behind her back.

'Is there not virtue in our silence, Sister?' she says, but Hannah ignores her and starts a warbling version of 'What a Friend We Have in Jesus'. A few of the others join in, but I don't. I watch the rain pouring down outside. If it carries on like this it will be damp and freezing in the Solitary, and that makes me worried, because I don't think anyone has been to visit there all day and I doubt Alex has enough blankets.

I don't want to ask, for fear of making myself look interested. Ruth and Margaret seem to have forgotten that they have been tasked to watch me. They are too busy thinking about the Rapture and the fall of the world of man. They can't stop talking about it with Hannah, especially the destruction part, I can tell they are pleased to know that all the people that have ever caused them harm will suffer and die. They speculate about what heaven will be like, about the golden clothes and shining haloes and the fact they will get to meet the characters from the Bible again. Margaret is reeling off a list. 'Moses! I should like to talk to him – and Thomas and Luke!' As if they might walk into the room at any moment.

I wonder who I should like to meet from the Bible, but I can't think of anyone, apart from Jesus. And surely if the Rapture does come, then he will be here anyway. I think of all the Bible stories I know, but there are no girls like me in any of them and I wonder if heaven will just be full of old men with long white beards.

I excuse myself to go to the outside toilet, but I can hardly *see*, the rain is so intense.

Across the other side of the yard I can make out a figure — Micah, I can tell from the slope of his shoulder. He has Job the sheepdog with him. He's holding him by the collar and is bending down to the dog, speaking to it. I know how he loves that dog. He's trained it since it was a puppy to round the sheep and come when it is called. But then, in a sudden, terrible instant, he holds the gun to the dog's head and fires.

I think I must cry out, because immediately he looks up at me and shouts, but all I can see is the limp body of his dog, fallen into an unnatural heap at his feet.

'What is it, child? You're like a ghost!' I bump into Hannah as I fly through the door.

Mary frowns at me. 'What was that noise?'

'Micah,' I say, the blood draining from my face. 'He shot Job.'

There is a gasp. 'But he loves that dog!' Margaret says.

'Which is doubtless why he did it,' says Hannah. 'How much crueller to leave him behind to fend for himself.'

'Are there dogs in heaven, do you think?' asks Margaret.

I am distracted for a moment by her idiocy, but then give way to the howl of protest building up in my heart and the floor seems to melt beneath me. 'But . . .' I say. 'But . . .' They will leave Alex to fend for herself, but not an animal?

Mary grabs my arm. 'A word,' she says, pulling me out of the kitchen into the tack room where the dead chickens hang plucked from the ceiling, naked and defenceless. 'Shush, Rebekah. Shush. Don't make a fuss.'

'But why not?'

'It's not our place to ask why.'

'But they've killed all the livestock and now Job! And Alex is in the Solitary, in this weather! You know it's wrong.'

'I've paid for it.' She touches her cheek.

'I *must* see her!' I say, looking at her pleadingly. 'We can't just leave her over there in this weather.'

'You can't go,' she says. 'Not now. It will be noticed.'

'I don't care if it's noticed!' I say rashly. 'She should not be out there tonight, alone in this weather.'

'What you say is true, but she is probably drier there than we are – the Solitary is safer than most places here. I know. I've spent time there. If you want to see her again, you must not be seen to want it.'

Defiance takes hold of me that will not be extinguished with reason. All I can think of is Alex, cold and alone in the raw weather, lost in the night with no comfort. 'But what has she done wrong?' I say out loud. 'She'll get sick and die!' The thought that I might not see her again consumes me with a fear that is almost too painful to contemplate. Mary puts her hand on my arm to still me.

'We'll find a way. Just not now. You must be obedient, even if it kills your heart to do so. Alex will be OK, you'll see. But if you go out tonight you will be followed, and if you're followed you might come to harm, and then I can't protect you.'

Her words surprise me. 'Protect me? Why should I need to be protected?'

She tuts and looks at the ceiling as if to ask God Himself for patience. 'Rebekah, do you trust me?'

'Yes.'

'Well, then you must be quiet. For all our sakes.' She lowers her voice still further. 'Hannah and Margaret are watching and they do not mean you well.'

This I understand. 'You mean they will tell Father?

'Yes, but worse than that.'

We do not say his name. To say his name would be to make it real, this fear that we both carry. It would be a heresy, and also a truth, and we are silent because we are afraid.

I nod slowly. 'Do you think the Rapture is coming on Tuesday?'

Mary bites her lip. 'I don't know, Rebekah. Some of us might be grateful for the glory. I watch and pray. So should you.'

'Micah shot the dog . . .' I can't get the image out of my head.

'For what Micah has done he will have to answer to the Almighty.'

When we walk back into the kitchen, Hannah is there with Bevins. He is flushed and agitated, full of a kind of happiness that is almost manic.

'Live for the Victory!' he says, his face shining with sweat. 'Live for the Victory!' And he needs to borrow a pan, although he doesn't say why.

I stare at him. When he looks at me the excitement leaves his face, which becomes set, his eyes like stones. He seems not like the kindly father sent to lead us to the promised land, but a lost man, wandering through a wilderness of his own creation, not leading us anywhere at all.

# TWENTY

# ALEX

I fell asleep and woke up not knowing where I was. It was so dark that for a moment I thought I'd gone blind. I waved my hand in front of my eyes but all I could feel was air against my face.

Then I heard a sound, like someone clearing their throat.

'Hello?'

But there was no reply. I listened really hard. I heard it again.

'Hello?' I sat upright, pushed myself to the back of the bed, clutching my knees to my chest. There was someone in the room with me, I was sure of it.

'Who's there?'

I sat there listening, staring into the dark until my eyes hurt. Nothing. They had come and prayed with me all of last night. Droning on and on while I fell in and out of awareness. You are a sinner; you must repent. On and on and on until I thought I was going to explode. Now I was alone and I couldn't work out which was worse.

My thoughts became pitiless. There was something wrong with me. I'd always known it. I mean, you don't end up in care because you're a good person. She didn't even want me enough to fight for me. Perhaps if I'd been more normal then all these bad things wouldn't have happened. The scars on my arms started to itch.

Bevins was right; I did have a devil inside of me. A chattering monkey that never shut up, that always wanted to do the wrong thing. The more I thought about it, the more I realised it was true – I came from badness and to badness I would return, and the thoughts and feelings I had about other girls were *unnatural*, just like everyone said all along. I was here because I *deserved* to be here, because I was a sinner, because what happened between me and Rebekah was a terrible thing.

I was so thirsty. I rubbed my head against the wall, pressed it in, hard until I could feel the rough stone scratching my scalp. Bevins left me with a bottle of water, but I didn't trust it, it smelled bitter, poisoned. I took a tiny, tiny sip, just to wet my tongue. But it made me want to vomit.

They said that she wouldn't have felt a thing. The drugs would have sent her into a deep sleep, her heart slowing until it stopped. And then she was gone, switched off like a light. It was two days before they found me, running around in a filthy nappy trying to wake her. Apparently I had opened the all the kitchen cupboards and taken out all the bleach and the sugar and the flour and the washing powder and was trying to make a cake with it on the kitchen floor.

After she died, everyone handed me on, like a pass-the-parcel nobody wanted. I was the accident that she wasn't ready for. The reason that she relapsed. If I hadn't been born, maybe she might have lived. Before she had me she'd had hard times but she'd cleaned up, got her life together. It was me and my weirdness that messed everything up. If only I had been an easier baby.

And then the crack that had opened in my mind just seemed to get bigger and bigger until it became a deep black hole and I took the flask of dirty water and I drank it all down in one go.

The cell quickly became too small and too hot and the walls shrank and suddenly I was too big, swelling up so that I filled each corner of the space, my skin rubbing against the rough surface of the walls, and I thought I might burst out like a giant born from a tiny egg and then the room seemed to explode, shattering into a million pieces, and then I was floating on the little bed of planks, a life raft in a huge sea and I was really tiny and the vaulted ceiling above me became a sky full of stars and above my head a whole firmament, which split open, clouds parting, and through the gaps came bright shafts of light illuminating the darkness. And there was an island in the middle of the sea with a tree full of angels, all sleeping, their faces folded into their wings like birds.

'Alex? It's me.' Rebekah's face smiling. I reached out a hand. I was so happy to see her again I wanted to cry, but then she turned her back to me and when she turned round it wasn't her at all, but an old woman with evil sharp teeth who was laughing at me.

I blinked and slapped my face. This couldn't be real, I knew it couldn't be real, it was something in the water Bevins had given me. But even as I thought this another wave of nausea washed over me and I threw up and I was back in the room and there were dark shadows crawling the walls. They came close and then scurried away like spiders. So many of them. The room swarming with them. They massed around me, even when I closed my eyes.

'Make them go away! Make them go away!' I tried to brush them off me but they wouldn't.

'I can't. Only you can. They're inside you,' the Rebekah/not-Rebekah woman said.

'But I can feel them!' And my skin itched everywhere like someone had set it on fire.

Then there was a burning in my ankle, and when I looked all I could see was the eye of my tattoo. Except it was real and it blinked at me, the eyeball glossy like an egg, and the gaze followed me, and swivelled in its socket, and it spoke to me. *Alex*, it said, in a dark voice that sounded like him. *Alex, you belong to me.*

I found a sharp stone and started to scratch against it. Deep gouges, the skin coming away in strips. I wanted to dig it out of me.

And then he was there with Thomas and other men in the background. Everything was blurry and hard to see.

'Alex, we've come to cast it out of you,' he said. And they held me down and prayed over me, and when I closed my eyes these winged creatures flew around in my head like birds. And from the tree of angels came this white light and they fought with the dark shapes and he shouted and raved and I tried not to look, but the visions were everywhere around me and in me, and I began to see that what I was witnessing was some kind of mortal battle for my soul.

'You can see them all around you, I know you can see them, just like I can,' he said. 'It's only when you are truly blind that you can see.'

I looked at him. His face kept blurring in and out of focus.

'Are they real?'

'Repent, Alex! Repent!'

'I'm sorry,' I said. 'I'm sorry. I believe!'

I just wanted it to go away. I wanted to feel *clean*. I wanted my teeth to stop chattering, for my headache to pass. I wanted the angels to win. By the time they were finished I would have believed just about anything Bevins told me.

'You have been reborn,' he said. 'You will come with me to heaven, just like in my vision and all of this will go away, and be as nothing.'

'Thank you,' I said, overtaken by sudden relief, a euphoric peacefulness. 'Thank you.' And I started to cry.

# TWENTY-ONE

# REBEKAH

I keep dropping off, waking up with a start, terrified that already it is morning. Finally I decide, it must be time. The whole house lies under a thick blanket of silence. It has stopped raining and the sky has cleared to a clear black that is full with the pinpricks of stars. I slowly make my way downstairs. Each creak in the floorboard makes my heart wither. I can hear loud snores coming from the front bedroom, where Micah and Mary sleep. I stand at the top of the stairs and hold my breath.

I tiptoe my way through to the kitchen. The room still carries some of the warmth of the day, though a chill draught breathes through the cracks and under the door. I search the larder for food, but there is none. Some flour, an egg — I can't take her any of these things. There are coats in the tack room. I take one even though it is not mine. Maybe Micah's or Jonathan's. It is dirty and ripped and smells of the goats but at least it will keep me warm.

The wind bites, making me glad of the extra layer, but aware that it will not keep me warm long unless I am moving. The wind blows with a stinging insistence. I can't walk hard or fast enough to overcome it and I wish I'd worn more clothes.

I follow the path out to the lake before I strike a match to light the lantern, just in case there's someone watching. The air is still, a fingernail of moon shines through the thin clouds. The air carries the smell of the harvest, and the coming autumn chill.

I'm shivering in spite of the heavy coat. I hurry along the narrow track, stumbling over the tussocked grass, my feet slipping into the puddles of mud. The lantern throws out a meagre light, which shines no further than a step in front of me. Without the sheep the fields are too quiet and my heart quickens at a rustling in the hedge. I don't look.

When I get to the flat rocks I can just make out the shape of the Devil's Seat above me, glowering down at me in the night sky. My heart pounds so fast I'm afraid it will jump out of my chest. I daren't look too hard in case I should see the devil on his seat. I imagine he must have a fork in his hand and a long tail and cloven hoofs like a goat's. When I get to the top I wish I'd taken the lower path through the marsh instead. Every rock seems to hide the shadow of a demon.

I hurry and stumble and fall, hurting my knee. The wind howls through the gaps in the boulders, I put my head down, not daring to look. I can just make out the horizon against the sky and I run down the slope, my feet skidding and sliding over the damp turf. I can hear the sea again too, the loud roar and boom of water hitting the cliffs.

There's no sound when I get there. I tread quietly around Naomi's cell in case I wake her and she tells someone I was here. I don't know which cell they've put her in and my blood roars in my ears as I open the hatch on one of the doors. I lift up the lantern, but it throws only shadows against the wall; there is no one in there. I try the one next door. This time I can see a shape hunched up against the wall under a blanket.

'Alex?'

She doesn't move.

'Alex!' I say more loudly. She sits up in her bed, and for a moment I think I must have got the wrong cell, that this is Naomi, not Alex. Because her hair is wild and her dress is ragged and torn and on her leg, where her tattoo used to be, there is a bandage that is dark with blood.

*No*. I wish I could just break through the door and get her. 'What have they done to you?'

She doesn't answer. Instead she shields her eyes from the light. 'Rebekah?' She sounds strange; her voice is deeper, slurred.

'It's me,' I say. 'I'm going to get you out of here.'

She gets up from the bed and walks slowly, like an old person, towards me. All over her arms and legs are livid scratches.

'What's wrong with you? What happened to your leg?'

'All bad,' she says. 'All bad.' She scratches at her skin with her nails. 'We had to take it off. Get rid of it.'

'Get rid of what?'

'The bad eye. It's how it got in. It's the reason everything got so messed up. They're coming. Rebekah. I saw them. So many, they filled the sky, like birds.'

'What did?'

'Devils. I saw them. I really saw them . . .' She trails off. 'Who are you?' She looks at me blankly.

'Alex, it's *me*, Rebekah. What happened to you?'

'He came and he forgave me. But he can't do anything. My badness, it's inside. I can't ever be rid of it.' She shakes her head. 'I've got to stay here and pray.'

'Don't be silly! We're going to get you out of here, remember?' I reach out to take her hand but she swats me away.

'Get off!' Her face is glazed with sweat and she smells strange. 'You're dirty!'

'Are you sick? Why are you being like this? You're acting really weird.'

'I'm fine.' She leans her head against the door so I can see her face close up. Her eyelids suddenly droop. 'I've seen the light, that's all. It's so obvious. I should have seen it all along.'

'Did they hurt you?'

She shakes her head. 'I *told* you. He forgave me.'

'Who?'

'Bevins.'

'You saw him today?'

She nods. He's done something to her. She sounds like she's speaking from underwater, and her movements are slow and treacly. I think about when we first got here and Jonathan was weird and the twins were fast asleep and she said they'd been drugged.

'Did he bring you anything?' I ask.

'Just water,' she says. 'It made me feel sick.'

'Alex, listen to me,' I say very slowly in the hope that she will hear me. 'I'm going to get you out of here, OK, but if he gives you any more to drink, throw it away. They killed all the animals today. In the barn – all the sheep and the goats, even the dog. We need to get away from here. We need to get help.'

'OK,' she says. Then she wanders away from me back to her bed. 'It doesn't matter anyway. There's nothing you can do that will make any difference. Our lives are already written.'

I press my head against the door in despair. Now what? Slowly, like a creeping chill, the thought that I will have to find a way to get off this island by myself fills me with dread. All our plans. We are supposed to do this together. 'I can't do it without you.'

But she doesn't answer. She lies on the bed and pulls the blanket

194

up over her head and stays still and rigid until eventually I have to leave, a lump in my throat so hard it's impossible to swallow.

Cloud has descended on the Devil's Seat and the air is heavy with the threat of rain so I walk back through the bog. I don't care, even as my feet sink into the cold mud.

About halfway back it starts to get really deep and marshy – up to my knees in one place – and it is an effort to keep taking one step after another. I struggle forward, suddenly really cold, my teeth chattering, the lantern swinging wildly as I try to walk. Eventually I manage to bully my way through to firmer ground, but by the time I do I am worried that I have been gone long.

As I approach the farmhouse I can hear voices – there are people in the yard. Too late I realize I am still visible, my lantern swinging from my hand. I drop to my knees and quickly blow out the flame. There is a shout.

'Over there! I saw it, over there!'

Then someone else shouts, 'Get inside! Get inside!'

I run away down the path, over the gate into the field and push myself into the hedge, the hawthorn scratching my back and my arms.

They are coming, running along the other side of the hedge. Oh God, don't let them see me. *Please*. I close my eyes and grit my teeth. I hold my breath till I think I might explode. Then a voice shouts: 'This way!'

The footsteps run past me and further along the path and on towards Devil's Seat. I let out a long slow breath before pulling myself out of the hedge. I walk slowly and carefully back towards the house, taking the long way, squeezing between the vegetable garden and the wall, treading on the soft soil of the flowerbeds so as not to crunch the stones on the path. I run across the yard into the shadows, pressing myself against the wall, and turn the corner to the front of the house. Lantern light dances in the window and there is the sound of muffled talking: people have come back from church. I wonder if they even know that I am missing. I open the front door very slowly and quietly. If I can get as far as the stairs, then I can pretend I've been in the attic with the boys all along.

The house smells of woodsmoke and people. A lantern on the table by the door throws a dim light into the hallway. Everyone is awake. I can hear talking, then a scream from the kitchen and someone bursts into the hallway. It is Hannah, quickly pursued by Mary.

'Are you sure it's worth disturbing his sleep over this?' Mary is asking.

'But I must tell him what I saw,' she says. 'The girl walks abroad even though she is locked up! Jonathan and Ezekiel think so too.' She sees me and stops. 'And where have *you* been, Rebekah?'

'Upstairs,' I say.

But she furrows her brow at the mud on my legs, my boots, my blue-knuckled hands.

'Well, I went outside for a moment because I heard shouting. But I came back in because I was scared.'

'He is about us,' she says conspiratorially. 'Now. I have seen him. A glow in the marsh towards the Devil's Seat. A will-o'-the-wisp. A demon spirit. Many saw it. Jonathan and Ezekiel have gone to banish it. Mr Bevins must be told. Your father too.'

Mary Protheroe looks at me and raises her eyebrows. Hannah is so preoccupied with what she has seen that she's not looking at me. Quickly I walk past her towards the stairs. 'The noise woke me. I wanted to see what it was about.'

Mary Protheroe's lips twitch into a little half-smile and she nods at me.

'Go to your room, child, and pray,' Hannah says. 'We must bind cords of light around this house if we are to stop the devil from getting in. Cords of light.' She knocks on the door of the living room and enters. I don't stay to hear what she says.

# TWENTY-TWO

# REBEKAH

In the morning Mary is in the kitchen with the twins. She has given them small cakes made of potato, but there is no food for us. My belly grumbles. The light is the blue-grey of just-dawn and her frame appears shadowed against the window, thin and spectral.

She doesn't even ask me where I've been. 'Was she alive?' is all she asks.

'She's not herself,' I say. 'She's not well. What has he given her?' We both look at each other. It's like in the last few days a thought has grown between us that neither of us can say aloud.

Mary bites her lip. I want to cry like a child. 'What are we going to do?'

'*Ssshhhhh*. We'll talk about this later, OK? When did you last eat?'

I don't know. 'Yesterday?'

She goes into the store and comes out with a sugar cube. 'I am saving these for the boys, but you must have one.'

I suck on it and my bloodstream fills with the relief of a sudden chemical energy. It's going to be OK, I tell myself. You've just got to be brave. But I don't feel brave at all.

The other women come in — Hannah and Margaret and Ruth and Mrs Bragg. No one is sleeping much these days. Mrs Bragg says it's because everyone's hungry.

'Doing wonders for my waistline, this is!' she says idly,

before Hannah silences her with a glare.

Then she notices me. 'What is wrong with you, child? You look like you've seen the devil himself,' she fusses, placing her hand on my forehead.

'I had a bad dream,' I say.

'Perhaps it was a vision,' she suggests earnestly.

She's starting to sound more and more like a shadow of Mr Bevins. I look at her face. Even her features have changed, her mouth like his when she is speaking.

Mr Bevins has drawn up a rota that each of us must observe, a vigil of prayers in the church that we must keep until the Rapture comes. Hannah shows me a copy; her name is down for the evening, Mary at midnight tonight.

'A final farewell to our lives in New Canaan,' Hannah says. 'Our waiting is over at last!'

My head spins with the weight of everything I'm about to do and I have to hold on to the table to stop myself from falling over.

The men finish building the bonfire, a trench for water is dug around it and piled up with branches from the hawthorn and rowan. In the middle they have made a pen where they will drive the last of our livestock, and placed around it are some of the carcasses which they did not bury. The crows and the seagulls have discovered it too, and sit around in the field waiting for their chance to peck at the corpses. The first thing they go for is the eyes, so now several of the sheep's heads are grotesquely blinded. I stand and look at it when Mary sends me out to get some logs from the barn. Something in me hardens. This will not bring God down from heaven. How could something so monstrous be divine?

*

In the evening we gather even though there is no food. Bevins insists that we are to think about food, and about the meaning of our fast, but all we are permitted is a glass of water. All are here, expect Hannah who is keeping vigil in the church.

Mrs Bragg comes into the kitchen. 'He's asking for you.'

'Who?'

'Bevins.'

Even since yesterday he seems to have grown in stature. He towers over us all, even though he's physically shorter than most of the men. I take in the water and pour a cup for everyone present. The atmosphere is so serious it makes me want to laugh, a kind of fizz in my stomach that will not be quelled, and I am not hungry even though I know I should be starving.

'Did anyone visit the Solitary today?' asks Ruth.

I freeze.

'I have,' says Mr Bevins. My heart stops in my chest. What did they find? Was she there? I want to ask but I can't for fear of looking too interested. 'Thomas and I went over this afternoon.'

I stare at the floor. I daren't look at him, even though I am sure he is looking at me to search out my reaction. My face starts to get hot.

'I spoke with Naomi and she asked to be remembered in our prayers. She will come among us on Sunday.'

And what about Alex? I want to ask. He's deliberately withholding information about her, I know he is.

'And the girl?' Mr Bragg asks.

He sighs. 'She brings trouble. The devil is so deeply embedded. We're having to coax it out. There may yet be some damage to the vessel, but she is softening. Rebekah!' I jump. 'How are you?'

'I'm well, thank you.' What does he mean by damage to the vessel? What have they *done* to her?

'And are you looking forward to meeting your maker?'

'I am,' I say. I am realising how this is like a game where I have my appointed role and all I have to do is say the right lines.

'Look at me when I'm talking to you!' I look up. It's as if he's trying to see inside my head, so intensely does he stare at me.

'You're lying,' he says, 'but it makes no odds. We will see who is left behind on Tuesday. Then we'll know the truth. Call the women in.'

I go and get the others and we stand there at the door, our heads bowed. Mr Bevins then starts to tell us how he wants each one of us in white vestments on the final day. There's cloth that he has been keeping for this occasion, and the women are to make simple robes from it, enough for everyone. Jonathan brings in a roll of white cloth from I know not where. It is spotted with black mould along the bottom.

'It'll need to be washed obviously. But it'll give you something to keep you occupied.'

'What pattern are we to use?' Margaret asks.

He waves his hand as if he is being generous. 'That's not for me to say. You have more knowledge than me. Dressmaking is women's work, and blessed it is too.'

Then, out of nowhere ,Jonathan asks if he can go to the mainland.

'Just to see my ma again, like, before it all kicks off?'

Mr Bevins's eyebrows rise to his hairline. 'Brother Jonathan.' He puts his arm around Jonathan's shoulder. 'Brother Jonathan, would that you could! Would that I could take you there myself. We would all like to see our mothers again.' His voice is low and rich with fake sympathy. 'But God has called us to be separate. To be here. To be first!'

Jonathan nods meekly. 'Yes, yes, I know.'

'Don't think about leaving. Do not even let it cross your mind. It's just a vile temptation whispered by the devil, put there to distract you.' He swivels round to look at the rest of us in the room. 'Do any of you want to leave? Speak now!'

I look at the floor and pray that he doesn't pick on me. No one speaks.

'How could we think such a thing?! After everything you've done to bring us here! We will follow you to heaven!' Margaret of course, sucking up to him.

He seems satisfied then, and he takes Jonathan with him to the church to pray.

'It is going to take a lot of washing to get those spots out,' Margaret says, unrolling the fabric on to the kitchen table and scratching at the mould spots with her thumbnail.

'If it ever does come out. We need bleach, which we don't have. And a great deal of hot water,' Mary says, sighing. She asks me to fetch more buckets of water from the water butt which leans up outside the house. At least with all the rain it's full to overflowing, and we stoke up the fire to boil the water and get the tin bath and use some squares of hard soap to make a lather. Margaret cuts the cloth into thirty sheets; each one must be washed and scrubbed. I think about Alex. What did Bevins mean by damaging the vessel to get the devil out? My skin crawls with fear. She must be OK, she must.

The women talk on about the best patterns and designs. Soon the kitchen is full with squares of damp white material hanging from every space, on the backs of chairs, on a line that

Mary has strung out across the kitchen.

It's decided that if we cut a hole in the centre of each for the head to go through the rest can be worn as a kind of shawl. And with a few snips and pleats they can be hemmed and turned into serviceable garments, perhaps even tied at the waist with lengths of cord, which Hannah thinks will represent the way in which we are tied to the service of the Lord. She has some plan that she will sew brocade on each one, so that they will be like the raiments of angels.

'And where will you get your brocade?' Mary asks.

She's strangely silent and then she says in a voice that is quite tight, 'I brought some with me. It was the only thing I didn't give away. It was to be on my wedding gown.' There's a silence in the kitchen. No one knows what to say. 'Imagine if I had got married! I would never have come here and I would not be so blessed. The Lord really does work in mysterious ways, and to Him we should be grateful.'

'Amen!' say Margaret and Ruth.

'My first and final marriage to Jesus,' she says. 'It will be as my wedding was intended but so much better.'

She goes to her cabin and comes back with two heavy duffel bags full of material. 'It's in here somewhere. Might as well go through it all and see what might be useful.'

She tips the bags out on the table. And I see Alex's clothes tumbling out with all the piles of scraps and rags. Before anyone else can touch them, I grab her jeans and check the pockets. There's the crinkle of paper and I pull out the letter and hide it up my sleeve. No one has noticed because they are too busy looking at Alex's phone, which has fallen out on the table in front of us with a clatter.

Margaret and Ruth jump back.

'It's a sign of the beast!' Hannah pokes at it with a pair of scissors as if it's alive and might bite her.

Mrs Bragg picks it up and looks at it. She presses the buttons. 'I don't think it's got any power.'

'But how can you say that? It's the work of the Antichrist! We need to get rid of it!' Hannah hits it with her scissors, knocking it on to the stone floor. The glass screen splinters.

'Well, it's certainly broken now,' Mary says, picking it up and putting it in the pocket of her apron. 'I'll give it to Bevins when I see him.'

As the evening wears on I wonder when I will get to escape. I follow Mary when she takes the twins upstairs to bed.

'Don't go out tonight,' she says. 'Bevins suspects witchcraft. They have locked her door with padlocks and chains. He is going over there later to cast out demons – you will be seen. And he is already watching you. You know it.'

'But . . .' I can't bear the thought of her alone with him. Of what might happen.

She takes the broken phone out of her pocket. 'Do you know how this works? Can we get a message out on it?'

I shake my head. 'She said the battery was dead.'

She sighs. 'I'm sorry, Rebekah, that it's come to this. I . . . I have only ever tried to do the right thing.' She looks as if she's about to say something else, but thinks better of it. 'Promise me you won't go out.'

I look at her. 'I promise.' But I don't mean it, and Mary knows this because she sends Ruth upstairs to sit outside on the landing in case the twins don't settle but really I know, it's to keep watch over me.

Very slowly and quietly I pull the crumpled envelope out of my sleeve. The handwriting looks familiar. It's addressed to me, care of the Church of New Canaan. The date on the postmark is last year. I can see the shape of Ruth's skirt through the gap in the door. I slide the paper out of the envelope slowly, trying not to make any noise. The envelope is already open so someone – Bevins – has already read this. It's written on two pieces of thin notepaper.

*Dear Rebekah,*

*I hope this message reaches you. I don't know if your father is passing my letters on. I just want you to know that I think of you every day and pray that you are safe and well. I want you to know too how sorry I am for what happened. I never meant for things to end up like this. I am going to church in Falmouth. Everyone has been so sweet and forgiving, but I know I must bear the burden of what I've done, both to you and your father and to the community. I should have had more faith! Please know I only did this with your best intentions in my heart. The doctors said if I did not take the pills I would die. Bevins said if I took the pills he would cast me out. What could I do?*

The paper trembles in my hand. I don't understand. This is from my mother? My mother is alive? But all this time we've been acting like she was dead. *Father* has been acting like she was dead. All this time I've been thinking she was dead. All this time I've been lied to. Does Father know about this?

*Life in New Canaan might be hard, but I know it's for the best for you to be there with the people who can keep you to the path. I think of you all the time and wonder how you have grown. If you do get to see this letter, ask your father to send word, even if it's only a short message, just to let me know you are OK. There are some in the Church here who think I should be going to the courts. I'm not going to do that yet, but if I hear nothing by the end of the year I will look again at my options. It's not fair to keep me from you like this!*

*Your ever-loving,*

*Mum xxxxxxxxx*

I screw the letter up in my hand and try to stop myself from crying, but I can't help it. I make such a noise that Ruth knocks on the door.

'Are you OK?'

I turn my face away from her. 'Yeah, I'm fine.' I sniff loudly. 'Just tired.'

'Would you like me to pray with you? Is there's anything you'd like to confess?'

'I'm *fine*,' I say, through gritted teeth.

She stands there for a while as if she doesn't believe me but doesn't know what to say. I squeeze my eyes closed, hard, so hard that the dark behind my eyes turns red.

# TWENTY-THREE

# REBEKAH

Father and Bevins are waiting at the church with the whole community gathered, even Naomi. They have brought her from the Solitary, which means that someone must have seen Alex. I look at Mary, but she just raises her eyebrows and nods at me, whatever that is supposed to mean. Because she is a prophet, Naomi sits at the front with the elders in her frayed dress with a headscarf that is too big for her head, and she seems much older than she appears in the Solitary. Her eyes are big as blue saucers in her shrunken face, and she stares at me as I take my seat.

Bevins says that today he will be going round asking each of us in turn to commit any final sins to the Lord, to ask His forgiveness. That we might be pure in heart when the end comes and that we might take great gratitude in the suffering of the cross, which is what allows Jesus to return in all His glory to the earth and forgive us miserable sinners. I sense my determination beginning to seep out of me. A chill creeps through me, which becomes a nervous tremor. I have the letter in my hand; when my turn comes I'm going to read it out, and we'll see how many of them want to stay with Bevins then. All this time they've been treating me with such sympathy, the motherless child. As if I don't have a mother who is alive and well and living in a place called Falmouth. If I could I would be like Samson in the temple, I would bring the whole church crashing down about their heads.

'He did this that we might live! Our petty privations are as nothing in comparison to such suffering. Imagine! One man took all those punishments on your behalf. To cleanse *you* from sin . . .'

And so he goes on. Listing in detail all the sufferings of the cross, each wound vividly remembered, from the nails that were hammered through his hands, to the crown of thorns, to the spear that pierced His side. He describes it as if he was there and saw it himself, moment by moment.

An old fear strikes me that if He comes back tomorrow, He will see the darkness in my heart, how I have turned away from Him and that I have not witnessed to Alex, rather I have let her turn me away from the path. It makes me squirm and there is a clamour in my head like a ringing bell that makes it hard to think. But then I remember that my mother is not going to be in heaven waiting for me, but that she is in a place on the mainland called Falmouth, in a house. And everything Bevins says has the hollow echo of a lie.

He walks among us, asking for confessions. Father follows him, carrying the communion cup. He expects everyone to list all the bad things they've thought and done, that we might be forgiven and become, according to Father 'white as the snow and blameless when we enter heaven'. And, after we've confessed, we have to take a sip of wine from the communion cup.

Jonathan is on his knees, clutching his hands together so tight his knuckles shine. He says that he has been having immodest thoughts. 'This is why I can't be with the women, like,' he says.

Micah confesses that he has taken up violence against his wife and is sorry that it was so. There is a murmur from the women.

'But this is not a sin, Micah,' Bevins says. 'Between a man and a wife.' He presses his hands on Micah's head and says a prayer asking the Lord to help Micah to forgive Mary for her rebelliousness.

I look at Mary, her head bowed, her jaw clenched. *That's not fair!* I want to shout out, my resolve hardening again. Micah committed a sin against Mary – how is it *her* fault that *he* lost his temper and was moved to strike her? I am dreading when it comes to my turn. I need to think of what I will say.

When it comes to Mary she confesses her disobedience and they say long prayers over her that she may be humbled and accept the guidance of her husband without question, in trust and humility as the Lord would want.

Hannah breaks down sobbing and prostrates herself on the floor, her arms outstretched. It takes an age for her to stop crying long enough so we can hear what she has to say.

'I . . . have . . . stolen a comb from Ruth . . . and kept it as my own even though I knew it was hers. And . . . and . . .' Here she breaks off to cry some more although I am sure the good Lord in heaven gives not one small bit of anything for her stupid dilemmas and she will get into heaven by sheer persistence alone. '. . . I too have had lewd and lustful thoughts.'

Something in me recoils. I do not want to know this about Hannah. Dear God, if You are truly coming back to take us to Your own, can you put me in a different part of heaven to Hannah?

Thomas says he has been having resentful thoughts towards his parents; Ruth that she is jealous of Mary for having a husband; Gideon says nothing for a while, and then one word very quickly in his thick accent, that it takes me a while to decipher as 'sloth'.

They come to me last, by which point the morning is already nearly over, the light outside the church changes to bright sun, which shines through the window at the back.

'And what of you, Rebekah? What sins do you harbour in the dark corners of your heart?'

I stand up, my legs trembling. I know what I have to say, but I don't know what will happen when I've said it. Everyone needs to know that he's lying to us.

I hold the letter out in front of me.

'*Dear Rebekah . . .*' I read out the words that I have read and reread so many times since last night. There's a sharp intake of breath from someone – Hannah or Margaret maybe. I look up and I can see Mary shaking her head at me.

About halfway through I feel my father's hand on my shoulder; the communion cup in his hand smells strange, the same kind of smell that Alex had in the Solitary.

'Where did you get that?!' he growls at me.

My voice wavers but I carry on reading. I am aware that I am being shouted down by Mr Bevins.

'Disobedience! Disobedience! Not only have you broken into my room and taken my private papers, but you, like your mother, have a rebellious heart! She says it herself! Dead or alive, she will not be getting through the gates of heaven! She may as well be dead to you!'

He snatches the letter from me and presses his hand on my other shoulder. 'I want you to pray with me, child. Pray with me and your father and the whole of our community. Right here. Right now I am carrying you across the threshold into heaven. There is a war waging for your soul that I will win—'

'No! You're a liar! You're all liars!'

But he presses my shoulder so hard that I can feel the bones in his hands. I can't believe no one else is doing anything. They're all just sitting there, not moving, slow and obedient.

Father brings the communion cup to my lips.

'Drink.'

I don't want to. I don't like the smell. I close my lips but Mr Bevins pinches my nose so I open my mouth in surprise and father trickles some in my mouth. It tastes sweet and sickly, I keep it in my mouth, meaning to hold it there till I can spit it out, but it tastes so disgusting I have to swallow.

Almost immediately there is something odd in my body, a new lightness.

Bevins goes on and on while I kneel on the cold floor and all I can think of is her. Like a shield between me and Mr Bevins, the thought of her keeps me staring at the same spot on the floor, a little crack and a whorl in the stone that looks like the barnacles on the side of the whale. Mr Bevins's hand presses harder into my shoulder; the lighter touch of my father on the other shoulder makes me lopsided. And then Naomi comes and kneels next to me and starts mumbling and pointing her finger at me, and then Jonathan starts speaking in tongues and there are other noises, like the barking of a dog and the shrieking of a bird, and someone sings a hymn and the whole loud cacophony of it becomes like a roaring storm in my head. And I can see suddenly a pillar of fire and the shape of a cross and people making faces of fear and torment and the world of eternity, and figures that swarm about in my head, just like Alex said, and I'm frightened and the floor is melting under my knees and I want to scream.

The voices get louder and louder until Mr Bevins shouts, 'In the name of Jesus, Satan begone!' And he pushes me forward, and it seems to take a long time for the floor to rise up to greet my forehead, my body floppy as rag.

*

When I wake up I am in the corner against the wall, with Mary sitting next to me. Hannah is at the front reading from the Psalms. My head hurts.

'That was quite a bang,' Mary whispers.

I touch my forehead. It has a bandage tied round it and a crust of blood.

'You fainted in the Lord and you bled. Your father says it is a sign that you have been cleansed. Sit still.' She gives me a cup of water. I look at it suspiciously but Mary nods.

'It's OK, it's just water.'

Everything in the church is blurry; like when I was on the boat and got the sickness, nothing stays still. I can see Naomi at the front, prostrate on the floor, her arms spread out. Bevins and Father are kneeling in prayer. The day is already darkening.

'Did you know?' I stare at her. 'Why didn't you tell me?'

'Shhhh.' Mary shakes her head. 'I'm so, *so* sorry.' She grabs my hand. '*So* sorry. I did what I thought was best.' She turns round suddenly, fiercely, and holds my face in her hands. 'Whatever happens, I came here because I wanted a better life. I thought I was doing the right thing. You mustn't blame me.' Her face is beaten, weathered and sad, her eyes hazy with tears. 'I'm sorry.'

'It's OK,' I say.

'Don't try and run. Not now. You'll be brought back before you've got to the end of the path,' she says. 'Lie down, rest. We'll make a plan. I promise.' She folds a blanket as a pillow and pats it. I lie down and close my eyes again.

I must sleep again because the next thing Father is shaking me awake.

'Rebekah! Rebekah! You must wake up. It's your turn to read.'

I stare at him. 'No! Why didn't you tell me? Why have you made me believe all this time she was *dead*?!' I say this loud enough for Bevins to hear. He stands up.

'Rebekah, now is not the time,' says Father firmly. 'You heard Bevins – we're, you're, much better off without her. We couldn't risk our chance of glory.' But he won't look at me, just holds out his hand to help me stand up and looks nervously over his shoulder at Mr Bevins.

'I don't believe you!'

'Shhh. Rebekah, do you want to go to the Solitary?'

*I don't care*, I think. *You knew. You knew and you never told me.*

The room glows with candlelight; many are now lying on the floor, the chairs pushed back. Everyone except Mary and the boys, gone no doubt back to the farmhouse. Oh for a taste of that fresh air!

My head thuds as I try to stand up, everything strange and unsteady. One moment I am tall, the next shrunk to the size of a mouse. I stumble as Father leads me. Bevins is prostrate before the altar. Where I fell there is a stain of dried blood. I reach a hand up to my forehead and a large lump is emerging through the cloth and the whole side of my head is tender.

I kneel at the altar. Father gives me the Bible turned to the Book of Revelation. I am to read the whole book while everyone prays. I can hardly see the words on the page, my head throbs so much. I hear my own voice haltingly reading the words, but they make no sense.

Chapter after chapter it's all fire and conflagration and strange beasts and unnatural sights. It sets a fear in me, which is only made worse by my headache. I'm sure there's something I'm supposed to be remembering to do. When I get to the end I turn around and everyone's lying on the floor. There is a gentle snoring coming from Ezekiel.

I turn to the beginning and start again with the Book of Genesis. I'm halfway into Deuteronomy when Mary comes back.

'You need to make yourself ready,' she says, touching my head and frowning. 'Come.'

She leads me to the door and we slip outside. The air is like a blessing on my face. The early evening is calm, still, a mist of dampness in the air that soothes my face. We walk slowly up the path to the farmhouse.

'I've seen her,' Mary says.

I'm not sure who she is taking about. 'Who?'

'*Alex.*' Her name brings everything back into my body like a punch. I don't know how I could have forgotten.

'There was something odd in that communion wine,' I mutter.

She looks concerned. 'I know. Bevins thinks it brings us closer to God. I only took a small sip.'

'Is she OK?'

She makes a face. 'Bevins thinks he has won the battle. But she is not OK, no.' My heart turns even more against him. Gently she touches the bruise on the side of my face and winces. 'And you need to get that looked at. Here.' She gives me a key.

'Where did you get that?'

'Someone might have dropped something.' She winks at me. 'But you need to be strong enough to get that boat out of the harbour. If you can get it to sea, you'll likely be seen by someone, maybe a fishing boat.'

'Thank you.'

She shakes her head. 'Alex is not in a good way. You might have to leave her here. Do you think you can get the boat out on your own?'

'I don't know.'

I'm not leaving her here. Even if I have to carry her. I have to tell her about my mother. She needs to know that she was right, she needs to know that everything is going to be OK.

I look at Mary and wonder what she knows, but she is not looking at me. Just holding the lantern and staring ahead.

'Tomorrow just before Bevins lights the fire — you must go then. The men will be busy. I'll cover for you. You'll be in danger, the sea will be rough, and it's a long way to the mainland but I wouldn't say this to you if I didn't think that we needed help. Do you understand? I can buy you an hour, maybe a bit longer. You just need to get the boat out to sea. If Alex won't come with you, don't linger. You hear me?'

I nod. 'My head hurts,' I say, wanting to cry in relief.

When we get to the farmhouse Mary dresses it for me again with a fresh bandage; although it's not bleeding she says I need to protect it from getting knocked again.

She has packed a bag for me with spare clothes, a coat, some sugar cubes, dried apple, and hidden it in the wardrobe in my bedroom. She tells me to rest while I can. She says that the best time to go will be tomorrow after she has sounded the gong for supper, when everyone has gathered. I am to slip out of the front door and run to the harbour.

'What will you tell them?'

'Let me worry about that,' she says. 'The main thing is that you go. Fast as you can. And when you see your mother tell her —' she stops as if she can't think what to say — 'that I'm sorry.'

'But I don't know how to sail a boat! I don't know if I can do this on my own.'

'God will be with you.'

'And not with you?'

She laughs bitterly. 'He's always with us. When do we forget it?' And then we have to stop talking because Hannah comes into the kitchen, looking groggy and unkempt.

'Peace be with you, Sisters,' she says looking a little put out when I stifle a nervous giggle.

'What can I help you with, Sister?' Mary asks.

'I don't . . . I don't remember,' she puts her hand to her throat. 'I do feel a bit odd,' she says. 'Don't you?'

Mary gives her a glass of water, which she drinks in one go.

When Hannah has gone Mary says. 'You must be brave and you must get help.'

'Who from?'

'The police, Rebekah. You must go to the police.'

A shiver runs through me. This is serious now.

'I'm scared,' I say.

'I know you are, Rebekah.' She puts her arm around me. 'So am I.'

# TWENTY-FOUR

# REBEKAH

'Awake! Arise! Today is the precious day!'

Bevins is banging a gong downstairs to rouse everyone. It's not even light.

'How can you sleep? On such a day as today! All that we have hoped for, all that we have prayed for, finally come to pass! We are indeed blessed! *Blessed!*'

I groan and roll over. Ruth lies in bed, still awake, staring at the ceiling. My stomach growls with hunger.

She does not even acknowledge me when I stand up to dress.

On the way to church Mary walks beside me. 'How are you?'

'Afraid,' I say to her. 'Hungry.'

'Don't be afraid.' I look at her and the boys, who stare at me with their huge eyes. 'This is no life for them.'

'But we are going to the Rapture,' I say although I know we are as much going to the Rapture as my mother is dead.

'That we should be so lucky.'

Father walks ahead with the other men and I am not allowed to walk with them. I wish he would turn round and just see me. He is so deep in with Bevins that they are like brothers. Everything they say is analysed between the two of them, always hunched together, leafing through the Bible, talking.

I take my seat at the back next to Mary and we sit there for the rest of the morning, Bevins going through the Bible calling out passages and getting us to respond with the next one. Hannah has always been the best at this game and she answers all of them until Bevins gets annoyed and shouts at her.

'God hates a braggart, Sister. You are not permitted to speak.'

She drops her head abjectly. 'Forgive me,' she says.

'Sister, you know that I do this for you only because I love you. For your soul.'

She nods. And then he gets distracted by some pages from Leviticus, the book of the law, and reads aloud long, dry passages of rules from the days of long ago in the lands of the Middle East.

Then in the middle of the afternoon he dismisses the women to go and prepare the robes.

Hannah walks with us, between us. 'You were quiet this morning, Mary,' she says. There is something spoiled and pointed in her tone.

'You are just too quick with your answers, Sister.'

'Humph.' Hannah makes a noise as if she is not satisfied and then she says, 'If anyone was to leave, if any of you were to *try* to leave, you know that he has told me . . . he said, "Let any that would stray from me know: I will bring them back".'

Mary nods. 'Yes, I heard it,' she says, and we walk in silence back to the house.

When we get there she sends me upstairs to nap with the boys. 'Get them out from under my feet!' I lie in bed next to the twins stroking their hair and wait for her to give me the sign. They are quiet and hungry, their usual mithering replaced by a sleepy, starving exhaustion. In my pocket I worry the key that Mary gave me in my fingers. My heart races with what I know I must do. All kinds of frightening possibilities cross my mind: what if I wreck the boat on the rock getting out of the harbour? What if I get sick? What if Alex won't come with me? It feels like a lifetime since I saw her and the thought of her pale face, the scratches on her arms and legs, scare me. What if there is a big swell and the boat is capsized? I don't want to drown. Fear courses through my body. Maybe it's not so bad here, I think. Maybe if the Rapture doesn't come Mr Bevins will calm down and things will go back to how they used to be. And when the delivery boat comes I can get a message to my mother, get her to call the police. Maybe one of the others can take this on. Why do I have to be the one to do this?

By the time Mary comes upstairs I am nearly crazy with fear and hunger and I have almost persuaded myself that I don't need to go after all. The women are all sewing brocade and singing, the men will come to light the bonfire once it gets dark. Mary says she can protect me for about an hour, no longer.

'After that, they'll know you are gone.'

'But . . .' I *can't*, I want to say. I'm not strong enough.

'You *can* do this. You know Bevins. He isn't the type of person who will just let people go. He has to have everyone, or not at all. You *must* do this, for yourself, for Alex, for me, for your mother, for all of us.' She kneels beside me and puts her arms around me awkwardly. I feel like crying but I don't.

She takes the twins downstairs and I go and sit at the top of the stairs, frozen like the cormorant that fishes the harbour, waiting to strike. It will sit there for hours then suddenly dive, soundlessly breaking the water, returning with a fish speared in its beak. I can hear voices, the trudge of footsteps, the squeak of the kitchen door on its hinges, low conversation. Everyone is subdued, exhausted. I creep down the stairs until I could be seen from the hallway, and then I know I must go. Now or never.

*

Once I'm outside I run as if I have the wind in my heels. The evening is clear and the oncoming twilight sky full of emerging stars. Calm weather for boats. I tear along the path towards the lake, not stopping to take care on the rough ground, and I trip and go flying with a thump. The wind is knocked out of me for a second and the lump in my head throbs and the world swims red.

*Be careful now, Rebekah*. I hear her voice in my head, calm and steadying, my mother.

'I will,' I say, getting up slowly and walking more carefully, wiping the mud off my dress.

I reach the Devil's Seat just as the light is dipping towards the horizon, the sky pinking and the bright orange fever of the sun sitting on the horizon, big enough to take over the whole sky. I stop to breathe it in. I will miss this.

When I unlock her cell she rises sleepily from the bed. I run over and hug her, plant a kiss on her cheek, but she lies there stiff and indifferent. 'Is it time?'

'Yes!' I say, but her face seems changed. Her hair is matted and she's dirty.

'At last!' She falls on her knees and opens her arms wide. 'I give thanks to God.'

'What are you doing! You don't believe that shit!'

'Don't swear. And don't tell me what to think!' She even sounds like *them*.

I get her outside and we walk towards the harbour. She looks at me, confused. 'I thought the church was over there —' she says, pointing towards the Devil's Seat.

'We're not going there.'

'Why not?'

'We're going to get help. Remember?'

She laughs. 'It's the Rapture tonight. Tonight we go to heaven!' And she turns away from me.

'Where are you going?!'

'To the church! Mr Bevins said I could come. I thought you'd come to get me.'

I run back towards her. 'Alex!' I turn her towards me, but she's not really looking at me. She's got the same kind of face as the others, like something in her mind has been switched off. Like *she* has been switched off.

'Alex! What's happened to you?'

'I've seen the light, Rebekah! I'm going to go to heaven just like everybody else. I got rid of the evil eye!'

She points to the bandage on her ankle. I can't think what's underneath it, what she's done to the tattoo. There's a circle of blood soaked through, caked into a dark red crust.

'But . . .' *I can't do this without you.* My motivation sinks through my shoes. Maybe it was a bad plan, maybe I should just accept that Mr Bevins is right. But as I think that I remember my mother, and a molten anger fills my veins. Inside my head is a voice that pulses like my heartbeat and shouts louder than anything else – Hurry! Hurry!

But I need Alex with me. I try to give her a hug, but she pushes me away.

'Get off! I'm not like that any more!'

'Like what?'

'Like disgusting.' And her mouth twists out of shape, the thoughts in her mind mapped out on her face. Tears sting the corners of my eyes.

*But I love you*, I want to say. But I don't think it will make any difference.

'Well, you can stay here then!' I shout. 'I'm going to get help.'

I follow the path, quickly now. My breath in short bursts. I can't believe they have turned her! In the dusk I can just make out the outline of the land against the sea and the boathouse. The path becomes more solid and I start to hurry again. They must be missing me by now. There's a crackle in the hedgerow and I turn and shine the torch, but there's no one there.

The door to the boathouse is open. I enter into the darkness, and see the boat still on its trailer. I kick away the blocks from the wheels, meaning to pull the trailer out on to the harbour wall, although I'm not sure how I'm actually going to get the boat in the water. The tide is low, the tideline fringed with a slick of seaweed that lies about like treacherous hair. I can't just push the boat in – it will get broken on the rocks.

I undo the tarpaulin that covers it and throw my bag into the hull, and that's when I see the biggest problem in my plan: at the bottom of the boat is a huge jagged hole. Splinters of wood lie on the floor all around. It looks like someone did it with a hammer, viciously, recently.

I stare at it, not quite understanding. 'But . . . how . . . ?' Tears of frustration and realization catch in my throat. I look around wildly for tools, materials, something to fix the boat, knowing it is futile. Energy and hope evaporate. I can't bear it.

'There you are.' The voice that speaks is loud and close. I flinch. Thomas Bragg's face appears in the doorway. It takes me a moment to realize that he's holding the shotgun. 'Don't move,' he says.

'Thomas!' I wonder how he knew that I was here. Did he follow me?

'Don't move!'

I slowly raise my hands. 'OK,' I say. 'It's OK.'

He nods but keeps the gun trained on me. Would he actually shoot me?

'Thomas! You can't do this! What about the commandment? Thou shalt not kill. You'll go to hell! You won't be Raptured!' My voice sounds wheedling, hopeless. I stand up slowly. I have known him since he was a child; he was never this mean or this devout.

'Step away from me!' he says, then very quickly points the gun at the ceiling and shoots. There's a flash and a bang and a loud ricochet, and splinters of wood fall from the ceiling. 'Believe me, I *will* kill you. Bevins says I won't go to hell, because *you* are sent from the realms of Satan and must be contained.' He jabs the gun at me again. 'You're not real! You're a shadow, filled with the devil. If I shot you now, you wouldn't bleed, you'd turn to dust.'

'Thomas! It's *me*! Rebekah! What are you talking about?'

'The devil. She passed it on to you. It jumped from her to you. Except you can't feel it. No one that is infected with sin can feel it. Not till it's too late.'

'He's right.' Alex appears in the doorway. I look at her. What is she doing here with Thomas? 'I had the demon, but it went into her.'

'See!' He turns to me. 'Bevins said you'd been duped. He was right. But we are here! Warriors in Christ! Bevins will protect us because he has come to take us home.'

I look at Alex. She's not serious, surely. I bow my head. It's like someone has removed her brain.

'Alex! It's not true! It's just Mr Bevins talking!' But her eyes seem to look right through me. 'Alex! What has he *done* to you?'

'He's set me free,' she says.

Thomas comes close with the gun and jabs it close to my face. I stare at Alex, expecting her to laugh or wink at me, something, anything, a signal that she's still there inside.

'It's going to be OK,' I whisper. 'I know you're just going along with him.'

But she ignores me like I'm irrelevant and turns to Thomas. 'Come on, we've got to get back.'

'Alex!' I can't believe she's going along with all this.

Thomas motions at me with the gun. 'Walk!' he says, forcing me out of the boathouse and on to the path, back towards the farm.

He takes the torch from me and holds it, lighting our way, but I stumble.

'Do you really think that the Rapture is going to come tonight the way Bevins says?' I ask him. 'Don't you think he's mad?'

'Don't talk!' Thomas comes up behind me, prodding me in the back with the gun.

I drag my heels as we walk the path from the church, where the lights of the perpetual candles keep a dim glow shining through the windows. I wish it was possible to stop the clock so that there never would be another hour or another day.

# TWENTY-FIVE

# REBEKAH

When we get to the farmhouse everyone is already in the field stood around the fire. They are wearing the robes that Hannah and Margaret have made.

Bevins is standing on a hay bale, reading something from the Book of Revelation. He pauses when he sees us, but does not stop until we are close.

'At last, we are all here!' He claps his hands together. 'You know what it says: "Joy shall be in heaven over one sinner that repenteth." Well, here she is!'

I think he is speaking about me, but he walks right past me and embraces Alex. He holds her hand and lifts it to the sky. 'It's as I saw it, the sinner come to repent in the final hours.'

'Thank you,' Alex says quietly. 'Thank you. All of you.' She doesn't look at me.

'Praise God!' says Hannah.

'Of course there were those who were trying to thwart us,' he says, looking at me and shaking his head. 'But I have eyes and ears *everywhere*.' He sounds as if he is about to cry, but sucks it back in through his teeth.

Hannah shakes her head and tuts. Of course it was her. Snitching. Trying to gain favour. She must have been spying on me and Mary.

I look for Mary in the crowd. She is standing at the back with the boys. When I catch her eye she looks away, but in the light of the lanterns I can see the sparkle of tears.

'You thought you could leave and betray our birthright! Spoil what God had given us! But I know who you are! You who would betray us! But I am stronger than he who would destroy us. By the grace of God in me, you will not prevail! He sees everyone and everything!'

He pulls me roughly, and I wince. 'Let me go!' And for one moment I think he means throw me on to the pyre, but instead he drags me away and shoves me next to Margaret.

'You will repent when you see the face of your God! More terrifying and more glorious than anything you could ever imagine! I have seen it!' He's spitting at me now and he has that look in his eye that makes my stomach lurch in fear. I just stare at the ground. 'And then you will be left behind! That's when your suffering will start. Doubter! Liar! Who are you to think you can change the course of our destiny!'

He gives me one of the white robes. The square of cloth is rigid after the washing and it hangs stiffly like it is made of cardboard. Everyone is wearing one now.

Then he makes us stand in front of the pyre and recite a long and slow Lord's Prayer. It reeks of petrol, which makes me nauseous; the dead sheep and goats are shrunken now, and many have had their eyes pecked out by the birds. I try to hold my breath. I wonder where they got the petrol from – Bevins said we didn't have enough to run the generator. In the middle, penned in, are the live animals, scrabbling about and bleating.

When we are finished Bevins looks up. 'Time!' he shouts, turning to Jonathan, who holds a digital wristwatch close to his face, squinting in the dim light.

'Seventeen minutes past eleven!'

'Less than one hour!' Bevins says. 'Thanks to *my* guidance, *my* prophecy, we are here today ready to be Raptured! Light the offering!'

He nods at Father, who strikes a taper and throws it into the centre of the pyre which ignites in a whoosh, and the fire is suddenly blindingly ablaze. The livestock panic, try to clamber over each other, but they can't escape and soon they succumb to the heat and the flames. I can't watch. Everyone steps back, the flames are so loud and close and hot. Steam rises from the carcasses of the dead sheep, their wool heavy and oily, belching out a thick smoke which swirls around us, making me cough. A breeze catches the flames and sends a flare out towards the edge of the field. Hannah squeals and jumps back; her robe has caught fire on the hem. Quickly she rips it off and stamps on it.

'He's here.'

Bevins looks towards the sky, hands raised. Against the fierce light of the fire he appears as a shadow, hair blowing across his face like strands of wool caught in the hawthorn. 'He's coming for His children.'

He passes around the cup from which we must all drink, the murky wine that he says means we are now cleansed and ready to take our steps into the next world that waits for us. I take a sip, but this time don't swallow. It tastes like sweet mud, it makes me want to retch. I hold it in my mouth and when he has moved on down the line I dribble it out on the sleeve of my dress, letting the liquid soak into the material. I look at Alex. She is swaying on her feet, too close to the fire muttering to herself.

'I can hear trumpets!' Hannah says. 'The voices of the angels!'

'He's with us now!' Mr Bevins says. 'Brothers, Sister, come with me. It will be as if you have just passed through an open door!'

Before me the bonfire crackles and pops.

'Time, Jonathan!'

'Ten minutes to midnight,' Jonathan shouts over the sound of the blazing fire. Sparks rise into the sky and mingle with the stars.

'Only ten minutes!' Bevins says, falling on to his knees. 'So it begins.'

The flames rise higher, a white hot burning that draws in the whole world until it seems like the centre of everything.

Then Bevins breaks out into a chorus of 'Abide with Me' and is joined by Hannah and Margaret until everyone is singing. Jonathan has his eyes closed and is reaching his hands towards heaven and for a moment it seems possible that time will be snatched from us, and suddenly we will rise till we are above it all, like the angels. Alex holds her arms above her head.

But it is a long ten minutes that everyone is on their knees waiting, and the wet ground soaks through my dress and makes my knees muddy. The fire rises to its peak and then begins to die back. There is a terrible smell from the burning livestock, and deep in the heart of the fire there is still a heavy core of dead animal flesh which hasn't burned properly and which throws out an acrid smoke.

Jonathan checks his watch. 'Pastor, Mr Bevins, it is the hour,' he says.

I hold my breath.

Nothing.

Hannah repeats, 'Come, Lord Jesus,' over and over again, and Naomi wails, speaking loudly in tongues until Bevins turns and glares at her.

'Shut up, woman!' he barks. 'You're not helping to hasten the moment!'

Jonathan keeps staring at his watch, as if he cannot believe that time is still ticking forward. 'Perhaps my watch is a little fast, like,' he says, shaking it.

'Keep praying!' Bevins roars. 'Keep *praying*!'

He stands up and makes lifting gestures with his arms, as if he is trying to fan the flames that will take us to heaven.

'He must listen to us! We are here! We are ready. Oh Lord, come! Take us!'

And as the fire continues to roar and the sky turns slowly above out heads, none disappear or appear to be Raptured. Nothing comes down from heaven. Through the flames I watch the skeleton outline of a goat's ribcage, before it disintegrates into the embers.

'Time, Jonathan!' Bevins roars again.

He fumbles in his pocket. 'Quarter to one,' he says.

'Give me that!' Bevins snatches the watch from Jonathan and stares at it. 'This watch is still set to winter time!' He laughs. 'How could I doubt Him who loves us?! Even for one second!'

He gives the watch back to Jonathan, hitting him across the chest so that Jonathan winces. 'Fool!' he mutters.

He makes Jonathan count down the last ten minutes. Nine, eight, seven six . . . three, two one . . .

And the hour comes and passes, and again nothing.

Bevins is silent then, prostrate before the dwindling fire. No one moves until he stands up and begins mumbling to himself, running his hands through his hair, his face streaked with tears. A few people stand, Mary, Gideon, then Father and Hannah. Alex is on her knees praying as if her life depended on it. I go over to her and touch her on the shoulder. She half opens one eye.

'Alex. Alex, it's over, you don't have to pretend any more!' I whisper.

She jumps away from me. 'Get away from me! Liar!'

I flinch away from her. 'But . . .'

The others are all gathered around Bevins.

'Don't take it so hard,' Father says, embracing him.

'You are nothing but goodness to us,' says Hannah, reaching out and Joining their embrace. She holds him close for a long while and he seems to be sobbing in disappointment, until he pushes her away.

'I have such a headache,' he says. 'It's clouding my thoughts. Why did He not come to us? What have I overlooked?'

'You have not overlooked anything!' Hannah says.

'There will be another explanation to this. We must ask God to reveal His purpose,' says Father.

'How do you know?' He looks at them furiously. 'How do you know? He spoke to *me*. It's me who needs to find the answer. Me who needs to think! I need prayer!'

He clutches at his head, pulling his hair.

The fire is beginning to ebb, the warmth retreating back towards the centre. Instinctively we have all drawn closer together. Suddenly Mary is at my side.

'I *knew* it wouldn't come,' she says softly. 'Are you OK?'

'I'm sorry. I tried to get away,' I say croakily. 'But they've smashed up the boat. And Alex . . .' I nod at her pliant figure. 'He's done something to her.'

Mary nods. 'I know.' The twins are at her feet, sombre and quiet, their eyes half closed. It's unnatural for them to be awake so late; she could probably tuck them under a hedge and they would fall asleep. 'I'm going to put them to bed,' she says. 'And let's hope that this is the end of all this nonsense.'

'I need some water.'

'Of course you do,' and she moves to give me a draught from her flask. But then Bevins is standing in front of us.

'What are you doing?' he asks.

Mary bites her lip and does not look at him. 'I'm taking the boys to bed. They need their sleep.'

'They can sleep in the church!' he says. 'We are in the hour between this world and the next. We must all *listen* for answers. We must offer ourselves until there is an answer. We must find out why he has turned His face away from us. Come on!' He moves his arms like a herdsman, like we're just ornery livestock that need gathering up. 'Especially you.' He comes close to my face. 'Traitor!'

I look at his eyes. The piercing blue doesn't seem so visionary any more; they are desperate, watery.

'What did you do to my mother?' I shout at him now. 'Why did you keep all her letters? You're a liar! You can't see God!'

He stares at me as if he wishes he could set me on fire. 'Thomas, come here.'

Thomas lumbers over still holding the gun. When Mary sees him she starts to walk quickly away with the boys tucked in close against her body.

'To the church!'

'You heard him,' Thomas says, pointing ahead with the gun. 'Go on.'

I stumble forward, the path lit only by the dying embers of the fire, the kind of dark light that does not shine bright enough to illuminate the way.

# TWENTY-SIX

# REBEKAH

When we reach the church Bevins orders that I be sat at the front.

'The demon is still here – it has just jumped from one to the other.' He looks at Alex and then at me. 'It's because of *you* He hasn't come!'

'Let. Me. Go!' I fight against their grasp. 'I am not possessed of the devil, *you* are!'

Father bends to my ear. 'Examine your heart. You *must* confess,' he whispers loud enough for everyone to hear. 'It's the only way.'

'You're a liar!' I shout. 'You're all liars! You've let me think all these long years that my mother was dead!'

If Mother was here she wouldn't allow this, I know it. All because the Rapture didn't happen. Mother would have found a way, with Mary Protheroe, to contain them, to temper Bevins's manic enthusiasm, give him tasks to do, keep him level. I can see all that now, but I don't know what I can do about it.

Alex sits beside me.

'It's better if you confess,' she says. 'Just let go of all your stubbornness. Just let it all go.'

I look at her, close to me now, the freckles on her nose, the way her lips pinch into little peaks, the stray eyelash on her cheeks.

'Alex,' I say softly, as if I could reach through all the junk that Bevins has filled her with and find the real person inside, the one who kissed me in the barn. 'Alex. *Please.*'

'Don't be afraid, Rebekah. It's better this way,' she says. But when I look at her I think my heart will break.

'No, it's not.' And for a moment I think I see a flicker of the old Alex in her eyes, but just as quickly she closes it down.

Naomi comes to the front, points a finger at my face and makes a weird gesture with her tongue and then a kissing sound.

'Go away!' I hiss at her. 'Hag.'

I look at the others, everyone sitting obediently, hands in their laps. Why is no one moving?

Bevins clears his throat, raises his eyes and looks up. 'He is there in His heaven, looking down at us and waiting, *longing* to come, but that we would all let him into our hearts by renouncing the devil! But there is a blockage, something in the way that must be overcome. Another battle to fight. Another victory we must claim for him. What do you say? Do you confess?'

'I have nothing to confess! You're mad! Let me go!'

He comes towards me and puts his hand on my forehead.

'Rebekah, you're burning up! Satan himself is inside of you. Satan himself! Do you not see that you cannot leave? You *cannot* leave us. God will not allow it. *I* will not allow it.'

'You're full of shit,' I say. 'I want to see my mother.' Something inside me has broken. I don't care any more what they think. It won't make any difference. Who I am is not who they say. I'm just a chess piece to him, someone to move around the board of his mind.

He takes a step back. 'It's a strong one, Brothers! We must starve it out of her! We must exhaust it! We must break its will!'

His voice is hoarse, spittle and dirt in the corners of his mouth, his eyes aren't even focusing. I try to catch Father's eye but he's kneeling, his head bowed, his lips muttering prayers on over and over. Everyone is under Bevins's spell.

I close my eyes again and Bevins's voice drones on, reading from the Bible now, and the noise, this black sound, like a dark shadow against a red background, a persistent *blah blah blah* in my ear. I wish it would stop – I can't hear what it says any more, only that the constant noise makes it impossible to think. And he won't shut up, he won't shut up, he won't shut up, the whole time he just keeps talking to fill the silence, to fill everyone up with his talking, so in the end no one has enough room in their head to be able to think anything for themselves.

I drift in and out of awareness. Some people have fallen asleep. There is the sound of soft crying coming from behind me. A few mutters of 'Lord, please come'.

Next to me Alex is on her knees, and Bevins is prostrate before the altar, and Father is still kneeling where he was before. I have only been asleep for a few minutes. I am so confused. I can hear singing, maybe it is the Archangel Michael and all the angels, come to carry us home. For a moment my stomach lurches, and I'm thinking that perhaps it's true after all. Oh Lord, let me not be left behind. But then I think it sounds more like a folk song that Mary might hum in the kitchen, or a lullaby from when I was a baby, my mother in my memory, singing to me.

I jolt awake, realize I have been dreaming and look around the church. Everyone is still here, Mary at the back, with the boys sleeping under the chairs. Light has returned to the sky; through the milky glass windows a red dawn rises. Pink light floods the church. It's cold, my breath makes clouds and I pull my clothes tighter around me.

The cold seems to rouse Bevins and he stands up and shakes his head.

'Wake UP!' he shouts. A few people stand up, startled.

He opens his Bible and starts again, reciting verses from Revelation. He walks among us shouting that we are imbeciles, that we will suffer the lake of fire because we have not been taken. 'It is likely the whole world has been Raptured apart from us!'

He rocks backwards and forwards on his feet and moves right into the Lord's Prayer, and everyone joins in like this is just a normal service.

He moves to the back of the church and picks up a green can. The one he used to douse the bonfire in petrol. 'But now, together, Brothers and Sisters, together we will go to the glory. We will not have to wait. I have been sent to release you. In heaven we will be free!'

And he starts to slosh petrol all over the walls and the floor.

Then he grabs me by the arm and drags me to my feet. 'Come here,' he says, and pulls me the front.

'No!' I try to duck out of his grasp, but Jonathan is suddenly there, holding my other arm, tight.

'It's the only way!' he says.

He pours petrol over me, till my clothes are sodden and oily.

'No don't!' Some of it goes in my mouth and makes me feel sick.

'The time for talking is over! We are called to the glory!'

And he starts to sing 'Amazing Grace' and the others all join in except for me and Mary. The singing is loudly out of tune and the whole church now smells thick and greasy. I wriggle against Jonathan's grip but he won't let me go.

'It's OK, Rebekah,' he says. 'He's just taking us home.'

'Soon!' Bevins says. 'Brothers and Sisters! It will be like passing through a door from one world into the next. The disease of our flesh finally thrown aside, made holy, cleansed.'

He lights a candle and holds it aloft.

'Hallelujah!' Hannah says.

'Amen,' says Jonathan.

'We are soldiers of God! We have been faithful.'

Bevins walks among the congregation holding the flaming candle above his head. Micah and Jonathan kneel and begin to pray.

Mary stands up. 'Mr Bevins, I will not go to heaven under these conditions,' she says in a quiet, steady voice. 'A loving God would not take his children like this.'

Bevins pauses and lets out a long sigh. 'Mary, Mary, Mary,' he says, moving through the congregation. 'Are you afraid to meet your maker?'

'No,' she says. 'But I am not prepared to let the boys suffer.'

'You are an agitator, Mary.' He pinches the bridge of his nose and casts his eyes down as if seeking the patience to deal with her. 'You are sent to test me.'

'No, I am sent to speak the truth. There's no need for us to end this way.' She speaks, measured and calm, although I can hear a tremor in her voice.

'You're afraid.' Bevins says softly. 'I understand. But so were all the martyrs, all the many who have been called before us. What joy lies behind the veil! All our struggles ended! If you could see what I can see you would know that I tell the truth!'

Micah has moved to stand behind Mary. He puts his hands on her shoulders and pushes her back to sitting in her seat and Hannah starts to sing 'The Lord Is Calling Me Home', loud and out of tune.

I have this pressure in my chest so great it threatens to crush me so I can barely breathe. All it will take is for Bevins to drop the flame to the floor and the whole church and all of us inside will be consumed by fire. And I will never see Alex again and I will never see the world or Mother. I look at Mary. Fat tears stream down her cheeks and she clutches the twins.

'I confess,' I say.

'What?' Bevins comes over to me. 'What did you say?'

'I confess!' I say, louder. 'It's my fault we are not Raptured!'

Perhaps if I can keep talking he might listen and I might at least be able to blow the flame of the candle out. Somehow I need to find a way to slow him down. To force him to think of another plan.

'To my father. I want to confess to my father.'

'Do you hear her?' Mr Bevins kicks my father, who is kneeling at the altar. 'Wake up!'

He looks up, bleary, as if he doesn't really know where he is; everyone is so tired and hungry, the petrol fumes are strong.

'Rebekah.' He stands up stiffly, grabbing the altar rail for strength.

I look at him and wish that I had the power to get him to see for himself as clearly as I do what is at fault in this place. 'Perhaps we misunderstood? Perhaps our understanding of the prophecy was a mistake? There's no shame in that. We can't go like this. Mother would be so sad.'

'I believe—'

But Mr Bevins interrupts. 'She knows not what she says! It is not her that is speaking, but the devil in her. It is because of *your* faithlessness. As it says in the Bible if you come to me and cannot leave your family you cannot be my disciple!'

Father's eyes are blank, as if all the life inside him has been hollowed out. 'You heard him.'

'And you think he speaks the truth?'

He looks at me, and for a second I think he is about to stand up and claim the floor, cast Bevins out of the church and restore our peace and let us all go finally to bed and face tomorrow. But he does not. He just nods, slowly. 'I do. Yes.'

'But . . .' I don't know what else to say. 'Mother would not want it to be like this!'

When I mention her, there is a flicker in his eyes, like something he is remembering from a long time ago. But before he can think it the thought is snuffed out by Mr Bevins.

'*See?*' Bevins cannot contain his delight. '*See?*'

That noise, the insistence of his voice. 'You do not speak for me! Or for my father!' I struggle against Jonathan's grasp. 'You've been tricked! You all have!'

'Hear the devil who speaks with forked tongue!'

With every syllable he jabs his finger towards me. I am aware that Thomas has moved to stand behind me now, holding the gun. I close my eyes tight shut so I don't have to look. I am sure he will drop the flame to the floor.

There is a loud roar in my head, which becomes an actual roar from outside, a roar that is getting louder and louder. Through the hazy glass there is a monstrous shape and a noise so deafening that I think it might actually be the end of the world. Alex looks towards the window, and then at Bevins, her eyes wide and unblinking as if she's just been roused from a deep sleep.

'No!' she says, shaking her head. 'No, no, no, no!' She looks at me. 'Rebekah!' she says. 'Run!'

Bevins pauses and stares at her, panicked for a moment, then he closes his eyes and shouts:

'*Amen!*'

As the candle drops its light increases in momentum. A ravenous flame expands and expands until it fills the whole church.

# TWENTY-SEVEN

# REBEKAH

There's pain. The opening of a door, which seems to draw the fire, orange and terrible, towards me. I can see Hannah with tongues of flame dancing about her head, but she does not move, still she kneels, fingers knotted hard together, her lips moving in silent, determined prayer.

'*Alex!*' But it's so hot my words are taken from me, scorched and turned to ashes before they are even heard. I've never seen Father move so quickly. He jumps towards me, grabbing the cloth from the altar and throwing it over my head. And he's squeezing me tight, and saying a prayer over and over.

I'm surprised how calm I feel. It doesn't hurt. It is like stepping from one room to the next except the door is slammed shut behind you, no going back, as the room you used to live in is destroyed.

Everything is dark, muffled, then suddenly I can see everything. As if I'm above it all looking down. Mary and the boys running, Mr Bevins collapsing on his knees, Jonathan curled up in a ball beneath a chair. Father trying to push us through the flames to the doors, but it's too late. The wooden chairs have caught and go up in a wall of fire that forces him to step back.

I wonder what Mr Bevins feels right now? What does he see in the middle of his transformation? Does he see the welcome chorus of angels? The cherubim and seraphim? St Peter and all the prophets? Was it worth it? I think he is happy because he is not alone. Isn't that the point to take us all down with him?

In Mary's encyclopaedia it said fires need three things – heat, oxygen and fuel. And to fight a fire you need to starve it of one of these elements. This is what Mr Bevins understands so well: that all fires, whatever heat creates them, however much oxygen they receive need fuel to burn. Without the fuel of his congregation he is nothing but a lonely madman.

On the grass in front of the church is a machine, with thin blades and a body like a fat insect: a helicopter. I've seen them sometimes out at sea. Gideon said they use them on the rigs. Then outside the church two figures, one with a red canister that sprays white dust, fighting against the thick black smoke and the heat that keeps forcing them back.

'*Rebekah!*' Alex is outside, screaming, and then she's gone and I'm not in the church any more at all and the island beneath me becomes small and the world becomes bigger and bigger, the shape of the coastline like a jagged cut outlined by beach and cliff and patches of white surf.

There is a slow, hazy memory that I'm not sure is a memory at all. A hot afternoon, a river, light playing on the surface of the water, and a voice in the distance that I know belongs to my mother. I am a little toddler, I don't know where we are, maybe the park, I didn't even know I remembered this, and she is somewhere near me, her breath so close it tickles my ear, telling me not to be afraid.

# TWENTY-EIGHT

## ALEX

When I wake up I'm lying on my back looking at the sky and the clouds and I cough as if my lungs are coming up through my throat. I close my eyes and wonder for a moment if I'm dead, until a pain so sharp and searing burns up the back of my neck and I put my hand there to touch my hair but all it meets is a raw mess. Someone presses a wet towel to my head. I struggle to sit up.

I can't work out why I'm still here. I'm supposed to be Raptured. I'm supposed to be Raptured. The thought goes round and round my head, until I realize I'm saying it out loud.

'Shhhhh,' someone says. 'You need to lie down.'

A woman, close to my face. She has black and red burns on her arms, and her hair is matted and charred.

Mary, minus her headscarf. I hardly recognize her.

'Wha——?' My voice is a kind of strangled croak.

In front of me the twins and Thomas, sitting inside the open belly of a helicopter, drinking water from a bottle.

'Shhhhh.'

'But . . .'

There are shouts from further down the field, beyond the helicopter, and a plume of thick black smoke rising above the church. I can't work out why I'm here and not in there.

'Did Jesus come and leave me behind?'

Mary shakes her head. 'Shhhhh.'

I get up, although it feels as if I am standing on a sponge; any moment I could fall over. There is something important that I'm forgetting. It's hard to fit the pieces together. As if time has suddenly changed speed and life has jumped ahead into a new dimension that I don't understand.

Then there is a loud hiss and the roof of the church pops like the lid of a jar, flames licking through the plastic and the tarpaper and then the whole structure seems to melt, the wooden walls folding over and falling in on themselves, and the heat is so intense and fierce I can feel it even from this distance. Two men run towards me. One has a neat grey beard and a shaved head, the other, wrapped up in scarves to protect him from the smoke, is just a mop of thick black hair, but I can see his eyes are wild, his dark pupils huge.

'There was nothing we could do!' he says over and over. 'There was nothing we could do!'

'*Rebekah!*'


We are in the back of the helicopter while the men call for help on their radio. There are too many of us to go all at once apparently.

'Go where?' I ask, to no one in particular. My voice sounds hollow, almost as if it's coming from a different body. I realize I'm shivering, although I'm quite warm. One of them puts a silver blanket around my shoulders.

'To hospital! Those burns need treating.'

Thomas sits with his head in his hands, which are burned and raw. He won't look at me and he is mumbling over and over something that sounds like a prayer.

My body seems caught between wanting to run back to the church and the terrible, impossible truth that I can't. Anger rises up in me. I can't believe I ever fell for it. I can't believe I never saved her. I could murder Mr Bevins with my own hands, except I know he is already dead.

'It's *your* fault!' I say, my voice coming out like a shout, a scream. 'It's your fucking fault!'

Mary looks at me with drowning eyes.

'And yours! It's all your fault!' And before I can stop it I start to cry, loud and sudden.

Mary touches me on the shoulder. 'Alex —'

But I shrug her off and cry until everything hurts.

The men decide they will wait for more help rather than leaving some of us here. Mary looks relieved. 'I must stay with the children.'

They get their first-aid kit out and make me lie down, then spray something on my hair and legs and bandage them. They tell me not to move.

'How many of you?' the one with the beard asks.

'Thirty.' Mary says.

'How many children?'

'Four.'

I wrinkle my nose. 'No, two,' I say.

'Four,' Mary says again, 'but only three made it out.'

'Rebekah,' I say, it comes out in a pitiful croak. 'Rebekah.'

There is a long silence where the man looks at us and we look at him. He smiles uncertainly.

'Are you the Antichrist?' Peter asks. 'Or Jesus?'

He looks surprised. 'If I have to be anybody, then Jesus,' he says. 'But my name's John — and that's Duncan. Friends of the Earth.' He points at a logo on his jacket.

Mary nods wearily. John gets out a flask and unscrews the lid, offering it to me. Whiskey. It smells of peat and burns my mouth and makes me cough.

'We tried to land on the other side but it was too windy. We've been tracking that whale, the one that ended up on your beach?'

Mary nods. 'It was beached after the storm.'

'There have been a few these past months. We were hoping to find out why.'

'We didn't know anyone still lived here, like,' Duncan says; his voice has the same northern lilt as Jonathan's. I look at the church, still spewing out smoke and flames; even the wet grass around the building is singed. 'What happened?'

I look at Mary. There is a blank page where my thoughts ought to be.

'It was because of the Rapture,' I say.

'Because of the *what*?' The men look confused.

'The Rapture. It was supposed to happen last night, only it didn't,' I say.

'And what would that be then?'

Mary groans.

'The end of the world where Jesus comes to claim his own,' says Thomas.

'Religious, are you?'

I nod, but Mary does not. 'You could call it that,' she says.

Another helicopter arrives, bigger with more men in uniforms, Red Cross, police. We are quickly put to lie down in special stretchers. They have given me some painkillers that make everything seem far away, although I know that I will feel it later. There is a deafening sound and the helicopter seems to lurch up in the air, slowly, and then quickly, swaying a little as it pitches against the wind. Thomas sits beside me, solemn and shocked. I reach out a hand and touch his arm, and he leans towards me. I think he says sorry.

I turn away from him and start to cry. I know that in the future when people talk about New Canaan or ask me about my scars I will tell them about what happened and about Rebekah and they will ask me what I believe, and I will say that all I know for certain is that somewhere inside of me is this deep river, a flow of molecules and atoms, of water and blood, a precious current of electricity that moves through the muscles of my body, a sap that rises from the earth to fill me. The miracle that was inside me all along: life.

# ACKNOWLEDGEMENTS

Thanks to the friends who cheered me along with the writing of this book – Tina Jackson, Jean McNeil, Emma Forsberg, Lara Newson, Katie Sampson, Donna Mclean. But also especially to Emma Hargrave for all the close editorial help, my editor Rachel Petty for reading many drafts, and my agent, Hellie Ogden, for being visionary about this in the best possible way.

# MASS
# IVE

## JULIA BELL

'I'm *fat*,' I hear myself saying. I look in the mirror. My face has gone hot and red. I feel like I'm going to explode. 'I'm *fat*.' It sizzles under my skin, puffing me up, pushing me out, making me massive.

Weight has always been a big issue in Carmen's life. Not surprising when her mum is obsessed with the idea that thin equals beautiful, thin equals successful, thin equals the way to get what you want. And soon this obsession starts to take over.

When her mother sweeps her off to live in Birmingham – taking her away from her stepfather, the only good influence in her life – Carmen finds things spiralling out of control. And she begins to ask: if she was thin, could it all be very different?

'Exceptional – a superb portrayal of three generations of women for whom food is a problem' *Times Educational Supplement*

'Perceptive and disturbing' *Bookseller*

# MYKINDABOOK.COM

# LOVE BOOKS?
## JOIN MYKINDABOOK.COM
### YOUR KINDA BOOK CLUB

READ BOOK EXTRACTS

RECOMMENDED READS

 BE A PART OF THE MKB CREW

WIN STUFF

BUILD A PROFILE

GET CREATIVE

CHAT TO AUTHORS

 CHAT TO OTHER READERS